Dolores Gordon-Smith lives in Manchester, England, and is married with five daughters, three cats and two dogs. She's always been fascinated by the First World War and the 1920's and loves the Golden Age mysteries of Agatha Christie and Dorothy L. Sayers, an era which she re-creates in her books, capturing the glamour, style, intricate plotting and robust characters that have proved so compelling to so many readers.

She is the author of the Jack Haldean murder mystery series set in 1920's England, the Dr. Anthony Brooke WW1 spy stories, and the introduction to the classic crime novel, The Ponson Case, for HarperCollins. She hosts the How I Got Published column in the Warner Bros. Writing Magazine where she invites debut authors to share their journey to publication.

Dolores is a regular and popular speaker at Bodies from the Library, a day devoted to the Golden Age of crime fiction in the British Library.

Williams & Whiting (Publishers)

15 Chestnut Grove, Hurstpierpoint,

West Sussex, BN6 9SS

Dedicated to

Jessica and James Lewis

For your special year!

Also by Dolores Gordon-Smith

from Williams & Whiting

How to Write A Classic Murder Mystery

For information about this and other books
published by Williams & Whiting go to:
www.williamsandwhiting.com

Serpent's Eye

Dolores Gordon-Smith

WILLIAMS AND WHITING

Chapter One

Farholt, Surrey, September 1910

Agatha Eldon was dreaming.

The sea, pounding below onto jagged, vicious rocks, fountained upwards, drenching her with spray as the wind tore at her clothes and screamed in her ears. There was a horror on the rocks behind and the bridge was the only escape.

She clung desperately to the rickety wooden handrail, feet slipping, as the bridge, rotten with age, crumbled beneath her. Another plank fell away from the swaying bridge, spinning dizzily into the dark sea beneath. Beyond the end of the bridge a solid black wall of water, hundreds of feet high, rushed towards her. She couldn't go on but to turn back meant facing that evil creature on the rocks behind.

"Your tea, ma'am."

It was Dorothy, the housemaid. She put the tray with the pot of tea and slices of thin bread and butter on the dressing-table.

Agatha blinked open her eyes, her heart racing. For a few seconds she expected to see that terrifying wall of water and, even more terrifying, that awful figure behind, then blessed reality washed over her.

It had been a dream; only a dream. She was in her bed and Dorothy, God bless her, had woken her up with her morning tea. As Agatha Eldon saw her plump, comfortable face and kindly expression, she felt a rush of gratitude towards her.

"Adela Guthrie," she whispered. Adela Guthrie had been the figure – that dreadful figure – on the rocks behind. She knew it, with certain knowledge, yet why on earth should Adela Guthrie, of all people, appear in her dreams as a figure of horror?

Adela Guthrie wasn't hideous; she was a very beautiful woman. She'd even appeared in the more select of the shiny magazines on the strength of her beauty. Mrs John Guthrie at the Duchess of Glengowrie's reception... Mrs John Guthrie in her rose garden... Mrs John Guthrie cutting the ribbon to open the Houndferry Tunnel. Mrs John Guthrie...

Mrs John Guthrie, Agatha Eldon strongly suspected, was having an affair. The idea didn't shock her. She'd never have an affair herself – they were messy, awkward things and dear Frank would be bitterly hurt.

What had concerned her was that Adela Guthrie, who was clearly bored with her husband, would set her sights on Robert.

Agatha felt a wave of anxious defensiveness at the thought of her son. Robert was such a handsome boy, witty and carefree, with such charming manners, she could almost forgive anyone for setting their cap at him. Adela Guthrie, however, had found solace elsewhere. She still worried about Robert, though. Frank didn't understand him. It was too bad to complain that the boy ran through money, but to suspect, as Frank had done, that poor Robert had been responsible when those wretched diamond earrings had been lost last year, was plain wrong. Robert *couldn't* do anything like that.

2

At least she didn't have to worry about him and Adele Guthrie. Let the woman have her affairs. It wouldn't be the first illicit relationship that had happened at Farholt, not by a long chalk. Agatha loved her home but, she had to admit, the rarefied and, at times, highly charged, atmosphere of Farholt made affairs virtually inevitable.

When Francis Eldon had inherited Farholt, he had set about making Farholt matter in the political world. Without any ambition to take part in the hurly-burly of the political world, with hustings and campaigns and elections, Francis Eldon very much wanted to be one of the people who mattered.

He had done it, with Agatha's help, by turning Farholt into a political retreat, a behind the scenes meeting place where deals could be done and bargains struck. Agatha liked the company and the challenge and knew how much Frank relished being at the centre of things. She liked - she was honest enough to admit this – the sense of being important.

And that was why Adela Guthrie was here. Adela Guthrie, society beauty and wife of the brilliant civil engineer, John Guthrie, was here as part of the party with President Ramon Artiaga of Salvatierra.

Agatha only had the vaguest notion of where Salvatierra was. It was somewhere in South America and sturdy, adventurous sorts went there to find gold and emeralds and so on. She had been pleasantly surprised to find that President Artiaga (because they'd definitely had some odd types at Farholt over the years) spoke perfect English and had perfect manners.

Francis had been introduced to him in London and offered Farholt as an ideal meeting place for the President to bring together John Guthrie, who he wanted to build a railway which would open up Salvatierra, and the bankers that the President needed to finance the scheme. John Guthrie was, naturally enough, accompanied by his wife.

She liked Mr Guthrie. He was a sight too good for that wife of his, however lovely she was. He struck Agatha as solid and dependable and he talked about other things than politics and finance. He could even talk about other topics than engineering. He was fond of music and when she showed him round the gardens (a standard tour for guests at Farholt) he turned out to be a keen amateur botanist. Really, that walk had been positively educational.

Yes, she liked John Guthrie. The trouble was, he wasn't the only guest accompanying the President.

Count von Liebrich; apparently the President needed Count von Liebrich. The Germans, Frank had explained to her, had considerable influence in Salvatierra and the Count, who was polished and charming, acted as a useful liaison between the interests of the Imperial German government and President Artiaga's advisors.

The trouble was that the handsome, powerful Count had taken one look at the bewitching Adela Guthrie and the rest was practically inevitable. Unfortunately, John Guthrie clearly suspected what was going on as well.

The tension between Guthrie and Count von Liebrich had been contained at simmering point but if it boiled

4

over, heaven knows what would happen. Guthrie might be a decent man but he was nobody's fool. If he knew – really knew – that the Count had seduced his wife, however willing a partner she was, then there would be fireworks and no mistake.

Agatha sighed. She just hoped the fireworks wouldn't erupt at the ball …

She stopped, her tea cup frozen in her hand. The ball! Tonight's ball! For a fraction of a second she was whisked back into that terrifying dream. The solid black wall of water, the monstrous tidal wave in her dream, *was* the ball.

She forced down a sense of panic. This was utterly ridiculous. How many balls had they had at Farholt? At least sixteen and every one had been a success. What on earth could go wrong? She ran through a mental inventory; dress, guests, food, orchestra, staff.

Staff; she could rely on the staff. Dorothy had drawn the curtains and was now tidying the dressing-table. Agatha remembered the overwhelming sense of gratitude she had felt to her, minutes before.

"I'm afraid," she said, picking her words carefully, "that tonight's ball means a great deal of extra work for you and all the staff."

Dorothy turned to her, surprised but pleased. "Bless you, ma'am, it's no trouble. Well," she amended, her cheerful face contorting in thought, "I suppose it *is* extra trouble, but I do likes it."

"You like it?" questioned Agatha.

5

"Oh yes," said Dorothy reassuringly. "It's something to be part of Farholt, isn't it? I often sees Farholt in the papers." She beamed. "I keeps a scrapbook with us all in and sometimes there's even a picture with all us staff in it too. There was a bit of me in one picture," she said with innocent pride.

"You enjoyed that?" asked Agatha, amused.

Dorothy nodded vigorously. "I do. Then, there's always something extra in the wages for the trouble – generous, that is, and welcome, too, with the wedding coming up."

Dorothy was going to be married to Wilfred Banks, the coachman, an event which had enthralled the servants' hall.

She sighed happily. "Yes, it's a fair treat to see all the ladies in their beautiful clothes and gentlemen you read about in the paper."

Agatha sipped her tea. Ladies in beautiful clothes and gentlemen you read about in the paper. Dorothy obviously saw Farholt as a place of glamour and romance. It was odd to think that dear Frank thought about it in exactly the same way.

It suddenly struck her how much she liked Dorothy. "There will be something extra for all of you after the ball," she said. "And Dorothy, please tell the staff how very much I appreciate all the work you do."

The memory of that terrifying tidal wave was still very real. "If it all goes off smoothly tonight, it'll be a real relief."

*** *** ***

6

In the tiny police station of Farholt Parva, Inspector Summerskill was gloomily looking over a sheaf of paperwork. Inspector Summerskill usually worked in Guildford, not a little one-horse place like Farholt Parva, but there was, as the police had every reason to suspect, trouble brewing. There had been telephone calls from the Metropolitan Police which warned of that trouble.

President Ramon Artiaga might be assassinated. There were plenty of men in Salvatierra who would be happy to see the President dead. The programmes of reform which the President had vigorously instituted had left a lot of very powerful people very unhappy. One of those reforms – the right to form new political parties – had rebounded on him.

There were a lot of Germans and Americans in Salvatierra who had had things their own way for a long time and had joined forces with the landowners. Their new party, the Haciendistas, was the public face of some very ruthless types.

That much Inspector Summerskill knew from Scotland Yard. While the President had been in London, it had been fairly easy to keep tabs on him with a discreet police presence. Here in the country, it was a different matter. The President had flatly refused to have a police guard. His own staff, he said, were up to the job.

That was one headache. The other was, thought Inspector Summerskill with mounting irritation, was this ruddy necklace, property of President Artiaga, the Serpent's Eye.

It was worth God knew how much and if ever there was a target for thieves…

There was a knock at the door and Sergeant Benscombe, also drafted in from Guildford, came in. "We've had a report, sir, that Teddy Costello hasn't been seen in London for the past three days."

"Teddy Costello?" repeated Inspector Summerskill sharply. Teddy or Theresa Costello was a jewel thief and fence. She had been nabbed once and, having served her time, was now officially a blameless citizen. Privately, however, Scotland Yard had associated her with a string of jewel robberies.

He breathed a deep sigh. "I suppose we'd better add her to the list, Sergeant. That makes no less than four known jewel thieves in the vicinity, all trying to get their hooks on this blasted necklace." To say nothing, he added grimly to himself, of Robert Eldon.

The previous summer the wife of a Liberal politician had lost a pair of diamond earrings at Farholt. Francis Eldon had made good the loss and the lady was satisfied. Inspector Merrick had been in charge of that case and his considered opinion was that Francis Eldon was only so quick with his cheque-book because he was desperate to avoid scandal.

Inspector Merrick was certain in his own mind that the criminal was Robert Eldon, the Eldon's only child. Robert Eldon was, by all accounts, a pleasant, affable man with a wide circle of friends. Those friends included a very raffish crowd in London including, Inspector Summerskill remembered, Teddy Costello.

He sighed once more. He had visited Farholt and spoken to Sir Francis. The Serpent's Eye, he had been assured, was kept, together with other jewellery, in the safe. But there was this grand ball tonight. Would the necklace be on display? Inspector Summerskill winced. If any woman wore the necklace, she would be a real target.

Inspector Summerskill put down his pen and stood up. Francis Eldon had made light of his warnings so far, but perhaps he'd better have another word. Not that, he thought, it would do any good. Teddy Costello was missing from London, thieves had gathered and Robert Eldon was in the house.

The Serpent's Eye! It was a serpent in a nest of vipers.

*** *** ***

Despite all Agatha Eldon and Inspector Summerskill's forebodings, however, the ball was a huge success.

It was half past two that morning when John Guthrie walked into his wife's dressing-room. He had had, he knew, just a little too much to drink.

Adela's maid, Madeline, was brushing out her mistress's hair. John looked at his wife and his stomach twisted. Her hair was long, golden and shining, a perfect frame for her lovely face. Had the Count seen his wife like this? His stomach twisted again.

Adela, beautiful in her periwinkle blue chiffon negligee, looked up at him sharply. "Have you come to apologise, John?"

9

He rubbed a hand over his forehead. "Not exactly." He clicked his fingers at the maid, standing defensively by her mistress. "You. Leave us."

The woman didn't move. Adela put a reassuring hand on her arm. "You'd better go, Madeline." There was steely challenge in her voice. "Everything will be perfectly all right."

With a wary look at John, Madeline packed away the vanity case and left.

John flung himself heavily into an armchair and lit a cigarette.

"Shouldn't you ask my permission first?" asked Adela, the steel in her voice increasing.

John laughed. "Perhaps I should. But I know damn well that someone smoked a cigar in here last night and it certainly wasn't me. I smelt it this morning."

"You're mistaken, John."

"Am I?" He blew out a mouthful of smoke. "If you say so. You asked if I was going to apologise. What for?"

Adela sat up straight. "Let's start with the Serpent's Eye, shall we? You did your absolute best to prevent me wearing it tonight."

"The police said you'd be a target. I was thinking of your safety."

"Nonsense. You couldn't stand the idea of my being admired. You're ridiculously possessive, John, but you can back down now. The ball's over and the necklace is back in the safe."

"I wasn't being possessive," he said doggedly. "The police didn't want you to wear it. You were warned there

10

were thieves about and anyone who wore it would be a target."

Adela snorted in disgust. "That's complete nonsense! I was perfectly safe." Her eyes took on a dreamy expression. "It's a wonderful necklace."

"All the same…"

"All the same, just remember it was the President who insisted I wear it. You know why. You heard what the President said."

"I know," interrupted John. "The best setting for the Serpent's Eye is round the neck of a beautiful woman." He smiled cynically. "I'll say this for you, Adela. You carried it off beautifully. Even that crowd of hard-headed money men were impressed."

"I'm glad you think so."

"Did the Count think so?"

Adela's eyes snapped a warning, but she kept her voice level. "Of course."

"He had plenty of opportunity to tell you, didn't he?

"What's that supposed to mean?"

"I mean you spent far too much damn time with him. Alone."

"He was giving me advice on what to say to Mr Houblyn and his associates. Mr Houblyn of Houblyn's bank, remember? He's a very important man, John."

"And that's all you talked about, was it? How to impress a bunch of money men? There wasn't any mention of a little holiday you might be planning together, for instance?"

Adela looked utterly bewildered. "A holiday? What on earth are you talking about?"

John felt his certainty waver. If she was lying – and Adela could lie, he knew – she was doing it very well. "I heard him mention the sea."

"The sea?" Her frown deepened. "He must've meant the voyage to Salvatierra. Unless you've discovered a land route to South America, we will have to go by sea."

"You're lying," said John, but without the conviction he had felt seconds earlier.

Adela glared at him. "How dare you! Yes, I spoke to the Count. What's more, I was enjoying the conversation before you blundered in on it. If you had been listening properly and not making up wild stories, you would've heard him explain all about the railway - the railway you are so very keen to build – and the importance of obtaining a loan. The Serpent's Eye is the security for that loan."

"Banks and money," broke in John. "Yes, I heard him. The man's obsessed with money."

"As the President's chief financial advisor, don't you think he has to be?"

"He's got money on the brain."

"At least he's got some to think about."

"And I haven't, is that it? Well, let me tell you, Adela, that you have a very comfortable life. Even if I haven't got the money to throw about that Count von bloody Liebrich has, you have nothing to complain about."

"Kindly do not use coarse language in front of me."

"Get off your high horse," said John in disgust, chucking his cigarette into the grate. "All I can say is if you think the Count is your passport to riches, you're onto a loser. I know him, remember? He's a notorious womaniser who's had a string of mistresses. You're just the latest in a long line of conquests."

That hit home. Adela's eyes sparked with anger. "I can only imagine you're drunk. You burst in here, make a string of unfounded accusations..."

He crossed the room and grabbed hold of her arms. "Unfounded! I wish to God they were unfounded!"

She struggled to get free and the movement made something deep inside flare. He held her to him, feeling the closeness of that perfect body under the thin negligee. "I love you, Adela. I love you, understand? I've been through hell this past week, watching you with him. I'm your husband. You married me." Her face was buried in his chest. He forced her chin up, kissing her hungrily.

There was a brief struggle and then she responded with the passion he remembered. "You're my wife," he said shakily. "*My* wife".

***   ***   ***

Adela was gone. He rolled over in the bed but she was gone. A black suspicion engulfed him. She couldn't have gone to *him*, could she? He swung his feet over the side of the bed and sat hunched, knuckles to his forehead.

What the devil was the time? He pulled the cord of the curtains, letting a shaft of moonlight spill across the bed. She should be here, with him. Instead, she was... Where?

Darkness, a hot, blistering, darkness, rose up in him. He ground his knuckles into his closed eyes, seeing flames leap up in the darkness inside.

He dropped his hands and blinked. He was going to do it. He was going to find the Count and if Adela was with him, he would kill him.

Murder. He muttered the word over and over as he pulled on his scattered clothes. *Murder*. Murder with his bare hands. *Murder*.

He slipped out into the corridor. The moonlight flooded the passage and he leaned against the bannister.

Which was the Count's room? He didn't know, but if he waited, he would see Adela come along this corridor, back into her room, ready to pretend that nothing had happened. If he waited, he would have proof and, once he had that proof, he would commit murder.

A cold revulsion shook him. With glacial slowness, pieces clicked together in his mind. If he murdered the Count, he would be a murderer. And if he was a murderer, he would be caught, trapped and hanged.

Trapped. Waiting for death. Trapped. As he thought the word, he was nearly sick with horror. Trapped. He had been trapped once, in the tunnel at Houndferry. The tunnel had collapsed and he was trapped. He shook himself, wiping away the sweat that beaded his forehead with the back of his hand. Trapped.

Was it worth it? For Adela? He looked down at his hands, twitching in the moonlight. Adela was vain, acquisitive and ruthless. Yes, the hot darkness insisted, but she was his *wife*.

His wife, who wanted to be rich. Adela, who had delighted in acting as if she was rich tonight, dressed in pale green with the Serpent's Eye clasped around her perfect throat.

If he owned the Serpent's Eye he would be rich...

*** *** ***

The noise shook the house.

Francis Eldon jerked upright in bed. Scrambling for his dressing-gown, he tumbled out into the corridor. Doors slammed back all along the corridor as voices demanded to know what was going on.

Someone switched on the electric light and the guests blinked at each other.

Agatha put her hand on his arm. "Whatever is it, Frank? It sounded like an explosion."

A loud crack rang out downstairs. Agatha started back in fright.

"That was a shot!" called one of the guests.

"It came from the library!" shouted Frank. "Dash it, that's where the safe is! Come on!"

With all the guests and the household behind him, he led the charge down the stairs. The library was directly across the hall from the stairs.

Frank crashed open the door and switched on the light, then flung his arms back to stop Agatha entering the room.

The safe stood gaping open, its door hanging drunkenly by one hinge. In front of the safe, sprawled across the floor, lay the body of a man in a night shirt and dressing gown, an emerald necklace clutched in his hand.

15

He turned to find President Artiaga right behind him. "Keep the women out of the room," he ordered.

The President passed the command on then, together with Frank and the other men, went into library.

President Artiaga knelt by the body and turned it over, wincing as he saw the mess of blood on the white nightshirt. "It's Count von Liebrich," he said unsteadily. "He's been shot. He's dead." He touched the necklace clutched in the Count's hand. "It's the Serpent's Eye. He saved the Serpent's Eye."

Other jewel cases were scattered at the foot of the safe. "He saved all the jewels," said Frank in a gruff voice.

The curtains in front of the french windows were flapping open. Frank strode to the window, then gave a shout. "He's out there! The murderer's getting away!"

In the moonlight a man was running away from the house, over the lawn. Frank, the President and at least five other men poured out of the house and after the man. Although he had a good head start, two of the footmen, Eric and William, were keen amateur runners. They easily outdistanced their quarry and caught him.

He struggled frantically in their grasp. "Let me go, damn you! You're letting him escape!"

Frank panted up. "Mr Guthrie?" he said incredulously, looking at the struggling man in Eric and William's grip.

John pointed into the distance. "Look! That's the man you want!"

Frank clapped a hand on John's shoulder, following where he was pointing. "You!" he called to the shadowy figure in the distance. "Come back!"

He had shouted without thinking. To his complete surprise, the man stopped, turned and ran back. It was Robert, dressed in pyjamas but with outdoor shoes.

"So you've caught him, father," he said when he was a few yards away.

"Caught me?" countered John furiously. "What do you mean, caught me? I was chasing you."

"No you damn well weren't," said Robert. "I was chasing you, you murderer." He glanced at John's hand. "You've still got the gun."

"Give me the gun," barked Frank. John shrugged and handed the gun over.

President Artiaga strode towards them. He looked thunderstruck as he saw John Guthrie between Eric and William. "John? What the devil's happened?"

"I came downstairs," said John, still furious. "I found Count von Liebrich dead on the floor and the safe wide open. I looked out of the window and saw a man running off. I yelled for him to stop but he didn't, so I chased after him."

"That's rubbish," snarled Robert. "I found Count von Liebrich dead and this chap making a run for it." He glared at John. "It's obvious he's guilty. Look at him. He's fully dressed."

"That's true," agreed Frank. He rounded on John. "What's your explanation, sir?"

John was about to reply when he saw Adela's pale face looking out of the french windows. He swallowed, then stopped. "That's my business."

The President intervened. "Mr Eldon, this man is my friend. He cannot be a criminal."

Frank's mouth set in a thin line. "President Artiaga, I have the greatest respect for your judgement but it cannot have escaped your notice that this man and Count von Liebrich were at odds with each other." He too had seen Adela looking out of the window. "We will not go into causes, but as men of the world, we will all have our own ideas on the subject. One thing is clear. There is a murdered man in my library and we need the police."

***   ***   ***

Inspector Summerskill shut his notebook with a snap. They were in Frank Eldon's study. The women and most of the other guests had been asked to return to bed. Frank and Robert Eldon stood together while President Artiaga sat near John Guthrie. By the door stood two police constables. The room was very still, musty with the smell of old cigar smoke.

It was a relief when Frank Eldon drew the curtains and opened the window, flooding the room with the cold grey light of a chilly dawn. It was the sort of light, thought Inspector Summerskill, that filled the execution shed. From the half-open window, he could hear the sound of the horses harnessed to the police wagon, chomping the grass.

The trouble was, from his point of view, was that John Guthrie was the sort of man he liked and respected. He

18

had taken a completely unexpected liking to Robert Eldon as well. That, he reminded himself, was exactly what Inspector Merrick had reported the previous year when there had been that business about the diamond earrings.

However, at least on this occasion, no jewellery had been stolen. Frank Eldon and the butler, Hinton, had vouched that all the jewellery that should be in the safe was in the safe, including this ruddy Serpent's Eye. The Count had obviously stepped in to prevent a robbery. The question was, who was the robber?

Guthrie stated that he had heard someone moving downstairs and gone to investigate, when the explosion happened, followed by the gunshot. Going into the library, he'd found the Count dead with the gun beside him. He picked up the gun, then, looking out of the open window, saw a man running away. He couldn't say if it was Robert or not.

Robert Eldon stated that he was unable to sleep and had come downstairs for a book he'd left in the library. He was near the library when the explosion happened, followed by a shot. He ran into the library to find John Guthrie standing over the Count, gun in hand. Guthrie had escaped and Robert ran after him, but missed him in the dark.

Was it true? Inspector Summerskill sighed. By all accounts Guthrie had good reason to loath the Count. He had been told as much and Guthrie didn't deny it. Neither could he deny he had been caught holding the gun. What he wouldn't give was an explanation of why he had been fully dressed. Guthrie said he would tell the Inspector in private, but the Inspector wanted to know the reason now.

There was nothing for it but to take Guthrie to the police station. He might be a bit more forthcoming there.

"John Guthrie," he said formally. "It is my duty to arrest you on suspicion of having caused the death of Count Rupert von Liebrich. You do not have to say anything, but anything you do say will be noted down and might be used as evidence at your trial." He nodded to the two police constables who walked forward to stand on either side of Guthrie.

In the grey light, John's face turned to the colour of putty. "You're going to lock me up?" he said in a croak.

"For the time being, sir, yes."

President Artiaga put a hand on his shoulder. "It won't be for long, John. We'll soon get this mess sorted out."

Inspector Summerskill felt bound to intervene. "I'm afraid that's more than I can say, sir."

John's eyes were hunted. "Locked up?" He swallowed. "I'll be trapped. Trapped." There was a world of pain in his voice.

Like a man in a trance, he allowed himself to be raised to his feet, a police constable at either side, looking round the room as if bewildered.

Then, in an explosion of movement, he struck out, elbowing the constables out of the way, and made a dive for the window.

"After him!" yelled Inspector Summerskill, completely taken aback.

The two police constables, one reeling with a bloody nose, the other doubled up and gasping for breath, staggered to the window. Frank and Robert Eldon and President Artiaga got there first. Inspector Summerskill tried to force his way through as he saw Guthrie evade Robert Eldon's grasping hand.

"Get out of the way, man!" yelled Summerskill to a man blocking the window. "Out of the way!"

He caught the man by the shoulder and heaved. It was, he noticed with a sort of frozen horror, none other than the President who was blocking his way. The President struggled back, unable to move in the crush. By the time Summerskill got out of the window, John Guthrie had disappeared.

*** *** ***

"I'm afraid I have to report that the prisoner got clean away, sir," Inspector Summerskill said later that day to a very unsympathetic Superintendent Ross.

"And continues to evade capture," said Superintendent Ross grimly. "The whole business was shockingly managed, Summerskill. Why on earth didn't you arrest Guthrie at once?"

"I wasn't sure of his guilt, sir, and Guthrie's an important man. He was part of President Artiaga's party, after all, and we know there were other jewel thieves in the vicinity."

"Not sure of his guilt?" repeated Superintendent Ross in blank astonishment. "What proof do you need? The man's caught running away from the scene of the crime with a gun in his hand. The same gun, the experts assure

21

me, that was used to kill Count von Liebrich. That safe was blown apart, man! Guthrie's an engineer, dammit. He knows how to use explosives. He blew the safe and when this Count fellow came into the room, shot him."

"Without taking the jewels, sir?"

"He was interrupted," said Superintendent Ross with icy patience. "Interrupted by the Count who was murdered for his pains."

"What about Robert Eldon, sir?"

"What about him?" demanded the Superintendent. "I know perfectly well he came under suspicion last year but on this occasion he hasn't put a foot out of line." He tapped his pipe stem on the desk in irritation. "I can't believe you let Guthrie get away."

Inspector Summerskill coughed. "I haven't put this in my official report, but it's my firm conviction that President Artiaga deliberately hampered our pursuit. "

"Is it, by Jove. And what do you expect me to do about that, eh? Arrest the President?"

"You could ask him a few questions, sir," said Summerskill tentatively. "He was very warm in his support for Guthrie when I was interviewing the witnesses in the study. It wouldn't be a bad idea to keep an eye on him, President or no President. I think there's every chance Guthrie will turn to him for support."

"He'll have to turn a dickens of a long way if he does," said Superintendent Ross. "The entire presidential party – or what's left of it – has cleared out and are heading back to Salvatierra."

Inspector Summerskill gaped at him. "Heading back? Can't they be stopped?"

"On what grounds? The President was the victim of an attempted robbery. He's not the criminal. He's free to come and go exactly as he pleases. Besides that, I think he's got quite enough to think about without us questioning him. There was a revolt in Estrada yesterday."

"Estrada, sir?" asked Inspector Summerskill with a puzzled frown.

"You need to brush up your geography, Inspector. Estrada is the capital city of Salvatierra. The news came through this morning of heavy fighting round the presidential palace. The President stopped off in London to deliver the Serpent's Eye to Houblyn's bank and then caught the boat train from Victoria."

"He's skipped," said Inspector Summerskill blankly.

Superintendent Ross snorted dismissively. "He's gone to fight a war, man. I'd hardly describe that as skipping." He shuffled up the papers on his desk and boxed them together. "Forget the President, Summerskill. There's a murderer on the loose and," he added gloomily, "it's my guess if we don't lay hands on him soon, we never will. A man like that has connections. He'll use them, right enough."

Superintendent Ross's predictions proved to be correct. Despite all the police's efforts, John Guthrie was never found.

He became the footnote to a forgotten crime.

Chapter Two

London, April 1922

George Hankin nodded appreciatively as the Rolls-Royce glided to a halt outside the steps of the bank. A real gentleman's car, that was. Setting his face into the blankness expected of a commissionaire and shrugging his coat a little further back onto his shoulders, he started to walk ponderously down the steps to open the door, when his eyes widened in carefully concealed astonishment.

Mr Birch himself had appeared in the doorway of the bank and was now waiting to greet the visitor. Blimey, whoever it was must be important to get 'is Nibs out. He spared another glance out of the corner of his eye. Strewth! Not only Mr Birch but Mr Houblyn as well.

He opened the car door and stood respectfully to one side. If it had been the King, Hankin wouldn't have been surprised, not with that reception committee. As it was, a dark, athletic, young man, correctly but unexcitingly clad in full morning dress, got out followed by two similarly-dressed companions. Another Rolls-Royce drew up behind and George Hankin, conscious of being under the eyes of the great, walked to the car door.

Mr Birch had come half-way down the steps and was shaking the young man by the hand. "A great honour, President Artiaga," George overheard him say. "A very great honour indeed.

President, eh? That meant foreign and not even foreign royalty at that. George's respect lessened. Still, he must be *Someone* though, judging by the way Mr Birch was carrying on. Who the 'ell was it?

***   ***   ***

The someone was, as Mr Birch knew very well indeed, was President Enrique Ramon Alfonzo Artiaga, first minister of the republic of Salvatierra. A resounding title for such a young man, but one which had been earned. President Artiaga had come to power after a civil war which had been bitter, even by South American standards. Looking at the squarely-set shoulders and the brilliant blue eyes, Mr Birch wasn't surprised President Artiaga had won.

"Guts," thought Mr Birch to himself. "He's got guts. Mind you, think who his father was…"

As he shook the outstretched hand, Mr Birch remembered another man who had shaken his hand and met his gaze with brilliant blue eyes. "This is a real pleasure, your Excellency," he said, with genuine warmth. "I knew your late father, President Ramon Artiaga, well. I was delighted that he chose us to act for him in this matter."

The President paused. "You knew my father?" There was an odd wistfulness in his voice.

"Indeed I did, sir. He captivated London before the war and when we received the tragic news of his death, there were many who felt a deep sense of personal loss." Mr Birch led the way through the marble hall of the bank and through the steel door which opened onto the stairs to the well-lit vaults. "He was a very fine man, your Excellency."

25

He paused before the metal grill, waiting for the livered custodian of the vaults to draw back the door.

"This bank – it is very safe, yes?" asked one of the men with the President.

Mr Birch smiled. "Totally. I am glad to say that we have never suffered even an attempted robbery." The President looked round the steel-plated walls and murmured agreement. "Not only," continued Mr Birch, "are the walls and ceiling practically impregnable, but the floor is inlaid with a network of glycerine-filled pipes. Should anyone attempt to tunnel in, the pipes would be broken and an alarm would sound." The party paused before the stacked rows of metal safes. "Now, Your Excellency, I believe you have your father's key."

The door of the safe-deposit swung open and Mr Birch stood aside. The President gave his stick, hat and gloves to one of the men beside him and reached into the safe, bringing out a flat box of tooled red leather. He touched a catch and the lid of the box flew open, bringing a subdued gasp from the men present. He put in his hand and drew out a necklace of shining gold and green fire.

"Remarkable, truly remarkable," said the black-coated man at Mr Birch's elbow. He was Joseph Marcovitch, one of the finest goldsmiths and jewellers in London. "I have read the description and studied the drawings, of course, but to actually see it is a rare privilege. It is reputed to be one of the finest examples of Sixteenth Century Spanish work in the world, and to have such an important piece in our hands..."

His own hand moved involuntarily and, after the briefest hesitation, the President gave it to him with a smile.

As he took the necklace, Marcovitch's face clouded. With a muttered apology he whipped out a jeweller's eye-glass from his pocket and examined the jewels minutely, ending by delicately touching one of the emeralds with the tip of his tongue.

"What?" began Mr Birch, but Marcovitch waved him silent.

When he looked up his face was strained and he swallowed twice before speaking. "Gentlemen - Your Excellency - I am sorry to break the news, but I'm afraid that this is nothing more than a fake."

There was uproar. Mr Birch literally staggered and had to clutch at the wall for support.

In the clamour of voices came Joseph Marcovitch's steady, clear voice. "Look for yourself. Here - and here. Beautifully done, but a fake all the same. It's nothing more than gold and coloured glass. Know? Of course I know! Proof? It can be tested chemically, but any jeweller who knew his trade would confirm my opinion. It's an expert copy but it *is* a copy." He looked at the President with deep regret. "I'm sorry, sir, but apart from the value of the gold, it's worthless."

His Excellency President Enrique Ramon Alfonzo Artiaga leaned back against the wall, drew a cigarette from his case, tapped it on the back of his hand and lit it. "Well," he said, with a twist in his voice. "That has put the kybosh on things good and proper."

27

***   ***   ***

Sir Douglas Lynton, Assistant Commissioner of Scotland Yard, brought his fist down on the newspaper on the desk in front of him, as if trying to physically suppress the story on the front page. "We can't allow this, Brenzett," he said to the man on the other side of the desk. "Once the idea gets about that a bank such as Houblyn's can be broken into, then we can expect a spate of robberies."

Superintendent Brenzett shook his head slowly. He was a large, solidly built man, who looked as if he would be more at home behind a plough than in an office in Scotland Yard. "I don't agree, sir. I've had a good look at Houblyns. I have to say that it's practically impossible to break in, and an actual impossibility to do it undetected."

"So how was it done?" demanded Sir Douglas. "I can tell you that this affair is worrying a good many people. At a guess, rather more than half of the world's wealth is tucked under the pavements of London and it's there because it's thought to be safe. Let it be known it's not and the consequences don't bear thinking about. It wouldn't be so bad if we'd been able to keep it under wraps, but the newspapers are full of it. If President Artiaga was blessed with any sense he would have hushed the matter up but he's gone straight to the press with it. He seems to have had no *idea* of the scandal it would cause..." Sir Douglas broke off expressively.

The Superintendent took his pipe out of his pocket and absently stuffed it with tobacco. "You can't blame him for feeling sore. However, I don't believe the jewels were taken from Houblyns at all."

28

"They're not there now."

"No..." Brenzett put a match to his pipe. "But look at what a theft from Houblyns implies, sir. How their safe-deposit set-up works is like this; there are two keys to every box. One's kept securely by the bank. I've seen the arrangements and they *are* secure. The other's kept by the depositor. When the owner of the box wants to make a withdrawal, he's accompanied by bank officials to his box which is kept in the vaults. The vaults are locked and guarded day and night. I think it's a practical impossibility to break in. I don't think it can be done."

There was a note of helplessness in Sir Douglas' voice. "But it *was* done. Unless..." Sir Douglas sat forward thoughtfully. "Unless the emeralds - the real emeralds - were never in the box to start with."

Brenzett pulled at his pipe. "I really think that's the height of it, sir."

"A theft by substitution, you mean? God knows, we've had a spate of them recently." The sudden light faded from his eyes. "But damn it, man, that doesn't make any sense either. Those emeralds were deposited by President Enrique's father, Ramon Artiaga. Apart from his reputation as a thoroughly honest man, they weren't insured, so there isn't any way he could benefit from a fraud. I suppose he could have deposited them as a blind, but why? Once they were in the vaults of Houblyns they were safe."

"Could he have sold the real emeralds privately and deposited the false ones to conceal the fact?" suggested Brenzett. "That's been done before now."

29

Sir Douglas made an irritated gesture. "I'd have said definitely not. When I said he was an honest man, I meant it."

"Is his son, President Enrique Artiaga – is he an honest man, sir?"

"I've no reason to think otherwise," said Sir Douglas. "I can tell you there was a collective sigh of relief in Whitehall when President Enrique finally came to power."

"But is he honest, sir?"

Sir Douglas spread his hands wide. "As far as the Serpent's Eye is concerned, he's very much the loser. The emeralds were his own personal property, so the only person he'd be robbing would be himself. I can't make head or tail of it. If the real emeralds were stolen and false ones deposited in Houblyns, then they'd have had to be stolen twelve years ago, long before this current series of thefts. There's never been a whisper of stones of that quality coming on to the market, and I honestly think we'd have got to hear something. They could have been cut up into smaller gems but their value lies in the fact they're large, perfectly matched, and very nearly flawless. Any thief would be loath to shave thousands off the value by cutting them." He sighed. "Twelve years! How the devil do you investigate a theft that's twelve years old?"

"Twelve years," repeated Superintendent Brenzett. "The man who deposited them, this President Ramon, our man's father. What was he doing twelve years ago?"

Sir Douglas flicked open the file in front of him. "He was the guest of the Eldons at Farholt, in Surrey. Farholt was famous as a meeting-place for politicians, both British and foreign."

Brenzett glanced up. "Farholt? That's a name to take you back. I haven't heard it mentioned since before the war."

"You wouldn't have done. Eldon died about eight years ago and his wife outlasted him by a matter of months. Their only child, a son, had a very unsatisfactory reputation, but joined up at the start of the war and was listed as missing, believed killed, just over a year later. The estate went to a cousin, a man called Herriad. He has no interest in politics but twelve years ago Farholt was at the centre of public affairs. Directly before he deposited the emeralds, President Ramon was the principal guest at a very illustrious house-party." Sir Douglas looked again at the file. "I've got the names of his fellow guests. There's two cabinet ministers, four City bankers, including Houblyn himself, and a host of lesser luminaries. It was probably what happened at the house-party that made him decide to deposit the stones. There was an attempted robbery which ended in the murder of one of Ramon's right-hand men." He tapped the file. "The details are all here. The man suspected of the murder escaped and technically the case remains open." He glanced at his colleague. "What is it?"

"I was just thinking, sir," said Brenzett slowly. "*If* the real jewels never got to Houblyn's in the first place, then the obvious place for them to be taken was at Farholt. If that's the case, then I suppose they're long gone, but..." He pulled at his pipe, sending out a cloud of aromatic

31

smoke. "This man, this President Enrique - what's he doing now?"

A grim smile touched the corners of Sir Douglas's mouth. "There's a slight air of mystery about that. Sir Dennis Storwood took me to one side at the club last night. Why on earth the man couldn't come and see me openly is anyone's guess. Sir Dennis is worried about President Enrique. He finds matter, as he put it, for grave concern. As a director of Houblyns, I don't think his concern is completely altruistic, because the scandal has hurt them badly, but, to be fair, he has a point. To put it bluntly, there's a good few people in this world who wouldn't mind if President Enrique was an item in the obituary column. Officially, the President, who's a young man with a passion for sport, will shortly travel to Scotland as a guest of General Duridge at the General's estate on Loch Skail. Unofficially, as far as I could follow Sir Dennis, he seems to be going to Farholt."

Brenzett cocked a reflective eyebrow. "So the President himself is on the trail of his emeralds? There can't be any other reason for him to pay a visit to Farholt."

"It looks like it." Sir Douglas drummed his fingers on the desk. "I hadn't made the connection between Farholt and the robbery myself, but I was working on the premise that the emeralds had been taken from Houblyns. Mind you, by the time Storwood had finished buzzing down my ear I couldn't make out where President Artiaga was going. He seems to be attempting to be in two places at once, which is a good trick even for a politician, but there was one fact of which I was left in no doubt; if anything happens to him, it'll be our fault. Whether that's in Scotland or Surrey is up to us to guess."

"But how can we protect him if we don't know where he is?"

The grim smile widened. "We can't, so the obvious step is to put a man in both locations, and hope that one of them, at least, is correct. According to Dennis Storwood, the President doesn't take kindly to being followed, so it'll have to be done discreetly, which rules out staying in the house. Now, strictly speaking, you're in charge of locating the missing emeralds, but if you really think there's a chance you might pick up a clue at Farholt, then you could take on the job of looking after the President, if he's there. I was thinking of sending Hill, but two strangers would stand out in a place like Farholt. It's only a small village."

Brenzett sucked at his pipe once more. "Especially if both strangers are policemen. It's hard not to talk shop, however careful you try to be. I'll tackle this by myself, sir." He shook his head. "Twelve years! It's a long shot."

*** *** ***

Andrew Herriad, showing considerable nimbleness for one who would be fifty-six next birthday, jumped back into the doorway of the billiard room, but it was too late. Sir Dennis Storwood, C.M.G., who, in Herriad's opinion, fully lived up to the traditional reading of those initials ("Call Me God") had sighted his prey and was bearing down.

"Herriad!" he boomed, leaving his unfortunate quarry no chance of escape.

Herriad forced a smile. "Storwood, old chap. Nice to see you. How's things?"

Storwood's face took on the aspect of a doleful hippopotamus. "Dreadful. This appalling scandal has broken on us unannounced. Unannounced, I say! If we could only have had some notice of the impending crisis, then measures could have been taken...."

"Avenues found," muttered Herriad, who knew the language.

"And an incident averted. But, Herriad, although it grieves me to say it, I have no hesitation in stating that it has found us entirely unprepared. I may freely say that His Majesty's Government has the utmost confidence in the President's ability to rule Salvatierra in a way that will promote British interests in the region. Few, if any, would find fault with his policies both at home and abroad, but in this particular instance he has acted with a lamentable lack of discretion. By revealing the story to the Press he has caused grave embarrassment and run the risk of antagonising those elements, both financial and diplomatic, which he intended to ameliorate..."

"Storwood," broke in Herriad. "What the dickens are you talking about?"

Dennis Storwood drew back. "Why, this affair at Houblyns, man. You must have seen the newspapers."

"What, the big bank robbery? What on earth's that got to do with you? Or me, for that matter?"

34

Sir Dennis tapped Herriad on the chest. "It's a question of confidence. This could undermine trust in the leading British financial institutions with consequences that are potentially disastrous. Although you have never shown any taste for public life, Herriad, I felt confident in assuring the Minister that you would do everything in your power to help assuage the situation."

Andrew Herriad was frankly baffled. "What on earth can I do?" Light dawned. "Hang on a minute. Aren't you one of the big bugs at Houblyns?"

Sir Dennis inclined his head. "Although I would not describe myself in precisely those terms, I have that honour, yes."

"Bad luck, Storwood. I heard the City was having kittens over it, and I can't help but feel sorry for this bloke who's had his diamonds -"

"Emeralds."

"Emeralds pinched, then, but I'm dashed if I can see where I fit in. I haven't got any to give him."

Sir Dennis shook his head gravely. "This is no time for pleasantries. Have you never felt, Herriad, that the ownership of Farholt was given to you in trust?"

"In trust? What the dickens d'you mean? I inherited the place outright. There's never been any mention of a trust."

"Not a legal trust, perhaps," said Storwood portentously. "But a moral trust, certainly."

"What?"

"In trust for the nation," said Sir Dennis, so impressively that Herriad had to fight down an urge to giggle. "A great house, once at the very forefront of our civic life, has been shamefully neglected..."

"I'm damned if it has!"

"And here, at last, is a chance for you to prove worthy of the responsibility that your cousin laid on your shoulders when you inherited Farholt."

"Now hold on a minute," said Herriad, alarmed. "I can see where this is going. I'm blowed if I'm going to run Farholt as a sort of three-ring circus for a lot of blasted politicians who fancy a free weekend in the country. The Eldons enjoyed that sort of thing. I don't. And as for having a responsibility laid on my shoulders, it's a lot of nonsense and you know it."

Sir Dennis breathed deeply. "Perhaps if I were to tell you...." He leaned closer and whispered in Herriad's ear.

Herriad looked at him in astonishment. "You want what? *Why* does this wretched dago think anything of the sort?"

"The use of the term "dago" is, in the present circumstances, one I utterly deplore," said Sir Dennis with a look of outrage. "The President is a young man who, educated in England, has British interests firmly at heart. Besides..." He drew close and whispered again.

"So who is it you want me to invite to Farholt? Is it the President or is it this other feller?"

"I am not at liberty to say."

Herriad shook his head. "No, Storwood. I'm blessed if I'm going to butter up some South American Joe from a banana republic, no matter how pro-British he is."

"I will, of course, be present myself, and Eleanor will accompany me."

"Eleanor, eh?" For the first time, Herriad's face brightened. How on earth a lovely woman like Eleanor Redgrave had come to marry a pompous ass like Storwood, was, in his opinion, one of the great unsolved mysteries of the age.

Storwood firmly attached himself to his unwilling companion's arm. "I think, Herriad, we need to discuss this further over a drink. I happen to know the club possesses some remarkable pre-war whisky upon which I should value your opinion."

Herriad allowed himself to be led. He always found it difficult not to be led when Dennis Storwood was at his most adhesive, however apprehensive he may feel about the consequences.

At breakfast the next morning, while telling his daughter she would have to prepare for a house-party, he ruefully admitted he had underestimated Sir Dennis's powers of diplomacy.

***   ***   ***

"Aunt Daphne!"

Daphne Marston, trowel in hand, looked up from the box of tiny plants she was transferring into a large tub. "Over here, dear! By the candle-tree," she added, seeing that Sandy still hadn't spotted her. She smiled affectionately. She was fond of her niece, whilst disapproving of her short skirts, bobbed hair, cigarettes and what she distantly referred to as "Jazzing". In her day, as she was wont to say, young girls were content to stay at home under the careful supervision of their parents.

Despite herself, she smiled. The parent in question, her brother Andrew, was amiable, kind-hearted, self-centred and a million miles away from her stern ideal of the responsible father. If anything, Sandy looked after him, rather than the other way about. It wasn't, Daphne Marston reflected, right. The fact that it worked was simply an example of the irritating way in which facts ran contrary to principles.

Sandy Herriad walked through the conservatory, dodged an overhanging palm and stooped down beside her aunt. "What are you planting?"

"Daisies," said Aunt Daphne, getting to her feet, wincing slightly as what she always referred to as "My knee" registered a protest. "African daisies. Star of the Veldt. They're just about ready for pricking out. They should make the most glorious splash of orange here, with the candle-tree for a backdrop. I'm glad to say that the pelargoniums really seem to be coming to something this year."

She looked critically at the conservatory. "Ideally I would like to move the candle-tree and open up this whole corner, but I don't think it would take kindly to transplanting. I do wish the Eldons had thought more about where things should be sited and what sort of height and spread could be expected. It takes all the afternoon sun and would be far better at the other end of the house but, really, the thought of asking Hutchens to move the whole thing bodily is not on."

"I should say so," muttered Sandy, looking at the huge pot encased in ornamental stone. "You'd need a steam-roller to make much impression on that. I rather like it where it is actually. It makes a sheltered corner if you want to slip out after dinner. I know Dad hides here. I'm always finding his cigar ends."

"Yes," agreed Aunt Daphne grimly. Andrew Herriad's habit of using her plant-pots for ashtrays was one of his less endearing characteristics. "Was there anything you wanted, dear?" she added, her eyes straying back to her unplanted daisies, "because..."

"I've come to ask you about the final arrangements for the guest rooms. Sir Dennis and Lady Storwood will have the Amber Rooms, of course, and Tommy Leigh and what I may call the rest of the Storwood people aren't any problem, together with Dad's friends, but I don't know what to do about this Philip Brown. I'm not quite sure where he fits in."

"If you ask me there's something mysterious about Mr Brown," said Aunt Daphne, darkly. "*I* suggested to Andrew that as he's only a bachelor and secretary to this South American man, the end second floor back would be good enough, but it won't do. Your father said to put him in the Blue Room."

"Gosh," said Sandy, impressed. "That's like having your name in lights, isn't it? Private secretaries don't usually get that sort of lavish treatment."

"*If* that's what he is. However, Andrew thought it was a good idea, so we'd better go along with it. Apparently he's here to thresh out the ground-work for some deal

39

with Matherson, the banker, so it could be that he's more important than we've been led to believe."

"He may be the real thing, of course," said Sandy. "A proper secretary, I mean, not like poor old Tommy. I do wish Tommy would stop playing at work and get a real job. Sir Dennis treats him like an absolute slave and Tommy just puts up with it. If he could only get a chance..."

"How much of a chance does he want?" demanded Aunt Daphne. "He must be well over thirty.. "

"He's thirty-two," said Sandy defensively. She was very fond of Tommy Leigh.

"Well, however old he is, if a man hasn't got a settled career at his age, there's something not quite right. It shows a fundamental lack of purpose. I do know what I'm talking about, Alexandra. I remember crying myself to sleep because my father refused to agree to my engagement to a young man whom he said was unsuitable, but he was quite right. Then, fortunately, I met Edgar who was suitable in every way, despite being so much older than I was." She flicked a piece of earth off the trowel with her thumb. "It's about time you got married, you know. I said as much to your father the other night."

"I..." Sandy hunted for words but couldn't find them.

"If you ask me," continued Aunt Daphne, "you had too much excitement in the war. A nurse's training may be useful but..."

"There's not much I don't know about mopping floors and washing dishes," offered Sandy with the beginnings of a smile. "That wasn't desperately exciting."

"That isn't what I meant and you know it. If all you'd done was domestic service I wouldn't have any fault to find. It sounds a perfectly satisfactory grounding in the training necessary for running a household. But to take a young girl and to put her in a hospital..."

"A Casualty Clearing Station," Sandy amended.

"Whatever you call it, right at the front, where she cannot help but mix with all sorts of people is not my idea of a proper start in life."

"Oh, Aunty, we were very carefully segregated, you know. Any social mixing was very much frowned on."

"I'm glad to hear it. However, I still maintain that so much disruption and excitement at an early age is not good for any girl, or any young man, either, come to that. Since the war everyone seems so *restless*. When I was your age I would have no sooner thought of going up to London unaccompanied than I would of flying to the moon."

"You were married when you were my age, weren't you? And weren't you living with Uncle Edgar in Delhi or somewhere?"

"That only proves my point," said Aunt Daphne. "I was settled with responsibilities."

Sandy suddenly grinned. "Well, I've got the responsibility of looking after Dad. You're a dear, Aunt Daphne. I know you're only talking like this because you're worried about me, but honestly, I'm not going to

41

jump off the deep end and run away with someone I don't know from Adam, no matter how many times I go up to London. Even I want to know something more about a man than the fact they're a good dancer."

"I should hope so. Did you say the Storwoods are in the Amber Rooms?" She hesitated. "I hope Lady Storwood will be comfortable there. I must say, I never feel entirely at ease in her presence."

"She's too slinky for words," agreed Sandy. "I'd love to know what she spends on her dresses. She must cost poor old Sir Dennis a fortune."

Daphne Marston was mildly shocked. "Really, Alexandra, that is not a subject on which I feel you should speculate. Naturally, Sir Dennis would expect his wife to be adequately clad."

"There are limits."

"And being Sir Dennis, he would be most generous."

"You always did like him, didn't you, Aunty?" said Sandy, shrewdly.

"I admire his work. He reminds me of dear Edgar." She sighed. "I do wish I could get Andrew to take more of an interest in public affairs."

Sandy grinned. "Dad would hate it. He's no Dennis Storwood, Aunt Daphne, and you can't turn him into one. What shall I do about this Mr Brown? Shall I put him in the Blue Room?"

"If that's what Andrew suggested, you better had." Daphne Marston seemed grateful for the return to practicalities. "At least we're not faced with President Artiaga. That would mean opening up the West room. I

42

know the bed is supposed to have been slept in by Charles II, but I *cannot* think it's comfortable and all that carved wood and linen-fold panelling is so gloomy and harbours dust dreadfully."

"The Blue Room it is then," said Sandy cheerfully. "I'll arrange that, then I'm going to cycle into the village after lunch. Tommy should be the first of the guests to arrive, but I'm not expecting him till after four o' clock, which should give me plenty of time."

"Well, don't be late," said her aunt, frowning at the daises. "I would like some help at the tea-table."

*** *** ***

It was just on half-past three when Sandy toiled up the final stretch of the road on her bicycle out of the village. Remnants of Aunt Daphne's conversation had stayed with her all afternoon.

There was something absent from her life. She didn't want the war back - who could? - but she did miss the sense of purpose. She'd enjoyed nursing. There had been something very satisfying about having a definite job to do, and doing it well. Friends, too. You got close to people in a way you simply didn't at home. And yes, there was an excitement missing that no amount of fun could replace.

Farholt, of which she had dreamed of while in France, seemed... Well, dull. It's not really dull, she thought, it's me. I've got outside and I can't get back in again. Yet the country, the untroubled landscape of field and wood, bearing witness to thousands of years of patient labour of ploughing, sowing and reaping, hadn't changed. It's

43

peaceful, wonderfully peaceful, but it's a peace I can see but can't share.

She shook her head impatiently. Three hundred years ago this landscape hadn't been so peaceful. Farholt had held out for the King in the Civil War, and suffered as a result. And this very road she was on, The Switchback, as Farholt Road was known to everyone who lived in the village, was a Roman road which, regardless of contours, cut through the landscape like a sword-slash. That could neither have been conceived or constructed in peace. I want, she thought, something to *do*.

I want, she thought, as the last hundred yards defeated her, to get off this wretched hill.

Panting, she slipped off her bike and wheeling it up to the crest, stood for a few minutes to get her breath back.

This was, perhaps, her favourite view of all. Beneath her the road dropped away in an exhilarating swoop to the valley below. On this glorious day in early May the beech and oak woods which fringed the Farholt estate were a mass of delicate green and between the trees lay a carpet of ruffled blue shadow from the bluebells.

On the other side of the road the land stood open, a waving mass of green wheat, gently rolling away down the slope of the hill. At the bottom of the hill a white line snaked through the fields marking the footpath to Brosley Dean, where the train station was. Made by wandering Britons instead of marching Romans, the path curled out of sight, but its end was marked by a puff of smoke from a distant train.

A man, small in the distance, was standing by the footpath gate, holding a large piece of paper in his hands. A walker, presumably, consulting a map. Sandy, with the thought of the house-party before her, briefly envied him his freedom, then thought of Tommy Leigh and smiled.

A far-off hoot from the train made her glance at her watch and she guiltily re-mounted her bicycle. The London train had been due in at five past three, and although they weren't expecting anyone by it, there was just a chance that some early guests may even now be arriving at the house. She glanced down the road and froze.

A car had turned out of the road beyond the footpath and was now driving along the bottom of the valley. The walker had stuffed his map into his pocket and had stepped off the side of the wide verge. The car - it may have been a trick of vision for everything seemed to be moving horribly slowly - seemed to bear down deliberately upon him. At the last moment, the walker realised his danger and started back, but the car caught him and he was flung into the air. For a breathless fraction of a second he hung there, then with a thud that made Sandy gasp, crashed down onto the road. The car, unable to stop, hit him once more then, with an outraged squealing of brakes, slewed to a halt.

Sandy, feeling as if she was going to be horribly sick, leapt on her bicycle and hurtled down the hill.

Chapter Three

Her mad race down the hill brought her to the side of the crumpled man before the driver had time to get out of the car. Flinging her bicycle to one side, Sandy knelt on the road beside him. His forehead was deeply gashed and his face smeared with grit, but the blood was still welling from the wound. She gave a huge sigh of relief and reached out to touch his hand. The skin, under the hard calluses on the palm, was clammy and cold.

There was a footstep behind her. "Have I... Have I... Is he dead?"

She glanced up to see the driver of the car, a large, amiable, loose-limbed young man, his normally good-natured face contorted with apprehension. She drew in a sharp breath. "Tommy! Did you knock him over?"

Tommy Leigh nodded miserably and sunk to the ground beside Sandy and the man. "I simply didn't see him," he said wretchedly. "Then, when I did, it was too late. Is he...?" He paused, unable to say the word *dead*.

"No," said Sandy decisively. That head-wound needed bandaging right away. She felt in the pocket of her dress for a handkerchief. All she had was a small linen square. That was no use as a bandage. "Tommy, give me your handkerchief. A clean one."

He didn't move. "You're taking this very calmly."

He's suffering from shock, Sandy decided briskly, all her professional training coming to the fore. "I need your handkerchief, Tommy," she repeated, keeping her voice level.

He shook himself, gulped, and fumbling in his pockets, pulled out a large square of white cotton. "Will this do?"

"Not bad," she said, taking the hanky and tying it into a neat bandage round the man's head. "We need some pressure on this. Can you hold it here?"

Tommy gingerly reached out but his hands fumbled and the man groaned.

"Never mind," said Sandy quickly. "Leave it to me. Tommy, have you got a rug in the car? He'll need to be kept warm."

"I'll go and get one," he said but didn't move. Sandy bit her lip in frustration. The man's pulse was jumping under her fingers and he was lying very awkwardly. He definitely had a broken leg and there were likely to be other injuries as well. They needed a doctor as soon as possible but Tommy was obviously too shaken up to drive.

"Shouldn't we get him to a doctor?" asked Tommy, imperfectly echoing her thoughts. "If you took his legs, I could manage his body and we could get him in the car."

"No," Sandy said, speaking far more sharply than she intended to. "He'll need a stretcher to move him properly. "You'll have to stay with him while I take the car."

She looked up as the sound of another car broke in on them. She stretched out a hand to wave it down, but the red two-seater was already slowing to a halt. A dark-haired young man drew into the side and jumped out.

"Has there been an accident? Can I help?"

"Please," said Sandy quickly. "Can you take me to Farholt? We need a doctor right away."

"The house or the village?"

"It'd better be the house."

She broke off as the man in the road stirred. She turned to him once more, feeling his hand move in hers as his eyes fluttered open.

"Farholt," he said in a whisper. "Farholt."

Sandy felt his hand tighten. "Go on," she encouraged. "I'm from Farholt."

She saw his grey eyes, intelligent and alert, focus on her. "He didn't mean banks," he said, quite clearly. He had a clear, cultured voice. "He meant banks..." He moved feebly and coughed.

Sandy supported his shoulders, slipping the folded-up jacket which the stranger had given her under his head. The action was so unobtrusive, yet so helpful, she suddenly felt as if she no longer had to cope alone. "Sea air. You see? Buried in the..." He coughed once more.

"Quiet now," soothed Sandy. "Don't try to talk."

"No!" Even when weak his voice had a note of authority. "Count. Didn't mean banks..." His eyelids flickered and shut.

"He's still alive," said Sandy, feeling for the pulse once more. "We've got to get help. Tommy, you stay here."

Tommy Leigh shied away from the injured man. "What was he talking about?" he asked in a dazed voice. "He sounded delirious to me."

"Oh, goodness knows," said Sandy impatiently. "Do look after him, Tommy. I'll drive up to the house with Mr..?" She hesitated.

"Brown. Philip Brown."

Philip Brown? Sandy registered the name mechanically. This was President Artiaga's secretary.

He brought a rug from the back of the car and helped her put it over the man before walking quickly back to the driver's side of the car. "Jump in. We'll be as quick as we can, but you'll have to show me the way. I've never been in this neck of the woods before."

He gave her a quick, encouraging smile, and she felt an overwhelming sense of relief. She was tabulating in her mind what she would have to tell the doctor - pulse rate, obvious signs of haemorrhage and shock, visible injuries - but in the middle of all her anxiety the irrelevant knowledge registered that Philip Brown had a friendly smile and the most brilliant blue eyes.

"You'll have to turn the car," she said, forcing down these wayward thoughts, "and then it's the first road on the left."

"Right-oh," he said, slipping in the clutch. "I hope that poor bloke's going to be all right," he called over the sound of the engine.

Sandy bit her lip. "I don't think he's got much of a chance. I saw it happen."

"I say, did you? Are you okay? It never occurred to me to ask. You seemed to know what you were doing, so I left you to it." He spared her a swift glance. "Have you done this sort of thing before?"

49

"I was a nurse in the war," she explained. "I'll be all right until it's all over, I expect. Poor Tommy's really skittled out. He's not usually so helpless as he appeared just then."

"No? He looked as if he could do with a stiff drink." They were approaching the entrance to the house. "Is this Farholt?"

"Yes. Sorry, I should have said. I'll get out and open the gates. That'll save some time. Now," she said breathlessly as she scrambled back in. "Go like mad." She sat back and managed a small smile as they tore up the drive. "I'm Alexandra Herriad."

"Pleased to meet you," he muttered mechanically, bringing the car to a halt amidst a spray of gravel in front of the house.

They raced up the steps. Leaving Philip Brown to explain things to the butler, who was approaching the front door as they burst in, Sandy raced for the telephone in the hall.

Doctor Hayle was out on his rounds, but Jessie Banks, who manned the exchange from the post office in the High Street, helpfully and quite improperly, cut in on Sandy's conversation with Mrs Hayle. "He's at Miss Kitchener's, Miss. I've been watching out of the window here and I saw him go in. Shall I put you through to her house?"

A pause followed, then a brief few words, before Sandy put down the phone in relief, turning to Philip Brown and Larch, who were listening anxiously nearby.

"Dr Hayle's going to meet us out on the road," she said. "Thank God I managed to get hold of him."

"Would you like a cup of tea, Miss Sandy?" asked Larch, the butler, in concern. "I've just heard what's happened from this gentleman."

She flashed him a smile and brushed the hair back from her forehead. "No, thanks. I need to get back. Can you tell Aunt Daphne and Daddy what's happened? I expect we'll have to bring the poor man here." She glanced around the hall. "I think the sofa in the gun-room would be the most suitable place. Can you make sure it's clear, Larch? Thank you."

They drove back at a slightly less reckless pace than they had come. Intent on the road, Philip said nothing, and Sandy felt herself watching him. He was broad-shouldered with a firm chin and a profile saved from perfection by a small chip of a scar under his left eye. A smaller man than Tommy Leigh, there was a grace about him that Tommy lacked. Poor Tommy! He had been hit for six by the accident. Thank goodness this man had turned up. She had no hesitation about sharing the responsibility with him. As if aware of her scrutiny, he turned and gave her a sudden smile.

"Not long now."

Sandy, seeing those brilliant blue eyes once more, was suddenly aware that she liked him very much. They were *exciting* eyes - there was that word again - that seemed to invite challenge and risk. Did she want risk? She suddenly felt herself drawing back. She had relied upon him instinctively. Whether anyone with those dangerously exciting eyes could ever be wholly safe was quite a different matter.

Tommy's white face was clear from the moment they turned the corner onto Farholt Road. He had been sitting beside the man's body on the side of the verge, and as the car drew near, he got up and walked towards them.

"I'm afraid it's going to be all over soon," he said gravely, leaning on the car. "Poor bloke. He didn't say anything else, just gave a sort of gasp."

He reached out and restrained her as she made to climb out. "There's nothing more for you to do. God, I feel awful." His hand found hers. "To think that I... I..."

Philip had climbed out of the car and knelt beside the man. He looked up and shook his head. "I'm sorry," he said softly. "He's dead."

Tommy Leigh gave a wretching gasp. Sandy wondered if he was going to be sick. "Dead?" he muttered. "He can't be. He wasn't. He isn't, I tell you."

"Let me get you back to the house," said Sandy practically. "You look in a real state, Tommy." She raised herself in the car and slid across to the driver's side. "Mr Brown!" she called. "I'm going to drive back to Farholt. Will you stay here until Dr Hayle arrives?"

"Will do," answered Philip, settling down.

It was a sombre drive back to the house.

***　　***　　***

The gun-room bore all signs of having been hastily prepared for the patient. Andrew Herriad had been cleaning a shotgun when Larch had told him the news, and the massive oak table was heaped with old newspaper, oily rags, brushes, quills and bits of disassembled gun, thrust to one side to make a clear space for Doctor Hayle's things. The sofa lay ready with clean sheets, pillows and blankets. As Sandy and Tommy walked into the room, Aunt Daphne and Andrew Herriad rose to meet them.

"Oh, my dear," said Aunt Daphne, taking Sandy by the hands. "What a mercy you were there. I take back everything I said about nursing. Where's the poor man now?"

"He's still on the road. Mr Brown - the Mr Brown who's coming here - is with him." She hesitated and cast a brief glance at Tommy. "I think it may be too late."

"He's alive," insisted Tommy with weary persistence. "At least he was when I left him."

"You need a drink, man," said Herriad, with a sympathetic glance at Tommy. "Here, sit down and have this." He poured a generous measure of brandy into a glass from the decanter on the table and gave it to Tommy neat.

Tommy gulped it, coughing. "Thanks. He seemed to come from nowhere," he repeated plaintively. "I simply didn't see him."

"Do you want a drink, Sandy?" asked her father.

Sandy shook her head. "No. I want to have my wits about me for when Dr Hayle arrives. He might need my help." She looked up as the sound of car tyres scrunching on the gravel outside came through the open window. "Oh, blast! It isn't him, it's the Storwoods. Hell!"

53

"Alexandra!" said Aunt Daphne, shocked, but her niece was already at the door. Daphne Marston sighed and followed her.

"We'll have to tell them," said Sandy, on her way through the hall. "They'll need to know why the place is at sixes and sevens, and Sir Dennis always wants to organize everything. Thank goodness Lady Storwood's here as well. She might manage to choke him off."

Sandy ran lightly down the steps to the car. "Hello! Look, I'm awfully sorry, but there's been an accident. Not one of us. It's a poor man out on the road. The doctor should be bringing him here any minute now. We're all gathered in the gun-room waiting for them."

Eleanor Storwood, dressed in an exquisite travelling outfit of well-cut grey, stopped in the act of getting out of the Lanchester. "An accident?" She turned her head as the doctor's car, containing Doctor Hayle and Philip Brown came up the drive.

Sandy looked a question at Philip as he opened the door of the car, but he shook his head.

"It's all over, I'm afraid."

Doctor Hayle got out the car. "Hello, Miss Herriad. I'm sorry, but it was too late by the time I arrived. There was nothing left for me to do." He rubbed a hand through his thinning hair. "I've sent the body off to the hospital. I'll have to call there later, and I suppose the police better be informed. Mr Brown here tells me you saw what happened."

"Yes," said Sandy. She felt curiously empty. "It was horrible."

54

The doctor looked at her critically. "You look shaken up. Can we go into the house? I could do with getting some details. Did you recognize the man?"

"I've never seen him before." She led the way back into the gun-room. "He was a complete stranger," she added. "I assumed he was on a walking-tour. He had a map with him, so he might have booked in at the pub in the village."

They went into the gun-room. Sandy drew out a chair and sat down heavily. "I'll have that drink now, Dad, if you don't mind."

"I think we'd all be better off for something," agreed Herriad.

Sandy put her hand to her mouth. "I keep thinking there was more I could have done."

"I doubt it," said Doctor Hayle, reassuringly. He waved away the offer of whisky. "Nothing for me, thank you. I've still got work to do."

Eleanor Storwood glanced round the room and fixed on the unfortunate Tommy, nursing his brandy. "Mr Leigh! Were *you* responsible?" Tommy nodded. "What happened?"

"I can't really tell you, Lady Storwood," said Tommy, unsteadily.

"How fast were you going?"

Tommy shrugged. "Twenty - maybe a bit more. I don't honestly know." He looked round the room. "The road looked absolutely clear. I could have sworn it was clear. I don't think I was speeding. I'm sure I wasn't speeding."

"I have had occasion to speak to you before, Leigh," began Sir Dennis, but his wife waved him silent.

"Do be quiet, Dennis. This is no time for blaming anyone."

"Sandy knows what happened," put in Tommy defensively. "She had a ring-side seat from the top of the hill. She saw everything, didn't you, Sandy? You can tell everyone I wasn't speeding."

"Well, I..." began Sandy, then broke off.

Philip Brown had moved unobtrusively to stand beside her. "Can I refill your glass, Miss Herriad? 'Scuse me offering you a drink in your own house, but you've had a nasty shock."

She tried a smile. "That's all right. No, no more for me, thank you, but I'd like a cigarette." He produced his case and she took one, leaning forward as he lit it for her.

"What did happen?" he asked. "Don't talk about it if you'd rather not."

Sandy tried to smile again. "I'm okay really. It's just that it was all a bit of a shock. I was geared up for it in France but it's different here."

"I know exactly what you mean," said Philip softly.

She looked at him gratefully, then frowned. "I've been trying to put it all into order. I'd been into the village. As it's such a lovely day, I cycled in rather than take the car. I wanted to see a friend of mine, Edith Peverell, about a tennis party the Grant-Temperleys are organizing. I had an eye on the time as I'd promised Aunt Daphne I'd be home before anyone arrived."

56

As carefully as she could, she recounted the details of the accident. "I... I know you said you weren't speeding, Tommy, and really, it's hard to be sure, because everything seemed to happen so slowly, but you seemed to accelerate towards him on purpose."

"I didn't!" said Tommy indignantly.

"Yes, I know you didn't, but that's what it looked like. Then - it was horrible - the man seemed to realise his danger and leapt back, but the front passenger side of the car caught him. He was flung into the air and thudded down again. You swerved..."

"I was trying to miss him."

"I know *that*, Tommy, but what actually happened was that you ran over him again. You stopped the car, of course, and I shot down the hill on my bike." She looked at Doctor Hayle. "I didn't honestly think he had much of a chance, but he was still alive. I knew there was no hope unless he saw a doctor as soon as possible. Then, fortunately, Mr Brown arrived and helped me get a rug round him. He drove me to the house..."

"Hang on a minute," said Philip. "You're missing out all the stuff the chap said."

"He *spoke*?" asked Doctor Hayle.

Sandy looked at him. "Yes."

"But..." The doctor stopped, then shrugged. "It's just that with those injuries I'm surprised to find he wasn't killed outright. I certainly wouldn't have expected him to be able to speak. Was he rational?"

"More or less," replied Sandy, but Tommy interrupted her.

"No, he wasn't, not really. He was talking about sea air and things. That didn't sound very rational, did it?"

"What did he say?" asked the doctor, practically.

"Well..." Sandy frowned once more. "I'd mentioned Farholt - I'd asked Mr Brown to drive me to Farholt - and that seemed to stir the poor man. He repeated the name "Farholt" and I can't quite remember what he said after that. It was something about banks and counting."

The doctor tried to make sense of this. "Maybe he worked in a bank?" he offered.

"That's not quite right, Miss Herriad," said Philip. "As I recall, he said the name "Farholt" and you held his hand and told him that's where you were from."

"Yes," said Sandy slowly. "It's all coming back to me. I was holding his hand and it struck me that his voice sounded odd. That's it. It was an educated voice, if you know what I mean, with authority in it."

"A gentleman's voice?" asked her father.

"Yes, I suppose it was. But his hands weren't the sort of hands you'd expect to go with the voice. They were all rough and hard, like a workman's hands. When he spoke, it startled me. I'd been expecting an accent, I suppose, a Cockney accent, as I'd assumed he'd got off the London train. Come to think of it, his clothes were wrong for a workman's clothes, but it's hard to tell sometimes, isn't it? His eyes, too. He looked at me.... oh dear, this is difficult to explain, but he looked at me as if I were an equal. His hands didn't fit his voice or the way he looked at me."

"What did he say?" asked her father. "Farholt"?"

"Yes, that's right. I don't think he knew the house, though - he might have meant the village, of course - because he'd been looking at his map, but the name certainly stirred him. Then he started talking about banks."

Philip shut his eyes, concentrating. *"He didn't mean banks*. That's what the chap said. "He didn't mean banks." Then he contradicted himself and said "He meant banks"."

Everyone in the room looked at each other. "It doesn't sound particularly rational," said Andrew Herriad. "The poor man was obviously wandering." He looked at his daughter. "He mentioned counting, you say?"

"Well, he actually said "count". And then there was something about being buried."

"Being *buried*?"

"Yes, in the sea air."

Andrew Herriad shook his head. "He sounds a bit rocky to me, Sandy." He glanced at Philip Brown who had suddenly opened his eyes very wide and drawn his shoulders back. "Yes? You looked as if you were about to say something."

Philip gave a deprecating grin. "Sorry. It's nothing really. Just an idea about what the poor bloke said. I don't suppose for a minute I'm right. Forget it."

Sandy gave him a quick glance. *What the poor bloke said*. Was that it? She shook her head impatiently. No, that didn't seem to fit. Something, somewhere had jarred and she couldn't pin down what it was. Something that wasn't quite right... Was it to do with Mr Brown? Maybe it would come to her later. She dismissed the thought and turned her attention to Doctor Hayle.

The doctor was frowning. "I'm still surprised that he said anything at all. *Sea air.* I suppose he could want to be buried at sea, but I must say it doesn't sound very convincing."

"He sounded rational," said Sandy, defensively. "I thought he was trying to tell me something, not just mumbling nonsense."

"I had that impression," put in Philip. "As if what he was saying was very clear to him and he simply didn't have the strength to get it across."

The doctor put down his glass. "Well, what he actually meant is anyone's guess." He looked at Andrew Herriad. "I'd better be off. I'm sorry I wasn't in time to see the man alive, but I can hardly credit he lingered as long as he did."

Tommy Leigh licked his dry lips. "I hope you realise how truly awful I feel about this. I'd give anything to have missed the poor bloke. Will there... D'you think there'll be a charge?"

"That's for the inquest to decide," said Doctor Hayle stiffly, then, seeing Tommy's look of patent suffering, relented. "Have you ever been involved in anything like this before? No? Then I really think that you'll have nothing more than censure to face. You may very well be prohibited from driving for a time."

"I never want to sit behind the wheel of a car again."

Doctor Hayle glanced at him again, but Tommy's look of acute misery didn't lighten. "Cheer up, man. It was an accident."

"I'll never forget it," said Tommy with a shudder. "I can't do anything about it now, I suppose, but I wish I could."

Doctor Hayle clapped a hand upon his shoulder. "That's something we can all say at some time during our lives." He looked at Andrew Herriad once more. "I really must be going. There'll have to be an inquest, of course, and I imagine the police will want to talk to various people, but there should be nothing to worry about."

"You're still coming to dinner this evening?" asked Herriad, walking with the doctor to the door.

"Lord, yes." He grinned. "It'd take a braver man than me to go home and tell Cynthia it's all off because some poor unknown happened to get run over. She's been looking forward to it. Eight o'clock, I believe the invitation said?"

"Oh dear," said Daphne Marston as the clock in the hall sounded. "It's half past five already. I'm afraid it's too late for tea."

***   ***   ***

The conversation at dinner that evening was rather like an exercise in controlling a moorland fire.

The locals, who included Mr Peverell the vicar, and his family, the Grant-Temperleys, Lieutenant-Colonel Waldrist, the Chief Constable, and various neighbouring worthies, wanted, naturally enough, to discuss the incendiary topics of accidents, sudden death, the growing

61

menace of the motor-car, and (this from Mrs Mortimer-Doulting who was known to have Evangelical leanings) the importance of Being Prepared. For, as she justly, if tactlessly, pointed out, it was not given to us to know when our time had come to an end and the transition to another, and hopefully better, world was at hand. Tommy Leigh was seen to writhe visibly.

The home party, like keepers provided with buckets of water, were on hand to damp the fire down and attempt to keep it in safer channels. It was a gallant but doomed attempt.

Eleanor Storwood, whose devotion to her appearance was such that she had persuaded her husband to buy a controlling share in what could be called a Health Camp but what she described as a Kurhaus ("really radical new treatments.... most marvellous new man... equilibrium in mind and body...") got a thin audience for her views on Science and Beauty. Daphne Marston fell back, as she put it to herself, on spring bulbs to restless neighbours and Andrew Herriad was unable, for once, to draw Colonel Waldrist on the subject of modern husbandry with particular reference to the care of pigs. All were tried and all failed, and still the accident remained.

No sooner would Mrs Henrietta Peverell, say, mention That Unfortunate Man This Afternoon, Daphne Marston, Sandy Herriad, or even, on at least two occasions, Eleanor Storwood, would send the intelligence hissing round the table that the unhappy perpetrator was in their midst.

It never did percolate through to Colonel Waldrist, who had a granite-like impermeability to hints. Although careful to aver that the law must be maintained, his particular theme was the superiority of the French system to the English; the lack of speed restrictions in France meant that people looked where they were going, damn it, not like our namby-pamby Government who tried to pretend everything was safe and took the responsibility away from pedestrians to look both ways before they crossed a road.

Barking this argument out at Tommy Leigh, who was sitting opposite him, he was sublimely unconscious of that young man's misery, and was later heard to refer to the unhappy Leigh as a bit of a dull stick with no go in him.

The Londoners at the table, who included James Matherson, the banker, were frankly bored. "This theft of the necklace is a shocking business," he said to Philip Brown, in an attempt to steer the conversation out of the local morass. "It's bad for Houblyns and it's unsettled the City. You were actually there when the theft was discovered, weren't you?"

"That's right," agreed Philip.

There was a rustle of interest. If it was awkward to discuss a fatal accident (and, after all, the man *was* a complete stranger) the theft of an emerald necklace as described by an actual eye-witness was a pretty good substitute.

Edith Peverell gave a little squeak of excitement. "You were *there*! How thrilling! What happened?"

"I imagine they found the necklace was gone," said Mrs Mortimer-Doulting, repressively. She had been about to air the view that to witness a man cut down in his prime was A Lesson To Us All and resented the abrupt change of topic.

Edith Peverell opened her eyes wider. "But the necklace *wasn't* gone, that was the whole point. What's President Enrique like, Mr Brown? You're his secretary, aren't you? He's meant to be ever so good-looking, isn't he?"

Philip paused. "I've heard him called good-looking but you mustn't believe everything you read in the papers, Miss Peverell."

"But I *want* to believe what I read in the papers. Things of that sort, anyway. He's not very old, is he? For someone like that, I mean."

"He's about my age," admitted Philip.

She gave Philip a penetrating stare. "D'you know, that picture they printed of him in the papers... He looks a bit like you, doesn't he?"

"Superficially, perhaps. If you saw us together you wouldn't think we were particularly alike."

"He married an actress. A real one, I mean, a Hollywood star."

"Jane Lehman."

"That's right. It was terribly romantic and awfully sad. They married in secret but it all went wrong and she went back to Hollywood without him and he's suffering from a broken heart which he cloaks under a mask of gay living."

"As I said, you mustn't believe everything you read in the papers. He's certainly married but it was never going to work. She didn't want to give up her career and

Salvatierra isn't Hollywood. It's probably better for both of them that it's virtually over."

"If he's made his bed he should lie in it," observed Mrs Mortimer-Doulting, then blushed as she saw Philip's wicked grin.

"The necklace..." said Philip, throwing her a life-line, and was interrupted by a happy sigh from Edith Peverell.

"Yes, the necklace. Do tell us about it, Mr Brown." She gave a little wriggle of pleasure. "I read in the paper that it had a *desperately* romantic story attached to it. It's called the Snakes' Eyes, isn't it?"

"Damn silly thing to call a necklace," grunted Colonel Waldrist.

Philip Brown disagreed. "Not really, sir. There's a legend that if a snake stares at an emerald it goes blind. The legend is that emeralds are actually the fossilized eyes of snakes. Most famous jewels have a name and the principal stone is called, in Spanish, *el ojo del serpiente*."

"Gosh," said Edith Peverell, completely enraptured.

"The name, the Serpent's Eye, is a pretty good description of the quite wonderful stone at the heart of the necklace. I wish - you don't know how much I wish - that I'd seen the real thing but the copy gave me a good idea. The eye of a great snake; green, unwinking, and oblivious to human emotions."

He glanced at Edith Peverell. He was, in Sandy's opinion, richly enjoying her reactions. "Unfortunately, the great stones, as well as being beautiful, are the focus of jealousy. And jealousy and greed lead to crime."

If Edith Peverell, thought Sandy, had been a great snake herself, her eyes couldn't be wider.

"And it did," breathed Edith. "Lead to crime. The sort of crime you read about..."

"In the papers?" put in Philip.

"In the magazines," corrected Edith. "It's all so wonderfully mystery-making, isn't it? Who would put a false necklace in a safe-deposit box? You don't think the President could have done it himself, do you? That's the sort of thing which happens in stories."

Philip's smile widened. "I think I can assure you that he didn't."

"It's a gang, then," said Miss Peverell definitely. "I read there was a gang after him and although he goes in constant threat of his life, he won't have any guards or anything. He must be *awfully* brave."

Sir Dennis Storwood looked rather shocked. "I believe," he said, "that these matters may be safely left in the hands of the official authorities whom you may rely on to take all proper precautions. No useful purpose can be served by idle chatter on the subject. I am glad to say though, Mr Brown, that President Artiaga has now completely exonerated Houblyns of any blame in this sorry affair."

"It's still a bit tricky," said Matherson. "While the necklace is still missing Houblyns are implicated, like it or not. The other complication is the effect the theft'll have on Salvatierra. I'm not saying we can't work round it, but..."

"It'd be a lot easier if President Enrique had the necklace in his pocket," finished Philip Brown.

"I don't understand," said Edith Peverell.

Philip smiled at her. "It's quite simple, really. This missing necklace is worth an awful lot of money. Salvatierra is a very poor country."

"It didn't used to be," put in Andrew Herriad. "When I was your age people were always popping off there to try and find gold and diamonds and things. It was one of the few places in South America that one had actually heard about. Exports, you know, and shipping and so on."

"But that was before President Ramon Artiaga was deposed." Philip finished the last of his potatoes and put down his knife and fork. "You see, from everything I've heard, President Ramon - President Enrique's father - was a good bloke."

"Splendid fellow," agreed Sir Dennis.

Philip gave him an oddly wistful glance. "Did you ever meet him, Sir Dennis?"

"I'm afraid I never had that honour, but his reputation was very sound."

"I see...." Philip shook himself. "Well, one of the things he was keen on was to try and put the economy of Salvatierra on a sound footing. He opened up a lot of the interior to farming, and tried to develop mining and quarrying on modern, scientific lines. There's a lot of copper and other minerals in Salvatierra which could be very profitable. However, where he went wrong was in making a choice lot of enemies. For the last couple of centuries the country had been run by a handful of men who owned most of the land and the mineral rights. Ramon wanted to put the money back into the country, but that didn't suit the landowners. Once the peasants got richer, they argued, then the more likely they were to refuse to work at starvation wages for them. The big landowners, with some justice, saw President Ramon as a threat, and decided he should be removed."

"How?" asked Eleanor Storwood, sharply.

"They started a revolution themselves. Very quietly to begin with and nothing to ring any alarm bells. They formed a new political party, the Haciendistas. President Ramon had guaranteed the right to form new parties and the leaders of this bunch were all men who were well known in Salvatierra. However, behind them lay a much more sinister crowd, composed of Germans, who had the secret blessing of the Kaiser, and a collection of Americans, most of whom were wanted on various counts at home. The Haciendistas bought their way to favour, and a lot of the money came from Germany."

"Bad show," grunted Colonel Waldrist. "We always had good relations with Salvatierra, as I recall."

Philip nodded. "That's right. It's was on the strength of those relations that the President turned to Britain. He had pinned his hopes on building a railway between the copper mines in the north to the River Alcañices, which would, when it was in place, open up the whole country. He came over here - he was a frequent visitor - and negotiated a loan to fund the railway. Now naturally enough, a lot of hard-headed bankers aren't going to dish out money without security, so a deal was agreed with various rights to minerals and so on, but the actual, tangible, security for the loan was the Spanish necklace which was President Ramon's own property."

"*The* necklace," said Edith Peverell, with a sigh of relief. "I wondered when you were coming to that."

Philip smiled. "Yes, *the* necklace. Now, of course, this didn't suit the opposition's book at all. They arranged an uprising and President Ramon put the necklace, or what he thought was the necklace, in Houblyn's Bank and hurried home, leaving his son, Enrique, to be looked after in England. It was a short, fierce struggle, but it ended, I'm afraid, with Ramon's death. The Haciendistas, led by a man called Andrade, took over, and, as you'd expect from a bunch of gangsters and crooks, ran the country into the ground. Then, a couple of years ago, Andrade died and a group of Salvatierrans, who had always been loyal to Ramon's memory, contacted his son, Enrique. He agreed to lead them, and, after more fighting, came to power determined to carry on his father's work. You mentioned a gang, Miss Peverell. I'm afraid you're right. There is a gang. I don't know if they want the country back, for they took everything of value they could carry, but for sheer spite it's likely they'd want to kill President Enrique. Andrade's wife would, for one."

"Is that Nancy Sterling?" asked James Matherson. Philip nodded. "She was meant to be utterly charming in private life, I recall, and her own collection of precious stones was remarkable."

"She was a thief and a murderer," Philip said shortly. "She married Andrade and ended up running the show. I honestly think she was the brains of the outfit."

"This necklace," said Edith Peverell, who had but a tepid interest in a country she'd only just heard of. "How valuable is it?"

Philip picked up his glass of wine and looked at it thoughtfully. "At a conservative estimate I should say round about half a million pounds. It could easily be more."

There was an awed hush.

"Half a million *pounds*?" repeated Mrs Mortimer-Doulting. "Half a million *pounds* for a string of coloured stones? Mr Brown, that is nothing short of immoral."

Philip shrugged. "As a matter of fact, the necklace consists of three strings of coloured stones and the Serpent's Eye. It's a lovely thing and if that's what it's worth, that's what it's worth. The President doesn't want it for an ornament, you know. He wants to revive his father's scheme to build a railway to the north, and the necklace would act as security for the loan. Isn't that right, Mr Matherson?"

Matherson nodded. "Absolutely right. It's a perfectly sound idea. If Salvatierra wasn't so chronically broke, the President would probably be able to raise the loan without the necklace. As it is, it's going to be tricky."

Andrew Herriad was still gazing at Philip Brown. "Are you honestly telling me that these emeralds are worth a cool half million?"

"That's quite correct, sir."

70

Herriad swallowed. "But... Good God, man, whatever gave you the idea that they're here?"

Chapter Four

There was a horrified gasp from Sir Dennis. "Herriad!" he choked. "That information was given to you in confidence."

"But where?" cried Edith Peverell in a rising squeak. She glanced wildly round her as if expecting them to materialize before her eyes. "I can't see them."

Philip Brown broke the tension with a laugh. "Yes, they're somewhere in the house, or at least I think they are. Cheer up, Sir Dennis. It would have had to come out sooner or later, although I would be obliged if everyone tried to keep it to themselves, otherwise every jewel thief in the country'll be dropping in to take pot-luck."

He cast another glance at the spluttering Storwood. "Really, sir, it couldn't remain a secret for much longer. Anyone with a bit of sense and a grasp of the facts would be able to work it out."

"So that's why you're here," said Sandy, thoughtfully. "I did wonder what the real reason was. I mean, you could talk to Mr Matherson about loans and things in London. You don't need to come down to the country to do it."

"But it's pleasanter in the country, don't you think?" asked Philip, looking at her with an amused expression. "And poor old Salvatierra really does need that loan."

Tommy Leigh had no intention of allowing the conversation to be diverted once more onto the woes of Salvatierra. On this point, if no other, he and Edith Peverell were in perfect agreement. "Hang on a mo. I mean to say, if the jolly old jewels really are kicking about, how come no-one's ever found them? And how come that President Whatsits, the one from years ago I mean, why did he leave them behind and put a load of false ones in the bank? It all seems pretty odd to me."

"I think I'd better explain everything," said Philip. Sir Dennis made a noise like a half-lit firework. Sandy saw Philip's delighted grin, but when he looked up, his face showed nothing but grave concern.

"The fact that I'm a guest here is due to Mr Herriad's kindness and Sir Dennis's good offices. When it became apparent that the jewels in the safe at Houblyns were fake, President Enrique made no secret of his suspicions that Houblyns were responsible. He very soon realised how unjust those suspicions were, but by then the damage had been done. Sir Dennis, in his capacity both as a government minister and a director of Houblyns, requested a meeting with the President." He broke off and looked at Sir Dennis. "I'd like to say again, sir, that I'm sorry you couldn't actually see President Enrique, but I hope I was an adequate substitute."

"No problem about that at all, Mr Brown," muttered Sir Dennis, mollified.

"Between us, Sir Dennis and myself worked out it would be as well to kill two birds with one stone, so to speak. If I came down to Farholt, then not only could I begin negotiations with Mr Matherson, but could also look for the missing emeralds."

"But why d'you think they're here?" repeated Tommy Leigh with dogged persistence.

"Well, it all goes back twelve years, to President Ramon's attempt to raise a loan. As I said, he visited England with the necklace to try and get the dibs. He knew the Eldons fairly well and they invited him to stay, together with all the sort of people he needed to talk to."

Andrew Herriad nodded vigorously. "That's exactly the sort of thing old Francis loved. I never visited Farholt in those days - we were out in Canada at the time - but his letters to me were full of politics and who he'd had to stay. Used to bore me stiff."

"Yes... Anyway, the President had various members of his staff with him, including, amongst others, his chief financial advisor, a Count von Liebrich and a brilliant young civil engineer called John Guthrie. The President left a diary which recounts what happened and that, together with various letters which were written at the time, has helped us to piece together what happened on the night of the grand ball."

Philip Brown couldn't complain of any lack of attention from his audience. The company were held transfixed as he recounted the events of that night.

"And so this chap, this John Guthrie, got clean away, did he?" said Andrew Herriad thoughtfully. "That seems to prove his guilt."

Philip shrugged. "Not necessarily. President Ramon continued to believe in Guthrie's innocence, even after he'd made a run for it."

Andrew Herriad clicked his tongue. "That seems very loyal of him. What about Francis's son, Robert? I never met him. Not since he was out of the nursery, anyway.

74

We were in Canada, but I always gathered there was something not quite right there."

"You're perfectly correct, sir," agreed Philip. "There had been some trouble earlier concerning a pair of diamond earrings belonging to one of his father's previous guests and it's quite certain that Francis Eldon bought him out of trouble on a subsequent occasion."

"Did he by Jove?" asked Andrew, with interest. "I never heard that from Francis, I must say. Mind you, he had a fierce sense of family pride. I know he was relieved when Robert joined the army. It sounds a hard thing to say, but it was probably all for the best when he got himself killed. That was in 1915. Francis wrote to me, of course, and I remember thinking that he seemed to be taking it all awfully well. It turned out later that the boy had been on the point of being cashiered."

Colonel Waldrist made a blowing noise. "Hard to pretend it's a tragedy with that hanging over them, what? Probably a blessing all round that young Eldon came to a clean end. Bad business."

"Great-Uncle Simon," put in Aunt Daphne in sepulchral tones. "Robert must have taken after Great-Uncle Simon. There was always that streak in the Eldons."

"What did Great-Uncle Simon get up to?" asked Sandy.

"Nothing that is relevant or suitable for the dinner-table, Alexandra. Do go on, Mr Brown. Our ancient family history can be of no interest to you."

"The next morning the news came through that fighting had broken out in the capital, Estrada. It was imperative that Ramon should return at once, so, hastily banking the emeralds in Houblyns, he sailed for Salvatierra that day. There were reports that Guthrie managed to get himself back to South America and died fighting beside Ramon, so it's possible that he really was innocent or, if guilty, managed to redeem himself in that way. Either way, no trace has ever been found of the emeralds and, until the safe-deposit box at Houblyns was opened, there wasn't the slightest suspicion that the emeralds the President banked weren't the genuine article. President Ramon certainly believed they were the real thing, and, as he had them valued in London before coming to Farholt, we know that the ones he arrived with were the actual emeralds. Therefore they must have been taken at Farholt but by whom is another question."

"I bet it was Adela Guthrie," said Edith Peverell. "I mistrust desperately beautiful women on principle."

"Well, really, dear," protested her father, mildly. "You have absolutely no grounds for such a suspicion."

"She'd worn the emeralds, hadn't she? What d'you think, Sandy? Adela Guthrie must've had had a paste copy made, then swapped them on the night of the ball."

"She couldn't have done," argued Sandy. "She'd have to give the real necklace to a jewellers to have a copy made and the President would hardly lend it to her for a few days, would he? Besides that, can you walk into a jewellers and ask for a paste copy of a necklace? It'd seem pretty fishy, especially if you hear the real one's been pinched a few days later."

"But the theft was never discovered," said Miss Peverell. "Go on, Mr Brown, what happened to Adela Guthrie afterwards?"

"I'm blowed if I know," said Philip. "Nothing to draw attention to herself, that's for sure."

"That proves it then," said Edith, happily.

"Not necessarily, Edith," said Mr Peverell. "Although it seems clear that the jewels really were taken here, we must be very careful before we assign guilt to any one person." The vicar cleared his throat. "Although I am aware that this is nothing but prejudice, my feeling is against the Count. However, as the poor man died in defence of the President's property, we must exclude him from blame. Robert Eldon's part in the affair seems open to question, but there isn't any evidence against him. Why should the police theory not be correct? I take it that Guthrie was not a rich man; the sight of the emeralds might have dazzled him, as the prospect of sudden wealth has led so many others astray. Perhaps he yielded to the impulse of the moment."

Colonel Waldrist disagreed. "Can't be that. The feller would've had to have had the false ones made in advance, just as Miss Herriad said. What beats me, young man," he said, glaring at Philip, "is why you think the jewels are still here. The place seems to have been crawling with thieves, both home-grown and imported. This Count could've come in and found the feller at it and

77

got shot for his pains. What's to say the thief didn't make off with the real jewels and leave the false ones, eh?

"Because no trace of them has ever been found. You could be right, Colonel, but the police assured President Enrique the other day that no stones of that quality have been offered for sale. Emeralds such as the ones used in the necklace are very rare and they believe that some report would have reached them. Even if they had been cut, they would still be notable jewels."

"Who d'you think took them?" asked Tommy Leigh.

Philip shook his head. "It's almost impossible to say. Any one of the people staying in the house could have been the real culprit."

"But if the Count..." began Sandy and stopped. Something in Philip Brown's eyes warned her not to continue with her original thought. "But how are you going to go about finding them?" she amended. "We can hardly tap walls and things. It'd take too long."

Philip laughed. "I was hoping for a clue," he said. "Because, I'm sorry to say, I haven't really got one. Maybe I could talk to any old servants who were here at the time."

Andrew Herriad pulled a face. "That's going to be awkward. What with the Eldons dying and the war and everything, there must be precious few left. I'm hanged if I can think of any."

"A treasure hunt," said Edith Peverell, dreamily. "What a pity we haven't got a map."

"Talking of maps," said Colonel Waldrist, seizing the conversation by the scruff of its neck, "reminds me of an

odd thing that happened in Rhodesia before the war..."
The conversation clanked into well-worn channels, but
Sandy was left with the definite impression that Mr Philip
Brown had held back a great deal more than he had said.

***　　***　　***

Sandy put down the newspaper and squinted in the
sunshine as Tommy Leigh came towards her across the
lawn.

"You've got yourself a nice little nook here," he
approved, sitting down on the bench under the cedar
tree. "What paper's that? Oh, *The Mail*. I couldn't find it
at breakfast."

"You weren't at breakfast," Sandy reminded him. "At
least you hadn't come down by nine o'clock." She looked
at him affectionately. "How are you? You looked pretty
shaken-up yesterday."

He looked away self-consciously. "Well, you know. It
doesn't seem the thing to carry on about how I feel when
that poor bloke's dead, but it was a foul thing to happen."

"Poor Tommy," she said quietly, letting her hand rest
on his.

He turned to her with quick gratitude in his brown
eyes. "D'you know, Sandy, I was so glad you were there.
I suppose I should have been able to cope with things, but
I felt absolutely bowled out. Having you to see to all the
running about made all the difference. Women," he said
feelingly, "are so efficient."

Sandy felt a warm glow. Poor Tommy! He really did
need someone to take care of him. He had never made

79

any secret of his liking for her, but it was difficult to take him seriously.

Perhaps? No. Life with Tommy would be nice, but it wouldn't be very exciting. There was that word again. Did she really want nothing more than excitement? That was very shallow and Tommy... She looked at him out of the corner of her eye. He was such a *big* man, and so eager and awkward, that he reminded her irresistibly of a Newfoundland dog. She was very fond of dogs.

His hand held hers. "Sandy.... I've been thinking..."

She looked up at him expectantly. She had been prepared for this moment for weeks. What if she said Yes? Could she bring herself to say Yes? Sandy hesitated. Whatever happened, she wanted to be kind to him and...

"Sandy..." he said again and suddenly broke off, his eyes glancing past her. "Good Lord, look at that!"

Rather annoyed, she glanced round. Philip Brown and Eleanor Storwood had walked down the steps of the terrace and now stood, heads close together, on the lawn.

"I wonder what Lady Storwood wants with that chap," he said indignantly. "They seem to be getting a jolly sight too friendly to me. Eleanor - Lady Storwood, I mean - doesn't seem to realise the effect she has on a feller. Now there's a really lovely woman. Clever, too. I mean, that beauty place, the health and hygiene show, or whatever you call it. Sir Dennis owns it but it's Lady Storwood who makes it tick. Everybody goes there and it's all down to her. It's desperately fashionable. He makes an absolute mint out of it."

"Is that so?" snapped Sandy.

"Yes..." Tommy frowned across the lawn. "I don't know if I trust that bloke. He's a plausible sort of character, and yet what do we actually know about him? We've only his word for it that he's President Thingimijig's secretary."

"Don't be ridiculous, Tommy," said Sandy, understandably irritated. "Of course, he's the President's secretary."

"Oh, is he, by Jove? Well, let me tell you that I've been Sir Dennis's chief organizer and sort of willing slave for over a year now and he's never trusted *me* to go and fool about with loans and what-have-you."

"You amaze me."

"No, really," persisted Tommy, oblivious to any sarcasm. "If these jewels are here it'd be a clever move to insinuate yourself, then all you do is trouser them and walk away. I think there's a lot more to that chap than meets the eye. What's to say he isn't what-d'you-call-him, Robert, The Hope of The House, back from the dead? He might be, you know."

"Don't be silly. Someone would recognize him."

"Would they? It's years ago and if a chap says he's a chap, you don't suspect him of being another chap, especially if the other chap's meant to be dead, do you? There seems to have been a mass clear-out of everyone who was around then. We've only his word for who he is."

"And Sir Dennis's," Sandy reminded him.

"Yes... I suppose so. Here's another thing, though. All that story he told us last night about that bloke, Ramon. How do we know he didn't pinch his own jewels and leg off back to South America?"

"Tommy! I don't believe for a moment that President Ramon stole his own emeralds. Why on earth should he? And if Mr Brown was a jewel thief he'd hardly come and advertise the fact that the emeralds are here, would he?"

"I don't know. It could be a clever plot or something. I'm always reading about things like that. He has us all looking for the jewels, then, when they're found, bags them for himself. And I don't like to see him getting so friendly with Lady Storwood."

"Why don't you tell him so?" demanded Sandy, getting to her feet.

Tommy scrambled up from the bench. "I say, you're not going? Sandy, you're not cross with me about something, are you? You look awfully put out all of a sudden. Is there anything wrong?"

"Nothing," said Sandy. "Here's the newspaper, Tommy. Try not to be late for lunch."

She stalked off, leaving a bewildered Tommy Leigh gazing after her. Stupid man! It was one thing more or less deciding to turn him down, it was quite another not to be asked at all.

Her progress back to the house was cut off by Philip Brown. Making a small bow to Lady Storwood, he followed her swiftly up the steps.

"Miss Herriad! Wait a moment, won't you?"

She turned. "Yes?"

He stopped, abashed. "I say, is this a bad moment? You look as if you could skin someone alive. Flashing eyes, chin up."

She glared at him, then caught his mischievous grin and laughed, brushing her hair back from her eyes. "I'm sorry. I was feeling utterly rancid, but it's nothing to do with you." She looked to where Tommy Leigh was now deep in conversation with Eleanor Storwood. "It's just - well - men are such fools, aren't they?"

"It's usual to except the present company when making remarks of that nature," murmured Philip.

She laughed. "I do, of course." She looked at him thoughtfully, taking in the intelligent blue eyes. "I wouldn't have said you were a fool of any description, Mr Brown."

"No? I owe it all to the adverts in the newspapers. I undertook a correspondence course in fourteen weekly parts all about how to develop an air of self-confidence and radiate an air of authority. I lost the final bit, which promised a gimlet eye and would guarantee a pay rise from the boss, but I spent ages in front of the mirror doing the exercises in part three on how to look bright and efficient."

"Idiot!" said Sandy, her bad humour ebbing away.

"I want to thank you," said Philip, taking her arm and walking along the side of the terrace, "for your discretion last night at dinner. I could see you were bursting to point out something about the Count and, although I didn't mind telling everyone what you might call the public facts, I was quite glad to leave his part in it unsung."

"Yes, I got that impression."

"You're a very perceptive woman," said Philip, warmly. "What, can I ask, were you going to say?"

She paused. "Well, it's just this, really. If the jewels in the safe-deposit box were false, then somebody had them made on purpose, as Colonel Waldrist said last night. Now although it's reasonable that President Ramon should have had that done so he could keep the real ones safely hidden, it's unlikely that he'd go to the trouble of banking them at Houblyn's before going back to South America. Unless you know he had the real ones tucked away somewhere?"

"No, he didn't. You can take that as gospel."

"Very well, then. In that case, the fakes must have been made by the thief in order to steal the real ones."

"So far, so certain," agreed Philip. "Next point?"

"Well, if you have fake jewellery made, you must be thinking of a substitution - that is, of stealing them without anyone knowing they've been stolen - which is, of course, what happened. And what *that* means is that whole episode of the safe door being blown open was nothing more than a blind. As President Ramon went back to South America the next day, presumably the actual theft occurred before the attack on the safe. I bet they were stolen at the ball. Mrs Guthrie's the obvious person to have done it because all she'd have to do is to swap necklaces. I'm a bit worried about what she expected to happen next, though. After all, what should

84

have happened is that they'd be taken as security for this loan and, presumably, whoever took them would have them valued again. An expert would see that they were false, and she'd be suspected immediately. So, really, I don't think she can be guilty. Robert Eldon sounds like a very dodgy character and I wouldn't be surprised if he were involved. John Guthrie might be guilty but I do wonder, you know, about the part the Count played in it all."

"Do you, by jingo?" said Philip softly. "That's very interesting. Go on."

"He was killed, I know, which on the face of it seems to make him innocent. However, he'd be in a perfect position to have the false emeralds made beforehand *and* to get the real ones from Mrs Guthrie. He could merely ask her for them at the end of the evening. Then he could arrange to blow the door off the safe a couple of nights afterwards as if a real thief had broken in and he'd be in the clear."

"And how d'you get over the fact he was killed?"

Sandy frowned. "He must have been working with someone. That's it!" She turned to him eagerly. "What if the other person was Robert Eldon? Eldon and the Count are in it together. I don't know how they knew each other, but they must have arranged to steal the necklace before the President came here. Now if they simply pinched the jewels, the theft could be traced to them, so they arrange for them to vanish at the ball, substituting the fakes. I imagine the original plan was to pass them to that woman who you thought was the fence."

85

"Teddy Costello?"

"That's the one, but she was being watched by the police, wasn't she? So Eldon or the Count hide the jewels in a safe place, intending to get them later. They arrange to make it look as if the safe was robbed by an outsider, but then Eldon falls out with the Count. Goodness knows why. Maybe he suspected the Count was going to double-cross him or frame him or something. Anyway, Eldon shoots the Count and runs off, leaving the worthless fakes, and leaving John Guthrie to take the blame." She looked up at him enthusiastically. "I wonder if I'm right?"

"It's a funny thing," said Philip, "but you are."

"*What?*"

"About Count von Liebrich, I mean. When Ramon Artiaga got back to Salvatierra he regained control of the presidential palace which had been in enemy hands. There he found proof that the Count had been hand in glove with the Haciendistas, plotting that the revolution should take place while the President was in England. The papers also showed that he had engineered the theft of the emeralds and it's certain he wasn't working alone. Whether his partner was Eldon or someone else we don't know, but he did have a confederate and Eldon certainly fits the bill. There was a coded cable from the Count, sent the day after the ball, stating that a certain item was secured - so it looks as if you're right about when they were pinched - and saying that he'd put it in the bank."

Sandy was conscious of a slight feeling of chagrin. "Why the dickens didn't you tell me in the first place instead of having me work it all out?"

"I was enjoying listening to you," said Philip apologetically. "You were doing it so well. I'm sorry. That sounds beastly patronizing and I didn't mean it to."

"I..." She stopped, baffled.

"There's another thing," he added hastily. "You've got so near the truth of the matter simply by thinking about it that I started to hope that you might be able to crack the rest of the puzzle as well."

"And what's that?"

"Where he put the wretched necklace." He waved a hand at the bulk of Farholt. "Here I am in a house with about a hundred and ninety-six bedrooms..."

"That's a slight exaggeration."

"And I'm looking for something you could put in a cigar-box," continued Philip. "I haven't got a clue where to start."

Sandy paused, making small indentations in the grass with the toe of her shoe. "There's the Count's own words," she said eventually. "He put it in the bank..." She broke off and raised her eyes to him. "You're holding out on me again," she said accusingly. "Yesterday - that man who got run over. He said something about banks. It meant something to you, didn't it? Who was the man, Mr Brown?"

Philip opened his mouth as if to speak, then closed it again, laughing with a resigned shrug. "All right, I admit it. What the poor bloke said did strike a chord, but I don't know who he is. Honestly, I really don't. It could be nothing but coincidence, of course."

"Nonsense," said Sandy briskly. "It has to be connected. For heaven's sake, he even *said* "Count!" Are you sure you don't know who he is?"

"No, I don't. I only wish I did."

"It has to be someone who knew the Count... Robert Eldon!" She clutched at his arm. "It was Robert Eldon. It has to be."

"But he's dead."

"He's *meant* to be dead. I bet he wasn't really. It fits, don't you see? He was on the point of being for the high jump – he was going to be cashiered, remember? – so he took the opportunity to vanish and has been lying low for years. All this time he's believed the jewels were safely locked away but now he realises there's a chance to get them after all. So he comes down here and... and..." Sandy swallowed. "I don't like to think of the next bit much. I liked him, you know?" She brightened slightly. "It always says in books that murderers are nice people who you'd never suspect, like the vicar or the solicitor or..."

"Or the urbane young man about town?" asked Philip with a lift of his eyebrow.

"Yes. Just like you, in fact. He was meant to be a charmer, wasn't he? And he might not be a murderer, not really," she added. "It could have been a proper fight and the gun simply went off by mistake."

"But, Miss Herriad..."

"Call me Sandy," she said with a smile. "Everyone does except for Aunt Daphne."

He answered the smile. "Thanks. About this bloke, though. I'm not saying you're wrong, but if he was Robert Eldon, why did he have a map? He'd know his way around."

"For camouflage?" suggested Sandy after a few seconds' thought. "He'd need a map if he was pretending to be on a walking holiday."

"He wouldn't need to look at it though, would he? Unless he thought someone might see him, I suppose." He let go of her arm and leaned back against the wall of the terrace. Taking out his cigarette-case, he offered it to her before thoughtfully striking a match. "For all I know you've hit on the truth," he said. "The problem is, I can't see it gets me much further in the hunt for the emeralds. Bank. Banks. What does the word "banks" mean to you?"

Sandy gave him a puzzled look. "Well, it means banks. You know, where you put money."

"Do you know the local bank manager? Well enough to ask him if a guest at Farholt made a deposit twelve years ago?"

"I suppose so," said Sandy doubtfully. "I can't see the point, though. Robert Eldon said he didn't mean banks."

Philip grinned. "First of all, we don't know it's Eldon. Secondly, even if it is, he might have been mistaken, and thirdly, we have the Count's own words and it's worth a try..." He broke off as Tommy Leigh came towards them.

"Er... Brown, old man," he started awkwardly. "About yesterday. The fact is Lady Storwood's just pointed out to me what a brick you were, coming to the aid of the party as you did." He stopped, looking from one to the other. "I say, this isn't a bad moment, is it?"

"That's all right," said Philip easily. "Miss Herriad and I were just discussing these missing emeralds. The word "bank" doesn't mean anything to you, does it?"

"*I know a bank where the wild thyme grows*," said Tommy, with an unexpected burst of poetry. "I remember that one from school. Bank? No, it doesn't mean anything special. Not more than the place where you get money from. And jolly sticky they can be at times, too," he added mournfully. "Why?"

"Because we're wondering if whoever pinched the emeralds in the first place put them in a bank."

Tommy pondered for a moment, then shook his head. "No, they wouldn't do that. I mean, it's a bit tame, isn't it? Shouldn't they be buried under a blasted oak? Actually, couldn't that be the sort of bank you're looking for? A sand-bank, I mean, or the banks of a river or something?"

"You might have something there, Tommy," said Sandy. "What other sorts of bank are there?"

"There's banks of flowers," he said brightly, glancing round the garden.

"Those are usually called beds," murmured Philip.

"It might be banks of switches," mused Sandy out loud. "Electrical switches, I mean. I say, they couldn't be in the cellar, near the fuse boxes could they?"

"It depends. Have you got banks of switches down there?"

"Well, not banks, exactly, just a couple of rows." She pointed to where the grassy slope ran up to the terrace. "What about here? The earth's sort of banked-up, isn't it? It'd take us forever to dig it all up, though, and I can't see Daddy approving. He can be very stuffy sometimes. She looked up as a maid approached. "Did you want me, Annie?"

Annie shook her head. "No, Miss, but there's a gentleman come to see Mr Brown. A Mr Brenzett. He didn't have a card, sir."

Philip frowned. "I'd better go and see what he wants." Throwing away his cigarette he followed Annie back into the house, calling over his shoulder, "If you have an inspiration, let me know."

Mr Brenzett was waiting in the hall. He got to his feet as Philip approached. "Mr Brown? I'm sorry to trouble you, sir. It's about this Houblyns affair. I tried to contact you in London but was informed you'd already left for the country."

"I see." Philip turned to Annie with a smile. "Is there anywhere we can be undisturbed? This gentleman and I have some business to discuss."

"There's the library, sir. No-one's in there at this time of day."

The library was cool and dark after the glare of the sun outside. Philip waited for a moment, but Mr Brenzett, though obviously amiable, waited for him to speak first. "So you're here about Houblyns." Philip sized up his guest. "You don't look as if you're from the bank."

Mr Brenzett's weather-beaten face crinkled in a smile as he produced a small leather card-case from his pocket. "Maybe that will illuminate matters, sir. I didn't show it to the maid as I know how these girls talk."

Philip took the case and read the contents, his eyebrows rising. "Scotland Yard, eh? I would never have put you down as a detective. If I had to guess, I would have said you were a prosperous farmer."

Brenzett's smile increased. "That's reassuring to hear, sir. This is one of the occasions when I don't particularly want to be recognised as a policeman."

"I doubt you ever would be. Well, Superintendent, how did you track me down?"

"Your staff told me to ask for a Mr Philip Brown."

Philip nodded. "That's as good a name as any under the circumstances. What can I do for you? Please sit down, won't you?"

Brenzett sat, placing his hands firmly on his knees. "It's about this accident yesterday, sir. I understand you were involved."

"I was on the scene, yes."

"The point is, Mr... Mr Brown, is this; how much of an accident was it? I don't need to tell you, sir, that we're extremely suspicious about any accident happening near you."

Philip looked startled. "You mean it should have been me under the wheels of that car?"

"It's an idea that occurred to us."

"No." Philip shook his head. "No, I can't see it. I arrived after it was all over. I grant you it's a possibility, but I honestly think you're on the wrong lines. If you're saying it was a premeditated crime, then surely London would be the place to pull it off. It would've been easy enough to shove me under a car in London. I really believe that the accident was just an accident."

Brenzett nodded slowly and drew his pipe from his jacket pocket. "If you say so, sir. Is it your opinion that the victim was simply an unfortunate passer-by?"

Philip hesitated, remembering Sandy's speculations. "Miss Herriad thinks there's a chance he was Robert Eldon."

Brenzett paused in the act of filling his pipe. "She thinks he's *who*? What on earth for? Robert Eldon died years ago."

Philip smiled. "I'm far from convinced about that side of it myself, but whoever the man was, he certainly knew something about the theft." Philip rapidly brought Brenzett up to date with the dying man's last words and their ideas about von Liebrich's role. "And that ties in with the cable the Count sent, you see."

Brenzett looked at Philip reproachfully. "There's nothing on the file at the Yard about any cable."

"Well, it was all so vague. He didn't write "I've swiped the emeralds," he said "A certain item is secure". There are other papers, too, that make sense once you know the emeralds were stolen but if you don't know, you're left guessing. It's this blessed roundabout way in which diplomats talk. I'd damned if I know what they're on about half the time. When the balloon went up at Houblyns, the last thing I thought of was the theft having taken place before the war. That's like ancient history. It was only later I put two and two together. I was getting there gradually and the penny finally dropped yesterday when we were going over what the dying man said."

Brenzett put a match to his pipe and pulled at it thoughtfully. "It'll be interesting to find out who he really was," he said eventually. "I suppose it might be Eldon. You're assuming the man was on his way here to look for the emeralds?"

"Don't you? He knew something about it, that's for sure. Whether that makes him Eldon or not is another matter. Salvatierra was in uproar for years. A great many people could have de-coded the Count's message - it was a standard code - and granted the publicity there was when the jewels in Houblyns were found to be fakes, then this man could have decided to take a pop at it."

"It's a shame," said Brenzett dryly, "that the Press got to hear of it."

"Yes," agreed Philip ruefully. "With hindsight I can't argue with you. Can you chase up the bank part of it, Superintendent? I don't know what the Count meant or even if he was telling the truth, but I suppose he could have simply have banked the real thing, either here or in London. Could you investigate that?"

Brenzett contemplated the idea unenthusiastically. "It'll be a lot of work, but we can. It's doubtful we'll get anywhere though." He sighed. "I can't hold out much hope we're going to recover the jewels, sir. We'll try, of course, but it's only fair to warn you the prospects are a bit thin. It's hard enough to make any headway with the current crop of jewel robberies, let alone one dating from twelve years ago."

Philip pulled a face. "That's rather discouraging. It's not simply emeralds that are at stake, it's the difference it would make to Salvatierra."

"I'm just being realistic, sir. I know you're doing some hard bargaining at the moment for this loan but if you're hoping to get the stones back, I honestly think you're going to be disappointed." Brenzett stood up. "I'll be getting along now, sir. I'm staying at the local pub, the Bird In Hand. If you get any more ideas about the emeralds, perhaps you could let me know. Any more papers that turn up, for instance."

Philip acknowledged the reproof with a twisted smile. "Point taken."

Brenzett smiled in return. "Just keep me informed. Any information may prove to be useful and you never know what might crop up. This man who got knocked over is the best lead we have, in my opinion. He clearly knew something. I'll be interested in what the inquest has to say about him."

"And so will I, Superintendent," said Philip. "Unless anything happens in the meantime, I'll see you there."

Chapter Five

The inquest was held three days later in the parish hall.

Sandy, squeezing into her hard wooden chair in the front row, was conscious of how incongruous it all seemed. The hall, which on happier occasions, was used for jumble sales, whist drives, mission teas and concert parties, was furnished with a low stage on which the fourteen jurors sat, seven either side, round a trestle table.

The stage had last been used by the Farholt and District Amateur Players for their production of *Trial by Jury* and as the Coroner took his seat, Sandy wouldn't have been very surprised if he had conducted his examinations in song. There was the same subdued buzz of expectation she associated with the theatre.

The body, she knew, was in the kitchen at the side of the hall. As the jury, after having been sworn in, departed to solemnly view the corpse, Sandy wondered if she'd ever feel the same about that kitchen again. It would be hard, wouldn't it, cutting ham sandwiches and helping to make tea from the enormous urn for Sales of Work without sensing something?

She suddenly realised it wouldn't. Perhaps it was because the man was a total stranger, but it was curiously hard to feel sorrow or regret or any of the other emotions she'd expected. That was what was missing. The rest of the - she wanted to call them the audience - were obviously in much the same state of mind.

She glanced round the room. Tommy Leigh was clearly uncomfortable, constantly re-adjusting his collar and rumpling his tie in the process, but there was no sorrow there.

Her father sat, placidly waiting, as if for the rise of the curtain. She half-expected a hidden orchestra to play God Save The King.

Aunt Daphne sat on the other side of him, fidgeting with her handbag. Her mind, Sandy guessed, was still on her garden. In the car down to the village she had forsworn bodies as a topic of conversation and talked about potting compost.

Sir Dennis Storwood sat, drawing attention to the fact that he was really far too busy to attend tuppenny-ha'penny affairs like this by continually glancing at his watch.

Eleanor Storwood, almost motionless, radiated the correct air of concerned interest. Really, her clothes were stunning. How many other people in the room could even begin to guess at the cost of such unworried elegance? Navy blue; in this, as in most things, Lady Storwood looked unostentatiously correct. Black, even Parisian black, would have pretended an emotion she couldn't possibly feel and a colour would have been out of place.

Philip Brown, resplendent in grey with a violet in his buttonhole, stood at the back of the hall, talking to a tweed-suited man who looked like a well-to-do farmer.

Philip surveyed the packed hall, wondering that so many people could find time on a Tuesday morning to attend an enquiry into a complete unknown. Alive, he doubted if most of them, himself included, would have noticed the man. Dead, he was an object of overpowering interest.

"By the way," said Superintendent Brenzett in his ear, "I very much appreciated the photograph of President Enrique in this morning's paper."

Philip grinned. "So did I. A glorious evocation of fishing in the Highland twilight without a single mosquito to mar the idyll. It was quite beautifully half-toned and indistinct. If it hadn't been for the caption you'd never had known who it was."

"My thoughts exactly, Mr Brown," returned Brenzett with an answering smile.

"Have you had any professional involvement with this affair?" asked Philip, indicating the room with a wave of his hand.

Brenzett shook his head. "This is very much a local business. I'm just a spectator."

Philip fell silent. Sandy, at the front of the room, noticed how tired he looked when he wasn't making the effort to talk. That wasn't very surprising. She'd seen little of him the last couple of days for he had spent most of his time with James Matherson.

The banker's forces had been augmented by two morning-suited men who had arrived yesterday and departed before dinner.

"It's this blasted necklace," Philip had said quite frankly over their bridge game last night. "They'll lend Salvatierra the money without it, but it's so tied up with concessions and mineral rights that it'll be years before the country can benefit. What? No, I don't think they're being hard-hearted," he said in response to a comment from Tommy Leigh. "They've got to protect their investors' interests. I think it's a sure-fire scheme, but looked at from their point of view, it's mere speculation. Fortunes have been lost in South America before now and they're understandably cautious. I've only got the deal I have because of trading on President Enrique's willingness to follow in his father's footsteps. I was told pretty bluntly that if all they looked at was the current situation in Salvatierra, we wouldn't be able to borrow buttons."

Sandy watched him rub his hand across his forehead. Yes, he was tired. Her attention was caught by a plump woman dressed entirely in black.

The woman took a handkerchief from her capacious and very shiny bag and dabbed her eyes, spotting the powder on her face. Here at last was someone whose chief emotion wasn't curiosity but sorrow.

Watching her, Sandy thought that her grief was rather assumed. That in itself wasn't odd. Plenty of people thought they ought to "Have a good cry" at the death of the most unlamented relative... No, not relative. The woman furtively drew out a powder-compact and dabbed her cheeks. Surely that man on the road with those clear grey eyes couldn't be related to this stout, commonplace woman. His old Nanny? Not old enough, Sandy decided. Who on earth was she, then?

She sat up, dismissing her thoughts as the jury filed back into the room.

To his obvious horror, Tommy Leigh was the first witness to be called. No, he hadn't been going very fast. Round about twenty, or thereabouts. Know the man? Good Lord, he should say not. What an idea! Never clapped eyes on the feller before. Shockin' business. He felt awful about the whole... Mr Leigh was briskly reminded by the Coroner, Mr Holland, a retired solicitor from Spaldhurst, that his feelings had no bearing on the inquest.

This reprimand effectively reduced the unfortunate Tommy to red-faced, stuttering incoherence. Ten minutes later and without having added greatly to anyone's store of knowledge, Tommy gratefully retreated to his seat.

Sandy gave her evidence as clearly as she could, hoping that she wasn't making matters worse for Tommy, and was complimented on her actions. Philip Brown followed, reinforcing what she'd said.

Doctor Hayle came next, briefly describing the results of the post-mortem and the dead man's injuries and giving it as his opinion that these were fully consistent with the accident as described. His only reservation was his surprise that the man had managed to speak.

When questioned by the Coroner, he was forced to agree that speech wouldn't have been an impossibility, but that he merely wanted to state that he found it unexpected in the circumstances. Having been curtly reminded that he wasn't an eye-witness and was not in a position to testify if the man had spoken or not, he was

100

asked if he, therefore, disagreed with the testimony of the previous three witnesses who had all heard the victim speak. No, of course he didn't disagree, he simply wanted to voice his opinion.

But that, the Coroner thought, was irrelevant to the matter in hand. With a resigned shrug, Doctor Hayle took his place in the hall. His comment that the Coroner was an old windbag was, fortunately, only audible to his immediate neighbours.

Sergeant Lydd of the County Constabulary gave his evidence with painful precision. Here, there was an excited rustle of interest, for, after going through the details which everyone knew already, he stated that they had managed, through an examination of the deceased's belongings, to ascertain the identity of the dead man.

His clothes had not been marked but his pockets had contained, stated Sergeant Lydd, who was not a man to be hurried, a half-eaten cheese and pickle sandwich in a paper bag, a pipe, a box of matches and tobacco pouch, a pocket-book with three pound-notes and four ten-shillings and a return ticket from Waterloo to Brosley Dean.

A large-scale map, of the sort commonly used by walkers, had been found near the body. The pocket-book had also contained a letter signed with the name "Emmy". It was dated from July of last year and the address was a house in Camden Town. The police had communicated with the address given in the letter and ascertained it to be from the deceased's sister, a Mrs

101

Emmeline Strickland. Mrs Strickland was present in Court and would give evidence next.

Mrs Strickland was the woman in black. So she is a relative, thought Sandy with a stab of disappointment. If this woman was the man's sister, he could hardly be Robert Eldon.

Amid a rustle of interested murmurs, Mrs Strickland carefully picked her way to the front of the hall and perched herself at the very edge of the chair, clutching her handbag like a shield.

"Now then, Mrs Strickland," said the Coroner with an ingratiating smile, "there's no need to be nervous, you know. All you have to do is answer my questions."

Mrs Strickland's lips quivered and she felt in her bag for a handkerchief. "It's very good of you, I'm sure."

Sandy sat up. She had been startled that Mrs Strickland should claim the dead man as her brother, but that she should do it in an accent that clearly marked her as Irish was a real puzzle. Surely the man hadn't had an Irish accent? His speech had been so broken it was difficult to be certain, but surely she would have caught the inflection?

Mrs Strickland stated, in a quavering voice, that she was indeed Mrs Emmeline Strickland of 43, Hilldrop Road, Camden Town. "Everyone," went on Mrs Strickland, applying the corner of the hanky to her eyes, "has been very kind to me. Even that young man - and see him now - who was driving the car surely didn't mean any harm."

Tommy gave her a look of pathetic gratitude which was frozen by the Coroner's reminder that that was for the Court to decide.

"When that policeman arrived at the house with the message that our Kevin had been struck down, I couldn't believe it," continued Mrs Strickland with a sympathetic glance at the suffering Mr Leigh. "I thought I was going to faint, so I did." She put her bag beside her chair and clutched her brow expressively. "I never thought I'd hear such dreadful news about my own brother especially as..."

Her lips quivered again and her arms rose in supplication to heaven. "Especially as we parted on bad terms." Her arms dropped. She was evidently a person who couldn't talk without gestures. "After the policeman had gone I had to lie down with the curtains shut but, as true as I sit here, I never had a wink of sleep, what with thinking I'd never look on his face again."

Here the Coroner deftly interposed a question. "But you have seen him, Mrs Strickland?"

"Lying dead and cold I have." Her hands sketched a table in the air. "And it's a terrible thing to see."

"Do you positively identify the deceased as your brother?"

"Indeed I do, my own brother, Kevin Murphy. His face is untouched, thanks be to God."

"When did you see him last?"

The handkerchief was brought into play again. It had been last summer. Gradually the story was told. The dead man was Kevin Murphy. If he had been spared he would

103

have been forty next July. He had never married and she was his only living relation.

Kevin Murphy had been in the Navy during the war, and him an Irishman too, and no obligation to join up, and been all round the world. The South Atlantic, The North Atlantic, up to Russia - everywhere that God Almighty had seen fit to put water, Kevin had been.

She didn't know the name of his ship because he'd served on a few and she'd taken little interest. They hadn't seen much of each other before the war and even less since, as Kevin had gone to America with, he had stated, the intention of making his fortune. Which part of America? She'd had a post-card from New York and another from Chicago and thought he was doing well, and she was that surprised when he turned up on her doorstep last summer, without a penny to his name.

Of course she'd made him welcome - that was what families were for - but it was money he'd wanted, and her struggling to make ends meet herself, what with being a poor widow, her husband having died of that dreadful 'flu, and a terrible time he'd had of it, and prices rising all the time, as everyone here could say, and she didn't know what they'd had the war for, as no-one seemed to be the better off for it.

The letter found in his pocket? Why, that was what she was telling the Court all about. Kevin had stayed for two days - and the appetite he had on him - and then - Mrs Strickland was very delicate about this part of the story - she had asked him to leave.

He had written a month later to say he'd picked up some work but was living in a seamans' hostel and could he come and stay with her again while he got back on his feet again.

"And I refused!" said Mrs Srickland in a trembling voice. "I refused my own brother, so I did." Her answer to his letter was the one he had been carrying with him when he was taken from them. Why had he kept her letter? How should she know? But she was the only family he had and maybe it served as a reminder of her address, as he could be terribly forgetful at times.

Why had he come to Farholt? She couldn't say, but he might have been trying to see an old friend or maybe he had come for a day in the country as he missed the country terribly, that she knew.

Did his last words mean anything to her? No, they did not, and she thought poor Kevin was rambling, but he'd talked about the sea, as was only to be expected of a sailor, and to think he should have met his end like this, after having travelled all over the world...

Here the Coroner brought Mrs Strickland to a reluctant halt and, dismissing her, addressed the jury.

Thanks, he said, to the very full testimony of the deceased's sister, there was no longer any question of who the dead man was; the cause of death was also perfectly clear; the task which now lay before them was to give their opinion as to whether the motor-accident was deliberate or ... er... accidental. If they thought there was insufficient evidence to decide, they could return an open verdict. Tommy Leigh gulped as if he saw the hangman's noose before him.

As soon as the jury left the room, Sandy went over to him.

"This is absolutely awful," he said, twitching his hands together. "My God, Sandy, I wish I could have a cigarette. If they bring it in that I'm responsible, then I'll die." The significance of this remark seemed to strike him and he turned a shade paler. "What I mean is, I'll never forgive myself. I just didn't see the chap. He was just there, you know?"

He broke off as Mrs Strickland approached them.

"I wanted to say," she began, "that I'm sure you didn't mean any harm."

Tommy swallowed. "That's awfully good of you."

"And you too, Miss," carried on Mrs Strickland, turning to Sandy. "I was glad to think, as I sat there, that my poor brother's last moments were helped by someone like yourself."

The accent was so warm and her smile so genuine that Sandy felt ashamed of herself for her doubts.

"If your time's come," continued Mrs Strickland, indicating the thought by chopping one hand into the palm of the other, "then your time's come. All we can do is be grateful that someone's helped to ease the path."

"That's very good of you to say so, Mrs Strickland," said Sandy. "I only did what anyone would have done in the circumstances."

"Ah, but you knew *what* to do, didn't you, Miss, and I'm sure it was a great comfort to Kevin, with his mind wandering, poor boy, and time slipping away." Her hand went to the lapel of her coat in a vaguely familiar gesture, then fluttered down to consult an imaginary wrist-watch. "With you having been a nurse in the war and all."

She was so sincere Sandy felt the impulse to make up for her doubts about Mrs Strickland's authenticity and set out to be deliberately friendly. After all, the poor woman had just lost her only brother.

"It's very kind of you to say so, Mrs Strickland." She hunted round for a neutral topic of conversation. "Have you ever done any nursing?" she asked with a smile.

A startled look leapt into Mrs Strickland's eyes and for an instant the impression of good-fellowship fled to be replaced by something a great deal more calculating. "Nursing? I... I... No, I never... Unless it's nursing my husband you mean, when he was taken bad. I thought for a minute you meant hospital nursing. Oh yes," she continued, gathering confidence, "I had my fill of looking after him, I can tell you, but I'm sorry to say it was all for nothing in the end. All we can do is to try our best and leave the final outcome in the hands of the Almighty."

The smile was back and so was the self-assurance but it was too late. For a fraction of a second she had been caught with her guard down and all Sandy's suspicions rushed back with full force.

"Do you happen to know," went on Mrs Strickland, "what I can do about burying poor Kevin? I'm not associated with any church in London and he might as well be laid to rest here as anywhere."

"You'd better ask the Vicar - but excuse me, Mrs Strickland, wasn't your brother a Catholic?" That, too, caught Mrs Strickland unawares and Sandy saw the little twitch of annoyance.

"Sure, he was. I'll have to ask the Vicar where the nearest Catholic church is. I'll have to stay for the funeral. I can't let poor Kevin goes to his grave unmourned." She sighed. "There's a lot to be done after a sad event and no mistake."

"I'll help you find the Vicar," put in Tommy. "He should be around here somewhere."

Sandy saw them go with a feeling of relief. She wanted time to think this out and was irritated when she felt a touch on her arm. Her face cleared as she turned and saw Philip.

"Can I take you away from all this?" he offered. "The jury shouldn't be long but I think we've time to go outside for a cigarette."

She followed him out into the warm sunshine. "Who was that man you were talking to?" she asked. "The one in the tweed suit."

"Brenzett? I suppose you could call him a business associate. He called to see me the other day, if you remember. He's staying in the local pub for a few days to get some fishing in." He felt for his cigarette-case. "What d'you think of the inquest?"

"It seems all right," she began, then stopped, conscious of his thoughtful blue eyes. "It's not," she said decisively. "That woman, the one who's meant to be his sister.   She's phoney, I'm certain of it.   I bet she's no more his sister than I am."

Philip's eye's crinkled in an appreciative smile.   "I do like the way you're so definite," he said.   "You try and say what you think you ought, then you look as if you're going to burst if you don't tell the truth.   Why do you think Mrs Strickland isn't the genuine article?   Are you still hankering after Mr X being Robert Eldon?   It made a much more exciting story the way you told it."

"It's not that.   At least," amended Sandy, accepting a cigarette, "I don't think it's that.   What did you make of her?"

He shrugged.   "She seemed perfectly genuine.   A bit of a gas-bag but that's neither here or there.   His last words seem a bit odd in the circumstances but I suppose it could be nothing more than a coincidence."   He drew on his cigarette, frowning.   "Why shouldn't she be exactly what she says she is?"

"Because she's all wrong.   The man we saw wasn't Irish.   He didn't say much, but his voice was English.   He was a different class, too."

Philip raised his eyebrows.   "You're on a slippery slope there.   He said so little I couldn't tell you what his accent was, and as for class, he might easily have been a petty officer or even had a commission during the war and had some of his edges knocked off.   He might have lost his accent in the process, as well."

"I know that," said Sandy in frustration, "but there's more to it.   I was chatting to her after the jury had gone out and she was going out of her way to be pleasant, when I happened to ask if she'd ever done any nursing. She hated that question, you could see. For a moment she looked really anxious, as if I knew something about her, and I could see that all the niceness was just a front. I felt I'd discovered something I shouldn't. There's another thing, too. She was talking about having him buried here, and when I asked if he was a Catholic, she was put out. She hadn't thought about his religion."

"Maybe he wasn't an assiduous church-goer. Why on earth did you ask her if she'd done any nursing?"

Sandy bit her lip. "There was something, I know there was." She thought for a moment. "I've got it! She was waving her hands about as she talked and she mentioned "time". As she said the word she picked at the lapel of her coat, looking for an imaginary watch. I knew what she'd done struck a chord." Philip looked blank. "Don't you see? That's where a hospital nurse keeps her watch. It was ever such a clear gesture, but I wasn't thinking of it when I asked her the question. I was just making conversation."

"But why shouldn't she be a nurse?"

"There's no reason on earth, although she couldn't be a nurse and be married, of course, but my guess is that she's only pretending to be that chap's sister and the nursing bit doesn't fit in with the picture she's drawn of herself. I wish you'd been there. You'd have seen exactly what I mean. Tommy was with me, but he's hopeless. He's so strung up about the inquest that he wouldn't have noticed if she was wearing a false moustache."

Philip nodded thoughtfully. "I think you might be onto something. Especially when you take the poor bloke's last words into account, this whole identification lark may be an attempt to lead us up the garden path. Would you mind telling my pal, Mr Brenzett, all about it?"

"Of course I don't, but why?"

Philip smiled apologetically. "Well, keep this under your hat, but I'm afraid I was tinkering with the truth when I called him a business associate. He's actually a Scotland Yard man come to keep a weather eye on the hunt for this emerald necklace."

"Good Lord," said Sandy, impressed. "Yes, of course I'll tell him, only..."

"Only what?"

"It sounds so trivial when I think about it. It's all right telling you."

"And it'll be all right telling him. You just see."

They found Mr Brenzett propping up the low, sun-soaked wall that ran round the church. He nodded as he saw them approach and lifted his hat to Sandy. "'Morning, Miss Herriad."

He pointed with his pipe-stem to the yew that stood on the other side of the lych-gate. "Marvellous tree, that. It must have stood here a thousand years or more."

"Never mind trees," said Philip briskly. "Miss Herriad is harbouring suspicions of Mrs Strickland and I thought we'd better come and tell you about them. To put it bluntly, Miss Herriad doesn't think the good lady is the real McCoy."

Brenzett smiled. "So she struck you that way, did she? I was thinking that her account didn't chime in with your ideas as to who the passing stranger was. What makes you think she's not what she's cracked up to be?"

Sandy hesitated, then plunged in. To her relief, Mr Brenzett didn't laugh, but listened carefully.

"An expression, you say?" he said when she'd finished. "Hmm. It's a pity there's nothing a bit more concrete. You see, on the face of it, she's perfectly okay. We went looking for her, not the other way about. On the other hand, there's the dying man's last words to try and account for. I may as well say that I wasn't too impressed with the lady. I thought she was a bit too slick in some of her answers and wonderfully vague about anything that could be checked. I mean, to say someone's an Irishman called Murphy is like saying you're an Englishman called Smith. There must have been hundreds of Murphys in the Navy. Without the name of a ship to go on we can't possibly disprove a thing she's said. However, it could all be true because if she's not Emmeline Strickland, who is she, and where does she fit in?"

"She must be part of the gang," said Sandy.

"Gang?"

"The gang who's trying to find the necklace." She clicked her tongue impatiently. "Look, for ages and ages everyone thought the necklace was safely in the bank. Then it gets out it isn't safely in the bank but hidden somewhere at Farholt. This man, who could be Robert Eldon, is hardly going to waltz up to the house announcing who he is, so he has another identity as this

112

Kevin Murphy, with a letter and a sister to back him up. He could have been living a double life for years. He gets knocked over and the gang have a crisis, or at least Mrs Strickland does. There might not be a gang at all, actually, it could just be him and Mrs Strickland."

"That's a possibility," admitted Mr Brenzett dubiously.

"It's more than that. She'd have to be in league with Robert Eldon - I'm blessed if I'm going to call him Kevin Murphy because I'm sure that's not his name - if her letter was in his pocket. It's important that no-one realises who he was because that'd give the whole show away, about them being after the necklace. So Mrs Strickland comes forward when asked and identifies him as her harmless brother who's simply out for a day in the country. I'm sure I'm onto something. Mr Brenzett, Mr Brown told me who you really were. Can't you do something?"

Brenzett sucked at his pipe. "The trouble is, Miss Herriad, that I've got no official position regarding the inquest. It was an affair for the local police." He pulled at his pipe once more. "Leave it with me. I certainly can't do anything now and I wouldn't really want to. If Mrs Strickland's innocent, I don't want to cause her any more distress, and if she's not, it won't harm her to think she's pulled one over on us."

He glanced at his watch, then knocked his pipe out on the wall. "I think it's about time we were getting back inside. The jury ought to be returning soon."

It all ended satisfactorily, and Tommy Leigh, in a tone of deep relief, was heard to remark that evening that he'd

"Got away with it." They were in the drawing-room after dinner and Sandy, chaffing at the unaccountable absence of Philip Brown, was trying to avoid listening to, for what seemed like the hundredth time, Tommy's graphic account of how he'd felt when the jury had given their verdict. She looked up with relief as Philip came into the room. After a little while he drew her to one side.

"I've just seen Brenzett," he said quietly. "Come with me." Then loudly enough for his voice to carry, "Do you fancy a stroll in the garden, Miss Herriad? There's a wonderful moon."

"I'd be delighted," said Sandy, looking up with a smile.

Tommy Leigh watched them go with a disgruntled look. "I'm dashed if I know what she sees in that feller," he said to anyone who cared to listen. "*I* didn't think the moon was so marvellous and there's a nippy wind."

There was. Out on the lawn, Sandy was shivering.

"Let me go back for your shawl," offered Philip.

"Never mind that. What did Mr Brenzett have to say? I noticed you'd disappeared after dinner."

"Yes, I went down to the Bird In Hand where he's staying. He got in touch with Scotland Yard after the inquest and, to cut a long story short, they've got no record at all of any Mrs Emmeline Strickland. As far as they know, she's a perfectly blameless citizen."

"Well, she'd have to pretend to be, wouldn't she? Go on. I can see there's more."

"Well, it's about the poor bloke. We're assuming that he came from London because of the ticket from Waterloo, so Brenzett asked if they'd had anyone

114

reported as missing. There's only one suitable candidate, a man called Alan Oliver. His description, such as it is, fits our man. He was noted as missing yesterday, after a visit to Scotland Yard from his friend, a Major Harold Hornby, who had become worried by his continued absence. Apparently Alan Oliver hasn't been seen since last Thursday."

"And the accident was on Friday," breathed Sandy. "We're really onto something."

"Well, we might be. He certainly isn't in any of the London hospitals, which was Major Hornby's initial worry. Now we *could* leave it all up to Brenzett, and I suppose we should, but I don't know. It might be a wild goose chase, but I've got a fancy to run up to London tomorrow in the car and see the Major for myself."

"I'm coming as well."

"I thought you'd say that. You realise this is probably all a waste of time?"

"Nonsense," said Sandy. "At the very least you can take me to lunch."

***   ***   ***

Major Hornby was relieved to see them. "I felt a bit of a fool going to the police, you know," he confided as he ushered them into the restaurant. "I kept on thinking old Alan will come strolling back and be fearfully ticked off that I'd made a fuss over nothing. Now you people are looking for him as well, it lets me out a bit."

Philip had telephoned the Major that morning. By getting up at an indecently early hour, he had been able to catch him before he left for work. How to pump a total

115

stranger for information required some delicacy. He didn't want to tell the Major the true facts of the case.

He had an uncomfortable feeling that Sandy's conviction that Alan Oliver and Robert Eldon were the same person was nothing but wishful thinking and he certainly didn't want to make the connection between the inquest on Kevin Murphy and Major Hornby's friend.

Weighing up various possibilities that suggested themselves to him, he plumped for describing himself as a solicitor and Sandy as his confidential clerk retained to trace the whereabouts of Alan Oliver in connection with a legacy. Pausing by the telephone after speaking to Major Hornby, he hesitated, then put through a call to Scotland Yard. Satisfied with the result, he had gone in search of breakfast.

Now, confronting Major Harold Hornby in person, Philip felt a twinge of guilt. Major Hornby was so obviously straight-forward that it seemed wrong to deceive him. However, having started, he had to see it through.

"Yes," said the Major, as they followed the waiter across the room to their table, "If Alan turns up now, I'll be able to put all the hullabaloo down to this legacy business. Who on earth's it from? Or aren't I meant to ask that? It's news to me that Alan had anyone to leave him anything."

"The legacy is from a Miss Rebecca Clarice Standworthy of Tullis Creek, New South Wales," said Sandy. This had been agreed in the car on their way to London.

"She was his aunt," put in Philip, adding another part of the story they'd decided upon, "but the two sides of the family parted as a result of a quarrel concerning the reason for Miss... er... Standworthy's father's sudden departure from England."

Major Hornby's eyes widened. "Good Lord! A criminal, what?"

"I would hesitate to use the word "Criminal", Major," said Philip, putting his finger-tips together in a legal way that nearly made Sandy giggle. "There are certain crimes the Law cannot touch."

"I say! What the dickens did he do?"

"That, I am afraid, I am not at liberty to reveal. The confidentiality of my client, you understand."

"Yes... I see," said the Major, much impressed. So was Sandy.

"We do have to ascertain, however, that the Alan Oliver mentioned in Miss Standworthy's will is the same man as your friend, Mr Oliver," continued Philip, smoothly.

If this really was a mare's nest, the last thing he wanted was to have an outraged Alan Oliver demanding large sums of money from a deceased, albeit fictitious, Australian. "Therefore, Major, in order to carry out our client's wishes, we have instituted a search for Mr Oliver."

"Perhaps you've seen the adverts in the newspapers," added Sandy, quite unnecessarily.

"And in pursuance of those enquiries," continued Philip, with a glare at Sandy, "contacted Scotland Yard, where we were given your name. I need hardly say we

117

would be grateful for any assistance you could give us with this matter."

"Oh, I'll do all I can," said the Major, cheerfully. "Hang on a mo, just bag the waiter, will you?"

When matters had been satisfactory settled in the form of one mixed grill and two lamb cutlets, Philip returned to the attack. "Have you known Mr Oliver long?"

"Absolutely ages," said Major Hornby, between intervals of French beans. "And really, don't you know, he's the last man in the world to simply vanish like this. I can't understand it. We were meant to be going down to Yarmouth on Friday evening. A friend of mine, Freddie Rossiter, keeps an old yawl there and we were going to crew for him and get in a bit of fishing. I spoke to Alan on Thursday afternoon and he was looking forward to it. However, on Friday morning I got a note by the first post to say that something had cropped up but he'd see me after the weekend." He hesitated awkwardly.

"Was that all he said?" asked Sandy.

"No, but I'm dashed if I can understand what he was getting at. He said to keep my fingers crossed because all he needed was a lucky break and he'd be a free man. Well, he was a free man. I mean, he wasn't married or engaged, so I don't know what he was talking about."

Sandy's eyes widened. A nudge from Philip's foot under the table warned her to keep quiet.

"Well, when I got back," continued Major Hornby, "there was no sign of him. When yesterday morning came along and there was still no Alan, I got a bit concerned, you know? I wondered if he'd been caught up in an accident or something, so, feeling a bit of a fool, I toddled along to Scotland Yard and told them all about it. I can't make out what's happened to him."

"No. It sounds very odd. You said you'd known him a long time. Were you at school with him?" asked Philip, ignoring the excited gleam in Sandy's eyes.

"School? No. Dashed if I know where he did go to school, to be honest. He never talked about it, or any of his early life, come to think of it. He'd obviously knocked about the world a bit, though. I first ran across him in the Army. I was in the Sappers, and he was the NCO in charge of a party of London Scottish that I'd borrowed. That was early '17, just before Vimy Ridge. Well, it didn't take me long to see that he was a nailing good man and absolutely wasted in the infantry. He'd done the usual patriotic thing and joined as a private, but his talents were being thrown away. Apparently he'd been in my line before the war, engineering, y'know, mainly working abroad, but he didn't have any paper qualifications. Qualifications or not, I knew he was the sort of man we needed, so my C.O. had a word with his C.O., arranged a transfer, and we served together for the rest of the war."

This was sounding less and less promising. "Do you know if Mr Oliver has a job at the moment?" asked Philip.

The Major nodded a brisk assent. "Of course he's got a job. He works with me. I ran into him a few months after we'd both been demobbed and he was at a loose end. It was the usual sort of story. I'd started working for my uncle's firm - Thompson and Coolin, the big firm of

119

civil contractors in Goodge Street - and I invited him to come along. My uncle was a bit dubious about an unknown man, but I vouched for him, and the firm decided to give him a trial. Since then he's done some big jobs for us, mainly abroad, and really proved his worth. He only got back from Malacca a month ago. I hope he's all right. I can't make out what he's up to, going off like this. He's never done anything like it before."

"Where did he live?" asked Sandy. "Would it be possible to see his rooms? It might give us a clue as to what his intentions were."

The Major looked doubtful. "Well, he lived at his club, the Cornelian in St James, when he was in England. I don't suppose the Secretary would mind frightfully, considering the circumstances. The trouble, Miss Herriad, is you. Strictly speaking, ladies aren't permitted."

"Oh, but I'm on official business," said Sandy with a dazzling smile.

Philip drew out a note-book. "Perhaps this will help," he said and scribbling down a name and number, tore out the page and handed it to Major Hornby. "If the Secretary rings Sir Douglas Lynton at Scotland Yard, he'll vouch for us."

"Good Lord, will he?" said Major Hornby, looking at the name on the paper. "This must be no end of a big legacy if Scotland Yard are involved. Whatever is it?"

"It's not so much the value of the legacy, you understand," said Philip, thinking on his feet, "but the political implications of where it is." He looked gravely at

Major Hornby. "I'm sure you will understand that it would be impossible for me to say more."

Just how impossible it would be, was fortunately something that Major Hornby had no way of knowing.

Sir Douglas Lynton's name, coupled with Major Hornby's introduction, did the trick. However, whether the trick was worth it was another matter. Alan Oliver was obviously a very neat and orderly man and horribly unlike the picture of the reckless, crooked, if charming, Robert Eldon Sandy had been busily putting together in her mind.

A square of Turkish carpet lay in front of the empty grate, with an armchair to either side and an ash-tray on a stand beside the right-hand chair. On the mantelpiece lay, in contrast to the tidiness of the rest of the room, a homely clutter of pipes, matchboxes and spills. By the wall under the window was a roll-top desk and a bookcase. In the adjoining room was a neatly-made bed and a marble washstand on which lay a toothbrush, a bar of soap, a shaving-brush and a razor. Philip gazed at this assortment. "Whoever Mr Oliver is," he said to Sandy in a low voice, "he certainly intended coming back."

"It doesn't look as if he planned on staying away for long, either," added Sandy, nodding at the razor. "He'd have taken his things, surely. I do wish," she said, glancing at Major Hornby who were standing in the sitting-room, "that he would leave us alone."

"He can't do that," said Philip, taking out his handkerchief and wrapping the shaving-brush in it.

"What if we pinch something?" He slipped the shaving-brush into his pocket and walked back into the next room.

"Found anything?" asked Major Hornby. "No? I didn't think you would. What are you looking for?" he asked as Philip crouched down beside the bookcase.

"Title-pages," said Philip easily. "If we find a book with say, "To Alan, love from Aunt Rebecca" inside it, that would be an indication we were on the right track. However, I don't think we're going to be lucky. Hmm. *A Naturalist On the Amazon* by Bates. That's a good book." He rapidly took the books down and glanced through them. "There's four on South America altogether."

"Yes, he'd been there before the war. He described it as a sort of paradise if you were interested in bugs and moths and things."

"He's also got," said Philip, ignoring Sandy's excited intake of breath that the mention of South America had called forth, "Darwin, Hooker and Wallace, all in cheap editions, and *The Flora of the Nile Delta* with notes and maps and so on. I take it he was fairly keen on botany and so on?"

"He was," agreed the Major. "He wrote an article on pond-life, or whatever you call it, that was published last year. I know he collected notes wherever he was posted. Perhaps they're in the desk."

He stepped forward and opening the desk, pulled out a collection of bound note-books. "Here we are." He opened the topmost book, revealing a collection of newspaper clippings.

"What's all these bits of paper?" asked the Major, thumbing through them. "I say, they're all about that big jewel robbery. Come to think of it, I remember Alan talking about it. I wonder why he kept them all? There's this, too."

"This" was a quarter page evidently cut from the more frivolous section of the *Daily Express* for the previous Thursday. It showed a picture of a man who was just recognizable as Sir Dennis Storwood, apparently sunk in deep gloom. Eleanor Storwood was poised by his left elbow, shaking hands with someone out of sight.

"*Sir Dennis Storwood,*" read Major Hornby,' "*in thoughtful frame of mind snapped at the reception for President Enrique Artiaga at the Salvatierran Embassy earlier this week. Sir Dennis, in addition to his other talents, is a director of the troubled Houblyn's Bank (see story page two). Sir Dennis, we're glad to say, can put all his cares to one side this weekend as he joins a distinguished party at Farholt, one of England's most gracious country houses. Still, it's not all play for Sir Dennis. A little bird tells us* - Good Lord, don't they write some rubbish? - *that one of his fellow guests has a South American connection.*" He put the cutting back into the note-book with a puzzled frown. "Who's this Storwood feller?"

"A government minister, I believe," said Philip, rapidly rifling through the rest of the desk.

"But Alan didn't know anyone in the government. He had no turn for politics at all. Deadly stuff. I agreed with him."

"There's probably a reasonable explanation behind it at," agreed Philip, straightening up. "Thank you for your time, Major. I might as well say that it seems unlikely that Mr Oliver is man who we're looking for, but I'm very grateful for your help."

*** *** ***

"What d'you think, Sandy?" asked Philip, as they strolled into St James' Square after saying goodbye to Major Hornby. "There obviously is a connection between Alan Oliver and our business, but the bloke Major Hornby described didn't sound like Robert Eldon."

"Of course he's not Robert Eldon," said Sandy. "I tumbled to it when you were looking at all those books in the room. The man we saw has to be John Guthrie."

Chapter Six

Philip stopped dead on the pavement. "Of course! That would fit in beautifully. He was in the Sappers..."

"And later in this engineering firm."

"He worked in South America..."

"And kept those clippings about the emeralds." Sandy's eyes were shining. "It also tells us what he was doing at Farholt. That thing about Sir Dennis was in the *Daily Express* on Thursday. Now if he really was John Guthrie he'd have assumed, like everyone else, that President Ramon put the jewels in Houblyn's bank. However, when he read in the paper that the Houblyn emeralds were fake, he'd guess that they were at Farholt. He knew the Count swiped them and hid them somewhere and, going off what he said before he died, he thought he knew where that was. He must also know that the guest with the South American connection - you - that the paper talked about is from Salvatierra and would be going to Farholt to look for them. He sounds like a nice man, Phil. He wanted to find the jewels to prove his innocence. He virtually said as much to Major Hornby. That's what he meant by being free. He'd have to move fast, otherwise there's a risk you'd find them before he did."

"He could have rested easy on that score. I haven't a clue where to look."

"Yes, but he didn't know that, did he? After all, as President Thingamabob's secretary, you might have had access to all sorts of secret papers telling you where the Count hid the jewels."

"You're right." Philip thought for a few moments. "Where does this Mrs Strickland fit in?" he asked eventually.

Sandy shrugged. "I don't know, but she obviously does. After all, if he's John Guthrie, he's wanted for murder. Maybe she found out who he was and was blackmailing him. That'd explain the connection. She must've seen the stuff in the papers about the emeralds and sent him off to get them."

She hesitated. "Perhaps I'm wrong about him being innocent," she said in a disappointed voice. "They could've been going to split the proceeds. Then, of course, it all went horribly wrong. She's got to cover up the fact she was a blackmailer, so she came forward and identified him as Kevin Murphy."

"If he was carrying a letter from her she wouldn't have much choice."

"No, but she probably wanted to establish that he really was Kevin Murphy, so no one would be go on poking around to find out who he actually was. After the inquest, the case should have been closed. What d'you think?"

Philip hesitated. "I think you're going a bit fast. After all, we don't know yet that our man is Alan Oliver, still less that he's John Guthrie."

"We can find that out, surely. What were you going to do with the shaving-brush you nabbed from his rooms?"

"Take it to Sir Douglas Lynton at Scotland Yard. With any luck there'll be fingerprints on it that the police can compare with those of Kevin Murphy, to give him his courtesy name. I'm not sure when he's going to be buried, but I bet we haven't got long."

"In that case," said Sandy, "we'd better go and see Sir Douglas now."

***   ***   ***

Sir Douglas Lynton looked up as a knock sounded on his door. "This should be my man now," he said to Philip and Sandy. He raised his voice. "Come in."

Detective-Sergeant Usborne entered the room. "Well?" asked Sir Douglas. "Are there any fingerprints on the brush, Sergeant?"

"Yes, sir," replied Usborne. "There's a nice clear thumb-mark and a good print of the index and forefinger. We should have prints of the photographs very shortly."

"In that case," said Sir Douglas, "we could do with getting you to Farholt to make a comparison right away before the corpse is put underground. The trouble is, that unless the County Police call us in, we've got no authority to act in what is, after all, one of their cases." He drummed his fingers thoughtfully on the edge of his desk. "I think, under the circumstances, that I'd better have a word with the Chief Constable. He's called Waldrist, I believe."

"I know Colonel Waldrist," put in Sandy. "He plays golf with Daddy. In fact - what day is it? Wednesday? I bet he's at Farholt now. He often calls in for tea after a game."

Sir Douglas raised his eyebrows. "It's nice to know our public servants keep their nose to the grindstone." He pulled the telephone towards him. "Farholt, you say, Miss Herriad? What's the number?"

Sandy gave it to him, smiling slightly as she heard Larch, the butler's, tinny voice come over the receiver.

Sir Douglas glanced away from the telephone. "He's there. The butler's gone to get him. Ah, Colonel Waldrist? Douglas Lynton here from Scotland Yard.... Yes, that's right. Yes. I believe you've had an inquest recently - a man killed in a motor accident on the Farholt Road. Murphy, that's the one. We've got reason to believe that he may be the same man who's wanted in connection with a capital charge. No, nothing to do with Ireland. Purely a domestic matter. Just in case he is our man, I'd be obliged if you'd let me send one of our officers along, a Sergeant Usborne. Oh no, nothing drastic. Just a question of fingerprints. As soon as possible. Today, definitely. If we do make a positive identification, we shall want to make an arrest, yes. Not at all. Obliged to you."

Sir Douglas rang off. "Well, that's settled. Usborne, after you've got the fingerprints, get in touch with Superintendent Brenzett and bring him up to date. He's staying at the Bird in Hand. He's undercover, so don't make a fuss about who you are. I'll warn him to expect you."

He picked up the telephone again and rang The Bird in Hand and, after a short wait, spoke to the Superintendent.

Philip and Sandy drew to one side while Sir Douglas gave his instructions over the telephone. Sir Douglas put the phone down and glanced at Usborne. "Off you go, man. You should be there in a couple of hours." He turned to Philip and Sandy with a smile as Usborne left the room. "We should know the truth by this evening with any luck. At least," he amended, "we should know if Kevin Murphy and Alan Oliver are one and the same. Tell me again why you believe he's John Guthrie."

He nodded as Sandy ran through her line of reasoning. "Yes, that's all quite sound as far as it goes. I wonder if there's anything in his record that'll point us in the right direction." He opened the drawer of the desk and pulled out a file. "These are the papers relating to the murder of Count von Liebrich. I had them brought up when Brenzett and I were discussing the case. It contains all we know about John Guthrie." He opened the file, read briefly, then smiled. "Well, well. Look at the man's full name." He indicated the place on the page.

"John Alan Oliver Guthrie," read Philip. "I say! *Alan Oliver*!" He glanced across at Sandy. "It has to be him. That's far too close a coincidence for it not to be."

"I agree," said Sir Douglas. "Well done, Miss Herriad. I really think you're on to something." Sandy looked understandably smug. "Congratulations." He closed the file. "If we could only work out what it was that he knew..." He looked thoughtfully at Philip. "I don't suppose you've remembered anything else that could be useful to us?"

"I'm sorry, but no. However, this Mrs Strickland might be able to tell us something."

"Absolutely. As soon as we get a positive identification of the body, we'll pick her up. She played a very bold stroke, coming forward to the inquest like that. Mind you, I don't suppose she had much choice in a way. If she disappeared then we'd have known something was wrong."

"I suppose she is who she says she is?" asked Sandy. "Mrs Strickland, I mean. Actually, she'd have to be, wouldn't she, because of the address on the letter."

Sir Douglas shrugged. "She might have another name, but she's certainly Emmeline Strickland all right."

He walked over to the bookcase and took down *Kelly's Street Directory*. "Here she is. Listed under the correct name at the correct address, which means she's been there for at least a year. There's nothing on record about her. That was all checked yesterday at Brenzett's request."

Philip got to his feet. "There doesn't seem to be much more we can do at the moment, Sir Douglas. I'll be in touch this evening to see what's happened." He glanced at Sandy. "In the meantime, we might as well get a spot of dinner somewhere, yes?"

*** *** ***

"Dinner," said Sandy, as Philip helped her into the red two-seater, "sounds a bit tame."

"I'm crushed. Can't I tempt you with the Savoy?"

"It'd have to be the Grill Room in these clothes. Philip, I don't want to eat, I want to *do* something."

"Oh. I thought..."

"Look, here we are in London. Mrs Strickland told me she was staying in Brosley Dean for the funeral. Why don't we go and have a look at her house?"

Philip stopped half-way round the car. "Where will that get us? It'll simply be a house, won't it? We know she lives there. I can't see what looking at the front door will tell us."

"I didn't want to look at the front door. I wanted to get inside. Break in, if you like."

"Sandy! This craze for other people's houses is growing on you. That'd be the second one today. Besides, what on earth do you expect to find?"

"I don't know." She tutted impatiently. "Secret papers or something."

"But what about the servants? There's bound to be a housemaid."

"Then we could pretend to be from the gas board or collecting for charity or looking at the drains. You didn't mind pretending to be a solicitor."

"That was different. Solicitors are easy. All you do is look severe and talk about Rex V. Kegsworthy or what-have-you in the year 1830. I don't know anything about drains or charity. Honestly, Sandy, I think it's a waste of time."

She looked at him appealingly. "Come on, Philip. It can't do any harm."

He got into the car. "All right. We'll go and have a look. I'm not breaking in, though. What would Sir Douglas say?"

*** *** ***

They left the car parked at the tube station and walked to Hilldrop Road. Cars, particularly scarlet roadsters, were not common in Camden Town and Philip felt that the less attention they drew to themselves the better. Hilldrop Road was tucked away in a warren of streets behind Camden High Street. One side was completely occupied by the sooty brick wall of a furniture depot, while the other consisted of a row of small semi-detached houses, each separated from the pavement by three feet of garden and a low brick wall. Pausing by the dusty laburnum which marked number forty-three, Philip looked at the house doubtfully.

"Well, here it is. What do we do now?"

Sandy was gazing at the window intently. "D'you know, I think it's empty. The curtains are shut. I can't see her keeping a maid in a house that size. I don't believe there's a soul in there."

"Don't you?" asked Philip unhappily. "Oi! What are you doing?" For Sandy had opened the iron-work gate and raised the knocker.

"Seeing if it really is empty, of course."

No one answered Sandy's thunderous summons. Much to Philip's relief, no neighbour opened their door to enquire what was going on.

"Let's try round the back," said Sandy after a few minutes had passed. Without waiting to see if he was following, she plunged down the narrow passage between the houses to the alley at the back.

Philip caught up with her as she was opening the gate through a high brick wall into the gloomy yard. "Sandy! You aren't going in there."

"Of course I am. Do be quiet, Phil. You'll have people looking."

She snicked the gate closed behind them. The yard of the house was in the shape of an L, with the kitchen and outhouses running down the side. Nothing stirred. Over the top of the wall they could see the lights from next door's kitchen window. The sound of voices and the smell of cooking onions reached them clearly. Sandy walked quietly forward up the yard. "I think this is the sitting-room," she whispered. "There's a crack where the curtains aren't drawn together." She pointed to the middle bar of the sash. "Look, that's not closed properly. I'm sure we could get in."

"I knew it!"

"Shush! Don't talk so loudly. All you have to do is stand on the windowsill and push. Then we can get in through the bottom."

"And what if it squeaks?" demanded Philip in an indignant whisper. "We'll have the police round."

"Stop worrying. All you'd have to do is mention Sir Douglas's name and we'd be okay."

Philip was appalled. "I couldn't do that. It's... it's bribery or corruption or something."

She gave him a melting look.

"Women," he muttered in an undertone as he stepped up to the window, "have got no sense of ethics."

He pressed his fingers under the sash and pushed. The window reluctantly rose a few inches.

Sandy beamed with pleasure. "That's splendid," she hissed. "Now get down and push it up just a little bit more... There!" And, in an undignified scramble, she wriggled through the gap. Philip, raising his eyes to heaven, joined her.

The room was dark, sparsely furnished and cold. Sandy shivered and, wanting more light, carefully drew back the heavy bobbled curtains. The rings scraped on the curtain-poles and she froze. The voices from next door continued unchecked and she relaxed with a sigh.

"Well," said Philip, in a louder voice than he had dared to use outside, "now we're in, what do we do?"

"Look round. I want to get some sort of idea of who she is." She glanced round and shivered again. "It seems awfully deserted, somehow."

It was a comfortless room. The sofa and two chairs, made of an uninviting imitation leather, shiny with much use, could, perhaps, have looked welcoming with bright cushions. The oil-cloth on the floor cried out for rugs and the mantelpiece was totally bare. There were no papers, books, ash-trays or ornaments; nothing to show that anyone lived here. Sandy walked quietly into the tiny hall and looked in the front room. That had furniture - a table, chairs and a heavy sideboard - but again there was nothing at all to give the room individual life.

Philip led the way upstairs, mindful of creaking boards. The main bedroom door stood open. A double bed without any bed-clothes, a cheap deal wardrobe and a chest of drawers, stained to look like oak, were the sole contents of the room. Philip slid open the top drawer. It was empty, lined with last year's newspaper. He rapidly checked the other drawers. They, too, were empty. He crossed to the wardrobe and opened the door. There was nothing inside. Leaving Sandy he crossed the tiny corridor to the other bedroom. That, too, was bare, save for a stripped bedstead. He reappeared at the doorway. "Sandy," he said thoughtfully. "I think she's hooked it."

*** *** ***

"I can't understand why," said Sandy. They were standing in the sitting-room once more. "I mean, why should she up and leave? She can't know we suspect her of anything."

They had been through the whole house and, although furnished, it was completely lacking any personal possessions. Only the kitchen cupboard showed any sign of occupancy in the form of a half-used quarter of Typhoo Tipps tea and an opened bag of sugar.

"I've got to agree. She's obviously left for good and it doesn't look as if she's coming back. It doesn't make any sense, Sandy. She's lived here for the last year, at least. Why on earth should she clear out now?"

"And where are all her things? The wretched woman must have *some* bits and pieces but all that's here is the tea, sugar and half a scuttle-full of coal." Sandy stooped down by the hearth and looked in the grate. "It doesn't even look as if she burned papers in here. If she had done we'd know she was trying to cover something up."

135

In the interests of thoroughness she pulled away the front of the grate and peered in at the little heap of ash below. "There *is* a bit of paper in here," she announced in slightly more enthusiastic tones. Using the hearth brush, she swept out the ashes from under the grate, then picked up a slip of charred newspaper. "...*ly Ex*...." she read. "*Daily Express*, d'you think? Obviously she used it to lay the fire. Damn!"

"There's another bit of newspaper," said Philip, pointing. Sandy picked it up carefully, laying it on the flat of her hand.

"....*ngford* - then there's a burnt bit - *ette*. Ette? Gazette, I imagine. I say, Phil, d'you think it's a clue?"

"It's not much of one if it is. 'Ngford Gazette. We can hardly scour England looking for somewhere that ends in Ngford. There must be thousands of places. You can't make out any of the rest of it, can you?"

"There's not much to make out," complained Sandy. "It looks like eggs, and then a bit missed out and another word *Orpington*. It's all about hens." She dropped the paper back on the ash and straightened up. "Let's go. This has been the most disappointing house."

***   ***   ***

Back in the car, driving into the centre of London, they debated what to do next.

"It's a great pity," said Sandy thoughtfully, "that it's too late to go to the house-agents. I'd love to know what Mrs Strickland told them. She's obviously moved out. I wonder if she left a forwarding address? Perhaps we can

136

try them tomorrow. What reason can we have for asking, I wonder? We can hardly tell them the truth."

"I can see my ethics are going to be permanently dented if I continue to associate with you. Why on earth can't we simply say we're looking for the woman?"

"They might not tell us. Besides that, it's a bit tame, isn't it? We'd better pretend to be Mrs Strickland's relations or say that we wanted to rent a house for ourselves and that number 43 was our dream home."

"I honestly think we'd better let Scotland Yard tackle it," said Philip, concentrating on the traffic. "It'd be far easier for them to find who lets the house and all that sort of thing. I mean," he added, sparing a quick glance at Sandy, "a house-agent would never believe you were seriously interested in a house on Hilldrop Road."

"Why shouldn't he? If you're saying I..."

"Not while you're wearing a hat like that. He'd be far more likely to suggest a flat on Park Lane or somewhere."

Sandy stopped, conscious that the wind had been taken out of her sails. "I didn't realise I looked so opulent. It *is* a nice hat but I could always change it for something plain. I can look very dowdy if I try."

"I doubt it," muttered Philip. "Sandy, we absolutely have to tell Sir Douglas about that house. Maybe he can work out what's going on." He glanced at his watch. "I could do with dropping in at my club to see if there're any messages. It won't take me a minute or two. Why don't we do that, then have dinner somewhere and afterwards we can go back to Scotland Yard? You'll still get to know what's happening."

"All right," agreed Sandy with moderately good grace. "Which club do you belong to?"

*** *** ***

There were worse occupations, thought Sandy, than sitting in a car by the side of St James' Park, but she was conscious of a feeling of anti-climax. After all, she'd spotted Mrs Strickland was a phoney. If it hadn't been for that, the police would have accepted her at face value and never dreamed of going near the house in Camden Town. She lit a cigarette. Philip was taking ages inside his club. There obviously was something wrong with Mrs Strickland. Quite apart from the house, there was that slip-up about nursing. Where did that fit in?

Maybe she'd nursed John Guthrie. John Guthrie and Alan Oliver *had* to be the same man. Maybe he'd been a patient of hers. That would account for her looking so startled when she'd been asked about nursing. It would seem as if she, Sandy, was hinting at knowledge she didn't actually possess. That would put her on her guard, right enough, but it didn't account for why she'd abandoned her house before the inquest. After all, she'd lived there for at least a year, so why draw attention to herself now?

What on earth was Philip doing? On the other hand, she might have been afraid that her story wouldn't stand up, and had made arrangements for a quick getaway. Sandy shook her head. That didn't add up... At last! Philip was coming down the steps towards her. He looked worried.

"I'm sorry I've been such an age," he said, cutting off her protests. "There was a note for me and I had to get in touch with the embassy. I'm awfully sorry, but I'll have to call in there." He climbed into the car with an apologetic smile. "I really am sorry about this, Sandy, but I honestly think the best thing would be for me to see you onto a train back to Farholt. There's been some sort of burglary where the President's staying up in Scotland, but they wouldn't give me the details over the phone. The trouble is, I know what the embassy are like. It'll take me ages to sort things out and I might end up having to go to Scotland. I hope not, but there it is. I feel rotten about having to skip dinner with you."

"It doesn't matter," said Sandy. "Never mind about dinner, I can have something on the train. Can you telephone me this evening? I'd like to know what Sir Douglas has to say and we'll need to know when to expect you back. Don't look so worried, Philip. If you drop me off at Waterloo, you can get off straight away."

"I can see you on to the train, at least," said Philip, putting in the clutch. "Burglary or no burglary, that's the least I can do."

***　　***　　***

The next train to Brosley Dean was due in thirty-five minutes. Sitting in the tea-room at Waterloo, Philip glanced at his watch. "I wish I knew what this burglary business was about. It doesn't sound as if anything was taken."

"That's a good thing, isn't it?" asked Sandy, filling up the tea-pot with hot water. "Why on earth do railway scones always taste stale?"

139

"I don't know. The burglary, I mean, not the scones. Try one of these cakes instead." He hesitated. "A burglar's one thing, but an intruder.... well, I don't like the implications. You see, without wanting to sound like that friend of yours, Miss Peverell, there really could be a gang after him."

"You're really worried about him, aren't you?" asked Sandy.

"Yes," admitted Philip. "Without him, poor old Salvatierra would fall apart. Despite being called President he's more like a king, really. He was born to the job, you see. He didn't particularly want to be President but he is." He shook himself in irritation. "Still, whether he wanted it or not, he's got to do it. That's what led to the break-up between him and his wife, but God knows what'd happen if he wasn't there."

"Dad says that no-one's irreplaceable."

"He's wrong," said Philip, shortly. "Sorry, that sounded a bit sharp, but if the President bought it, the whole country could go under. Let's talk about something else."

As usual, this request was followed by silence, during which the tea-room door opened, admitting a cloud of sooty air and a rush of customers. Sandy glanced up, then gave a little start of recognition, smiling at a plump, kindly-faced woman in a seal-skin coat. "Mrs Banks?"

The woman in the seal-skin, who looked like a cook but was in fact a retired house-maid, paused by their table. "Hello, Miss Herriad," she said in a rich Surrey accent. "Fancy seeing you here. Oh, don't get up, sir."

Mrs Banks gave a warm beam of pleasure as Philip disobeyed this injunction. "I've just got off the Brosley Dean train. Nice and quiet at this time in the evening." She chuckled. "It'll be a different story going back, I'm sure. I've come down to stay with our Gladys for a day or two. She'll have something ready for me, but I thought I must have a cup of tea before I tackle that bus journey. Do sit down, sir, don't let me keep you standing. No, I won't join you, thanks all the same. Three's a crowd, as they say."

Philip sighed slightly. Good manners and years of careful training forbad him to sit whilst any woman stood, and not only did he want to carry on talking to Sandy, but his tea was cooling rapidly.

"I've seen you before," said Mrs Banks, who was apparently happy to stand all evening. "You were at the inquest, weren't you? You gave your little speech very well, Miss," she added, nodding at Sandy. "I said to our Jessie, 'I'm glad *I* don't have to do what Miss Herriad's doing,' and Jessie said she'd die, rather. Terrible business, wasn't it? There ought to be some sort of law about these motor-cars, dashing all over the country and that poor young man, he looked so sorry about what had happened. I'm sure the coroner had no need to speak to him as sharp as he did. I felt quite sorry for him, and so did everyone else. Yes, it was very sad altogether, and it's shocking, isn't it, the way people carry on so. It's human nature, I suppose, and, as I always say, there's nothing like a wedding or a funeral to get people together. I've never been to an inquest before, but it was much the same, but without the food. It was nice seeing everyone, though, even if I did think there could have been a cup of tea, at least. I saw people I haven't seen for months and there was one, I said to Jessie, 'If that's not the dead spit of...'

"Good Lord!" said Philip. He had been listening with feigned and paralysed interest, but now his eyes were fixed over the frosted glass that ran along the bottom of the tea-room windows. "Sandy, it's her!" He snatched up his hat and made a dive for the door.

Mrs Banks and Sandy gazed at each other in bewilderment. "Whatever...." began Mrs Banks, but Sandy was fumbling in her handbag. She brought out a ten-shilling note. "Mrs Banks, I've got to go. Can you give this to the waitress for our tea? Thank you." Without waiting for an answer, she plunged out of door after Philip.

"*Well*!" said Mrs Banks. She sank down at the table. She'd always thought Miss Herriad was such a nice, reliable young lady. London, that's what it was, London. Changed a person, it did. She gathered her handbag on to her knee, frowning her disapproval at the Metropolis as represented in the Waterloo tea-room.

*** *** ***

Philip quickened his stride, trying to see once more the woman in the blue serge coat and the dark felt hat. There she was! He pushed through the crowd, indifferent to the clucks of annoyance. The woman glanced up at the destination board and Philip drew a quick breath of satisfaction. It *was* Mrs Strickland.

142

A porter with a wagon-load of suitcases trundled across his path. Philip dodged round him, catching a glimpse of his quarry a few feet away. The crowd cleared and for some reason she turned, catching sight of him. He saw her face change, then she disappeared behind a crocodile of school-girls.

Ignoring a scandalized cry from a school-mistress, he pushed his way through the line of girls, hearing their giggles. She was gone again. Hell fire! No... There she was, heading for the Underground. Damn this crowd!

He wriggled forward again. Why the blazes had the whole world come to stand on this wretched station? He pushed his way through to the escalator. Wrong side, of course. It would be. He had an infuriating glimpse of blue serge vanishing down the stairway, before thrusting his way through. "Here!" said a deep voice. "What's your game?" A burly workman, whose arm he had knocked against, caught him by the shoulder. Philip dug out with his elbow and had the satisfaction of hearing an outraged grunt before jumping onto the moving staircase.

There was a flash of white at the bottom as Mrs Strickland turned her face upwards, then she was gathered up in the crowd moving towards the Bakerloo Line. Philip had never hated his fellow-man as heartily as he did at that moment. He lost precious moments circling round two elegant ladies who had decided to hold a reunion at the entrance to the booking-hall, before once more catching sight of the dark hat in the middle of the slowly moving tide. He wriggled forward, catching the woman by the arm. "Mrs Strickland..." he began.

A total stranger turned her face to his.

Apologies were necessary of course. "So sorry... I thought you were a lady I knew... I do beg your pardon..." and, tipping his hat, he managed to get away, chaffing at the delay.

How many tunnels were there on this bloody line? He had no choice but to go forward, a part of the crowd. This was hopeless. The crowd thinned and he reached the booking hall, his eyes feverishly searching the people round him.

There! That was her, surely, vanishing through the gates. He couldn't chance following her without a ticket. That would mean endless arguments and delays at the barrier. Change, change, he needed change. The wretched man in front of him only had a ten-shilling note. God damnit, now he'd dropped his money! Move out of the way, will you....

"Destination?" asked the booking clerk, politely.

"Moorgate Street," said Philip, picking a name at random. He put a shilling on the counter and without waiting for his change, snatched his ticket. He wanted to run but was forced to walk forward in irritatingly small steps. Through the barrier.... God in heaven, how long was this tunnel? And if he did manage to catch up with her, what on earth was he going to say? "Mrs Strickland, you've left your house." ("And what if I have? What business is it of yours, young man?") "Mrs Strickland, we believe you gave false evidence at the inquest." ("Do you indeed? Officer, this man is annoying me.")

She'd never dare to do that. She'd left Farholt in a hurry and run away from him. She had something to hide and knew he was on to her. If only he could manage to find where she was. Was this tunnel never going to end? The crowd thinned and spread out onto the platform. Suddenly there was space to move. Philip drew away from the tiled wall and walked along the platform, his eyes darting across the stolidly waiting passengers. The world was full of women in coats. Green coats, black coats, coats with fur collars... any sort of coat but blue serge. There! No.

A rush of air and a low rumble announced the imminent arrival of a train.

***   ***   ***

Sandy stood on the station concourse. She'd lost him, of course. He could have gone anywhere in this milling crowd and she hadn't a clue where to start looking. Had it really been Mrs Strickland he'd seen? There surely couldn't be anyone else who'd he describe as "Her!"

Why had she come to London? Somehow she must have found out the police were looking for her but how could she have done? The only people who knew were themselves and the police. The best thing to do was to go back into the tea-room and wait. After all, Philip was bound to come looking for her, wasn't he? Ourselves and the police. The police wouldn't warn Mrs Strickland. She *must* have been warned. She knew she hadn't said anything. He'd spent ages in his club. Plenty of time to phone... Ourselves and the police. Ourselves...

She opened the door of the tea-room. Mrs Banks, now armed with a pot of tea, was still there.

"I can't see him," said Sandy hopelessly, feeling oddly close to tears. "He's run off and I can't see him anywhere."

Mrs Banks put the most natural interpretation on these words. "Now, you never mind, my ducks. Sit down here and have a nice cup of tea. A young lady like you, you don't want to be fussing with men that run off without a by-your-leave. *And* he left you to pay the bill. Drink up your tea while it's nice and hot. That's right. Now don't you think about him anymore. As I said to our Jessie when she got in such a taking about Bill Hinchcliffe from the White Hart, there's plenty more where he came from. In your case it's likely to be true, as well, which is more than I can say for Jessie with the temper she has on her *and* far too choosy for her own good."

Sandy gave a watery giggle and sipped her tea. "You don't understand, Mrs Banks. It's not like that at all. Phil - Mr Brown - and I aren't seeing each other. Not in that way, anyhow."

"Ah," said Mrs Banks with profound and unshakable disbelief. "I dare say. Who is he then, my ducks?"

"Mr Brown?" Sandy bit her lip. "He's staying with us." (What had Tommy said? *There's a lot more to that chap than meets the eye.*) Certain vague thoughts clicked into place. This was crazy, but.... "Mrs Banks, would you recognize Robert Eldon if you saw him now?"

Mrs Banks blinked. "What, Master Eldon? But he was killed in the war, Miss."

"But would you?" persisted Sandy. "If he was still alive, I mean."

"Well, I don't know as I would." Mrs Banks readjusted her thoughts. "It's so long ago, you see, and he was away at school a lot of the time. I knew what he looked like then, of course, but I wouldn't know what he looked like now, even if he had been spared. I knew him best as a little boy. Sweet little thing, he was, and could always get his own way just by looking at you. Mind you, he liked his own way. It didn't do to cross him. The mistress spoiled him, so some said, but he was a sickly child and her only one. The funny thing is I was thinking of him the other day. I suppose it was the inquest and that man dying so suddenly that brought him to mind. The poor mistress, I'm sure that's what saw her off in the end, brooding about him being taken from her, but it's all over now, God rest them all."

Mrs Banks shook herself. "You mustn't think too much about what can't be mended. Jessie always says to me, 'Aunty Dorothy, you live in the past,' and I suppose I do, in a way. We had some happy times and I like to think on it, but Jessie's right. I've got enough to do to think of the living, never mind those who've passed on, and so have you. Sometimes you can't help it though. That young man of yours now - he puts me in mind of someone but I can't think...." She clicked her tongue. "No. I can't call it to mind. Who did you say he was?"

"Philip Brown," repeated Sandy. She picked up her tea. Really, she was just being silly. She had no reason to think Phil wasn't exactly who he said he was. She forced

147

down the niggle of doubt. *Ourselves*... No reason whatsoever.

***   ***   ***

The rumbling roar of the train increased. Behind him, Philip felt the crowd stir like a restless, waking animal. He had worked his way up to the end of the platform, hoping to keep a watch on who boarded the train. Two men, city-suited, newspapers furled under their arms, walked smartly in front on him, then stopped, blocking his view. They ground their umbrellas into the asphalt, proprietorially marking the exact spot where the train would open its doors. This was hopeless. He moved round to the front of the men, wincing slightly at their irritated tuts of disapproval.

With a blast of air and a shriek of noise the train shot from its encasing tunnel. There was a cry from the rear, and one of the city men stumbled against him, clutching onto his arm. Philip fell forward, one foot scrabbling at the empty air over the platform edge. His muscles screamed as he tried to turn, forcing his body round and back.

The huge front lights of the train were level with him, knocking him out of the way with a giant's breath. His leg jarred with pain and he was rolling as in a cement-mixer, feet, hands, faces, floor, all jumbled together. Something thudded into his chest, there was shouting, a brief explosion of light, and then there was nothing at all.

Chapter Seven

There were voices which came out of the mist; *"Cor, that was a lucky escape...." "Straight over, 'e went..." "Pushed in the back..." "I thought he was a gonner, true as I'm stood 'ere...." "How on earth did it happen?" "They're 'orrible when they go on the live rail - all twist up, they do..." "I'm sure I was pushed in the back...." "It's a miracle no-one was hurt..."*

The mist cleared and revealed a sharp, bright-eyed man, his face very close, wearing a black uniform and cap with a silver badge. "You feeling a bit better now, sir? That's the ticket." Philip tried to speak and managed a grunt. "Give the gent a bit of air," said the porter. "'E's orl right. How d'chu feel?"

"Nothing to write home about, that's for sure." He put a hand to his forehead, wincing as he saw the blood on his fingers. He fumbled for his handkerchief and held it to his head.

"Nasty graze, that," said the porter. "Still, no bones broken, eh?"

Philip gingerly tested his muscles. "I - I don't think so. What on earth happened?"

"You were standing in front of me," said a clipped voice. Philip turned his head cautiously to see the speaker. It was one of the city men, minus his newspaper but with his umbrella still firmly grasped. "Someone behind me must have stumbled because I felt a sharp push in the back. I fell forward and knocked into you. The next thing I knew you had fallen into the path of the

149

train. Goodness knows how you managed to keep your balance, but it's a miracle that you did."

"Can you get up, sir?" asked the porter, reaching out a hand.

Philip became aware that he was sitting on the floor of the platform. "Yes... Thanks. I'll be all right now. Thanks a lot." His legs felt horribly unattached, but he forced himself to stand upright. "I suppose the train's gone now, has it?"

"It has. Next one along in a few minutes for Baker Street. Do you want that one, sir?"

"No..." He had a sudden, guilty memory of Sandy sitting abandoned in the tea-room. "No, I don't think I better had." He felt in his pocket and pulled out his wallet. "Here, thanks for all your help."

"Thank *you*, sir," said the porter, pocketing the ten-shilling note. "Now c'mon, Ladies and Gents, move along the platform, please. You sure you're orl right now, sir? Good. Move along there, *if* you would be so good, everyone, please. Let's have a bit of room here...."

***　***　***

With a self-conscious grin at his host and fellow-guests, Philip sank into the comfortable armchair, and took the glass which Andrew Herriad was holding out to him. He took a grateful sip. "That's better. Thanks."

It had caused a minor sensation when the powerful black car with a police driver had swept up the drive to Farholt. It was thanks to Sandy that he had arrived back at Farholt in such state. She had been on the point of leaving the railway tea-room when Philip had walked in.

150

She took one look at Philip's battered form and insisted on driving him to Scotland Yard. She refused to go to the embassy; he was, she said, in no condition to deal with anything of the sort, but Sir Douglas Lynton had to be told right away. After all, he had just survived an attempted murder.

Philip had demurred at this description, but when asked what else he would call it, had to agree. It was only, he said, such a rotten dramatic way of putting things. Sir Douglas Lynton didn't think it was overly dramatic. Attempted murder it doubtless was, and he took a grave enough view to provide a police car and driver back to Farholt. He didn't, he said, want to hear of any more 'accidents'. And now, bathed, changed and fed, Philip had come to face the assembled company in the drawing-room, which, to his surprise, included Superintendent Brenzett.

"I telephoned the Superintendent," said Sandy. "I thought he ought to know what had happened and Dad said we better invite Mr Brenzett up here so he could see for himself."

"There was a bit of self-interest at work," put in Herriad. "To tell the truth I wanted to know what would bring a Scotland Yard man to Farholt, but I suppose it's these emeralds, isn't it? Sandy tells me you've been at the Bird In Hand for the last few days, Superintendent. You'd be far better staying here if you want to tap walls and things." He looked at Sir Dennis. "I'm surprised you didn't suggest it, Storwood."

151

"Well, I..." Sir Dennis stopped, momentarily lost for words. "I can hardly tell you who to invite to your own house, Herriad."

"I'll remind you of that one of these days," said Herriad softly. "By the way, Brown, there was a phone call for you from the Salvatierran Embassy earlier on."

"I took the call," said Tommy Leigh. "They seemed jolly anxious that you should get in touch."

Philip groaned. "I'll have to ring them, but I'm going to have this drink first. I'll bet there's nothing I can do but they're quite likely to suggest I go to Scotland and I'm blowed if I want to." He touched the bandage on his forehead and winced. "I'm feeling a bit too washed-out to think about work, but I suppose I better had. I know those proposals for the loan need looking at."

"We'll see to it later if you're feeling up to it," said Sir Dennis. "There's not terribly much to do, Mr Brown, but if there is a chance you might have to leave us, I'd appreciate you going through the papers Matherson left."

"Never mind about that, Dennis," said Eleanor Storwood. She was gazing at Philip with undisguised interest. "Whatever's happened? Have you had an accident?"

Philip laughed ruefully. "I suppose you could call it that." He paused for a moment, before adding with odd deliberation, "I was pushed."

"What?"

"Pushed off the platform of the underground at Waterloo. Quite deliberately. Scotland Yard believe it was attempted murder."

Eleanor Storwood's eyes widened. "But why, Mr Brown? Surely there must be some mistake? Who could possibly want to harm you?"

"I know exactly who would want to harm me," said Philip. He gave a fleeting smile as he caught Brenzett's agonized eye-signals. "It was the woman who appeared at the inquest calling herself Mrs Strickland." Brenzett's look of horror made him bite his lip to stop laughing out loud.

"Called herself? Whatever do you mean, called herself? And why on earth should she, of all people, attempt to murder you? I'm sure you're wrong, Mr Brown. It all sounds so wildly improbable. Whatever gave you the idea in the first place? And why are you so sure it was Mrs Strickland? It seems most unlikely."

"Yes," put in Brenzett in a croak.

"No," said Philip firmly. "Not when you understand what's behind it all."

"And what is behind it all?"

Philip took a cigar and lit it thoughtfully. "I'd better tell you the whole story." Brenzett briefly put his hand over his face. "I'm frankly puzzled and if anyone can make any suggestions as to what's really going on, I'd be glad to hear them. You see, we've got plenty of good reasons to believe that the man who was identified as Kevin Murphy wasn't called Kevin Murphy at all. Now, as to who he was..."

There was a tortured intake of breath from Brenzett which Philip ignored.

"...we don't actually know..."

153

Brenzett looked up sharply, a gleam of hope dawning.

"...but we suspect he was working in tandem with Mrs Strickland to steal the emeralds."

Brenzett breathed a sigh of relief.

"But why do you have these suspicions, Mr Brown," said Lady Storwood. "Surely you must be guessing. What evidence can you have against her?"

Philip blew a smoke ring and took a sip of whisky. "Mrs Strickland made an error at the inquest. She gave the address of her house in Camden Town. I went there this afternoon and had a look round. I managed to get inside - never mind how..."

Daphne Marston let her unregarded seedsman's catalogue slip from her fingers. "Alexandra!" she said in awful tones. "Were *you* with Mr Brown?"

"She wasn't there," put in Philip quickly.

"I say," said Tommy Leigh, deeply impressed. "You actually managed to get inside the house? How? Did you break in? It sounds jolly sporting to me. Whatever did you find?"

Philip opened his mouth to speak, but then stopped with a glance at Brenzett. "I don't think I'd better say, to be honest. I haven't actually told the police about it yet. I should have done, but all I could really think of was what a perfectly foul headache I had. Sandy, did you say anything to Sir Douglas Lynton about what I found in the house?"

"Well, as I didn't know a thing about it, I don't see how I could have done."

Philip flashed her a smile. "Sorry. I didn't mean to leave you out in the cold."

"What the dickens did you find? Go on, tell us!" encouraged Tommy.

"The house was cleared out from top to bottom and there was just this one thing she'd obviously overlooked. It seemed innocent enough but with any luck it should give the clue to the whole thing. I didn't touch it, of course, otherwise I might have destroyed the evidence."

"Very proper, Mr Brown," said Brenzett. "You ought to report it as soon as possible, though."

Dennis Storwood looked puzzled. "All that might be as you say, Mr Brown, and, although I feel these things should be left in the hands of the proper authorities, doubtless you did discover something. However, I still fail to see the connection between you going to this woman's house and your accident on the railway."

"That," said Philip, "was nothing but coincidence. It can't have been anything else and I was either very lucky, if you consider there wasn't actually any harm done, or very unlucky, if you consider I had the worst few minutes of my life as a result."

"We had Colonel Waldrist here this afternoon, full of the fact that Kevin Murphy probably wasn't Kevin Murphy," said Andrew Herriad. "He had a telephone call from Scotland Yard which stirred him up."

"I was quite concerned," put in Daphne Marston. "After all, Colonel Waldrist does have some experience in these matters and he said he shouldn't wonder if this Murphy turned out to be connected with those dreadful people who go round blowing things up, and it makes you wonder why they do it because, really, all the Irish people one meets are totally respectable and so terribly good with horses."

Sandy appeared to be much moved by this reflection. "You're quite right, Aunt Daphne. It's dreadful to think of Mr Murphy and Mrs Strickland running round with bombs." Daphne Marston shot her a sharp glance as if not quite sure if she were being made fun of, but her niece's face was guiless. "Did everyone decide that Mrs Strickland must be a member of the IRA?"

"Well, not in those terms, young lady," said Sir Dennis. "Certainly not in those terms. I remember you, m'dear," he continued, turning to his wife, "thought that we were all jumping to conclusions far too rapidly."

"I thought," said Eleanor Storwood, taking a cigarette with languid grace, "that everyone was talking a great deal of nonsense based on nothing more than a perfectly reasonable request from Scotland Yard for further identification." She glanced at her watch. "Are you going to play bridge, Dennis, or are you really going to make poor Mr Brown wade through a heap of papers?" She yawned and glanced at her watch. "I think it's far too late to do anything this evening and I'm sure Mr Brown and Mr Leigh would agree with me."

"Nonsense, Eleanor. We'll be half an hour or so at the most, and I must go to London tomorrow. I've an appointment with Sedgwick from the Kurhaus and it would be convenient if I could take the Salvatierran papers up to Houblyns with me. Leigh, can you go and get

156

the relevant documents out for us and put them on my desk?"

"My desk," muttered Andrew Herriad, who, although prepared to sacrifice his study to Dennis Storwood, resented his casual assumption of ownership. "Will you be joining us later, Leigh?"

"I should think so," said Sir Dennis, answering for his secretary. "We'll only need him for a little while. Off you go, Leigh. Now then, Mr Brown," he said, as Tommy Leigh got up to go, "do you want to contact the embassy tonight? If so, Leigh can get them on the telephone for you."

Philip shook his head. "I'll do it later. I'm feeling remarkably lazy. Mr Brenzett, I believe you left your tobacco pouch when you called the other day. It's in the library. I'll just walk along and get it for you, then I'll join you in the study, Sir Dennis."

Brenzett rose to his feet. "I'll come along with you, sir. I think I know exactly where I put it. And that," he said as they went into the hall and closed the drawing-room door behind them, "was a very neat piece of work. I thought at first you'd taken leave of your senses, spilling the beans like that. I soon realised you were very much in possession of them."

Philip laughed. "I'm glad you think so. I take you gathered what I was up to?"

"I think so," agreed Brenzett, cautiously. "But I've only spoken to the Yard briefly. What did you find in the house?"

"Absolutely nothing to get excited about. Hold on a minute." He walked quietly down to hall to the study and stood for a few moments, listening outside the door. Then, just as quietly, he walked back to where the hall telephone stood in its cabinet and, very cautiously, lifted the receiver. He listened for a moment then, with enormous care, replaced the telephone on the hook. He looked at Brenzett. "We'd better go to the library," he said in a low voice. "It'd look a bit odd if we didn't."

Brenzett followed him with a puzzled frown. "What was all that about, sir?" he asked as he shut the library door behind them.

Philip flung himself into an armchair and took a cigarette from the box beside him. "I put a ferret down a rabbit hole and the rabbit didn't run. Damn!" He lit his cigarette and threw the match into the fireplace, before turning to Brenzett with a wry expression. "You asked me what I found in the house. I found nothing in the house, Superintendent, apart from a packet of tea and a bag of sugar and there was nothing remarkable about them, believe me."

"Then why...?"

Philip held up his hand. "Before I answer that, can I ask if the fingerprints you checked this afternoon matched up?"

Brenzett nodded. "They were a match all right, which means Alan Oliver and Kevin Murphy are the same man."

"And it's a racing certainty that Alan Oliver was John Guthrie."

"Absolutely, but who the devil this Mrs Strickland is, I don't know. I'd love to find out who gave her the word to skip. She obviously had been warned, that was clear enough. She'd been staying in the Mitre Arms in Brosley Dean, supposedly waiting for the funeral. However, by the time we got there, which was just on seven o'clock, she'd cleared out a good three hours earlier."

"Three hours?" Philip wriggled restlessly, then got up and walked over to the fireplace. "You see what that means, Superintendent? Miss Herriad and I were with Sir Douglas Lynton when he telephoned Colonel Waldrist. That would be about half-three or so. For her to scarper at four means that somebody here told the lady what was in the wind. I guessed as much earlier, but I'm certain now. There's an enemy in the camp."

Brenzett drew in a deep breath and dropped onto the arm of a chair. "You're right." He cocked an eyebrow at Philip. "And that, I suppose, is why you did that bit of digging in the drawing-room."

"Yes." He shook his head in disgust. "At first, you see, I'd thought that the mere fact that Mrs Strickland knew enough to hook it would lead us straight to the person who told her. Now we find that the good Colonel decided, for reasons best known to himself, to broadcast the information that a Scotland Yard policeman was on his way. You heard what everyone said. They all joined in the discussion about Ireland, and in the meantime, our enemy, Mrs Strickland's ally, knows exactly what your business was and must have guessed your next move would be to collar the woman."

159

"That's fairly obvious, as Mrs Strickland lied at the inquest about being the man's sister. But who d'you think her ally could be, sir?"

Philip shrugged. "Anyone here. Absolutely anyone. Even if they weren't in the room when Colonel Waldrist was holding forth, they could have been told."

"All the same, there's certain people who it's unlikely to be. Mr Herriad himself, for example."

"Why?" demanded Philip. "He might know that the emeralds are here, but not have a clue where to look. Then up pops Guthrie who, for a consideration, will arrange to find them. Those stones are worth half a *million*, Superintendent."

Brenzett sighed. "You could be right. You can't suspect Sir Dennis Storwood, though. He's the man who brought you here."

"And very good camouflage that would make, too. He's off to London tomorrow. All very above board and accounted for, with a meeting about his health place and another at Houblyns, but who else is he hoping to see? He might be absolutely snowy-white, but on the other hand, he might not. I don't know the first thing about the Storwoods' private lives, but simple observation tells you that Eleanor Storwood is an expensive addition to anyone's household. Sir Dennis above suspicion? Not ruddy likely and the same goes for Tommy Leigh, Lady Storwood, Mrs Marston and anyone else in the house, including the servants. I'll give you the same answer as I did about Mr Herriad; half a million is a lot of sugar. Miss Herriad is the only one who really is out of it. Not only was she with me all afternoon, but she's the one who had the bright idea about Guthrie in the first place and suggested having a dekko at Mrs Strickland's house."

Brenzett rubbed his hand through his hair. "This is the absolute devil." He paused as an uncomfortable thought struck him. "God help us, it could even be one of the police or Colonel Waldrist himself. Telling everyone what was in the wind like that may have been a way of covering his tracks before he gave Mrs Strickland the word to jump." He stirred impatiently. "Hell! Once you admit an accomplice you realise you can't trust anyone at all."

"I think I can help you absolve the Colonel," said Philip. "You remember I was very careful to tell everyone in the drawing-room I'd found something in the house in Camden Town?"

"Which, apparently, you didn't. What was that all about?"

"It was a trap, Superintendent. We believe, don't we, that someone here is in league with Mrs Strickland? That, after this afternoon's performance, can be taken as read. Now if that person thinks that Mrs S. has left something in the house - an incriminating something - what are they going to do about it?"

"Get in touch with Mrs Strickland," said Brenzett slowly. "By jingo, sir, if they do that, we've got 'em!"

"And so what does everyone do? Nothing, damn it, nothing at all. Sir Dennis ordered Tommy Leigh out of the room, which, I may say, caused hope to blaze. But does Tommy Leigh bound to the phone? No, he does not.

Instead he goes and innocently fools around in the study. The telephone in there is on the same line as the one in the hall, which is why I checked it, and got nowhere for my pains."

"Don't lose heart, sir. The ally will have to alert Mrs Strickland. I'll get onto the Yard right away and make sure there's a couple of men at the house, ready to pick her up."

"That's true." Philip brightened. "And if it happens tonight, you can be sure that whoever gave the message is someone in the house and not an outsider such as Colonel Waldrist. You'd better ring from the study. You can be undisturbed in there. I'll get rid of Leigh, if he hasn't finished, and stand guard over the phone in the hall in case anyone fancies listening in."

***   ***   ***

Tommy Leigh had indeed finished in the study. The neat piles of documents laid out on the desk showed him to have done exactly what had been asked of him and, presumably, nothing more. Philip left Superintendent Brenzett to contact Scotland Yard then went to hover round the telephone in the hall.

From where he stood he could hear the conversation in the drawing-room. *With no ace and only one king, you should have played two diamonds rather than two no trumps...* Lady Storwood giving some advice on bridge. She didn't sound worried. *So I thought I'd try Higgin's ideas and have new sties built...* Andrew Herriad on pigs. It was all so innocent, damn it! And yet surely his reasoning couldn't be wrong.

A ting sounded from the hall telephone as Superintendent Brenzett replaced the receiver in the study. Philip waited for him before going back into the drawing-room.

"That's all settled," said Brenzett in a low voice, when he had joined Philip in the hall. "I spoke to Sir Douglas at home and he's putting two men on to watch the house right away." He cocked an eyebrow at the open drawing-room door. "Has anyone moved?"

"Nobody, worse luck."

Brenzett grimaced. "Don't worry, sir. It was too much to hope we'd get a bite straight away." He raised his voice. "Well, thanks for my tobacco-pouch. I'm glad to have that back once more. I'll just say my "good-nights" and be on my way."

They walked into the drawing-room together. Everyone was still there. If someone's panicking, thought Philip in disgust, they were hiding it pretty well. He'd have to ask Sandy if anyone had left the room, but he was willing to bet the answer would be no.

Brenzett stood politely by the door, waiting to attract Andrew Herriad's attention, but Herriad was still describing the merits of his new pig-sties to a restless Sir Dennis. "...And by starting from scratch, I've been able to incorporate all the latest ideas, such as a properly drained, concrete floor in the outer court, which makes it a great deal easier to keep clean."

"I've been meaning to ask you, Andrew," said Mrs Marston. "Now that the men have finished the sties, could you get a couple of them to repair the church wall?

163

I noticed last week that two of the coping-stones on the south side are dangerously loose. All that corner could do with tidying up. There's a self-seeded dogwood bush which really needs grubbing out. It's right up against the church and should never have been allowed to grow. It has beautiful colours in the autumn, but it makes the wall terribly damp and, if we're not careful, the plaster on the inside will start to flake." She sighed. "I must try and get some new helpers in to clean the church. Mrs Horrocks is far too old, although I'd hate to hurt her feelings by telling her so. Alexandra, did Mrs Banks say how long she'd be away? I must see her. I'm sure she'd be delighted to help."

Sandy gave a start and gazed at her aunt. "Just say that again, Aunt Daphne."

Mrs Marston gazed at her in mild surprise. "The church cleaning, dear. I was wondering if Mrs Banks would help."

Sandy shook her head and turned to Philip with gleaming eyes. "Did you hear it? *Mrs Banks... See her.* Doesn't that sound familiar?"

"By George," said Philip. "You're right! *Mrs Banks... See her.* Sandy, you're on to something!"

"What the dickens," asked Herriad, plaintively, "are you talking about?"

"It's the dying man's last words, Dad," explained Sandy. "Don't you remember? We thought he said, *"Banks... Sea air,"* and we've been bending our brains to try and work out what he meant. But what if it was *Mrs*

164

Banks he was talking about? And he was telling us to *see her*. That would make a lot of sense."

"Would it?" asked Tommy Leigh. "Why should the poor bloke want to see this Mrs Banks, whoever she is? Unless she was his mother or something."

"Don't be silly, Tommy," said Sandy. "He wouldn't call his mother by her surname. Besides that, he was far too old to be her son. As far as I know she never had a son."

"She never had any children, dear, only nieces." Mrs Marston counted on her fingers. "There's Gladys, who lives in London, Enid, who is married to Ernest Stebbing and has the ironmongers, and Jessie in the post-office. Oh yes, and Gertrude who we don't talk about."

Ignoring this fascinating side-issue, Tommy returned to the attack. "But why would he want to see her? Who is she?"

"She was the senior housemaid here for years and years," said Mrs Marston. "Not for us, for the Eldons. None of the Eldons' servants stayed on, which was a considerable inconvenience. Having said that, the house was closed for months after Agatha Eldon died, because Andrew had to put all his affairs in order in Canada, so I can scarcely blame them. Mrs Banks would have been a great asset, though. She was married to Wilfred Banks, who was first of all coachman and then became the chauffeur - he's dead now, of course - and when the Eldons died they were remembered in the will and bought the ironmongers in the village. The Banks are a very pleasant, respectable family, which is why Gertrude was such a shock to them."

Daphne Marston lowered her voice conspiratorially. "She ran off with an Italian ice-cream seller. The fact he was foreign made it worse, somehow. Anyway," Mrs Marston coughed. "It was all very distressing and such a shame for the family and for Mrs Banks, who is always most obliging."

Once more Tommy ignored Gertrude. "She used to work here? I say, I wonder if she knows where the emeralds are?"

Andrew Herriad laughed. "I wouldn't think that was very likely. She's a perfectly ordinary woman, the last person to be mixed up with stolen emeralds. Nice woman, if a bit of a gossip. I've placed her now. She always gives respectfully at the knees when I go in the shop, then keeps me for hours talking about the old days here at Farholt. I think she must remember every blessed soul Francis and Edith ever had here. She even had her scrapbook out the other day. Full of cuttings and pictures of the parties before the war with comments written beside them."

"I've seen that scrapbook," said Mrs Marston. "I went to buy a new trowel and was told all about the Home Secretary's wife in 1908 or whenever."

"So she could know about the emeralds," said Tommy triumphantly. "Sandy, we'll have to see her."

"We can't, she's in London."

"When she gets back, then."

Philip yawned. "Excuse me. I don't know about this Mrs Banks. I can't help feeling we're barking up the wrong tree. Sir Dennis, if we are going to do anything this evening, we'd better start now. Mr Herriad, Mr Brenzett was just leaving."

Herriad got to his feet. "Were you, Superintendent? I'll get Larch to show you to the door."

"I can see myself out, thank you, sir."

"If you go out of the side door you can cut across the park," offered Philip. "It's a much quicker way. I'll point you in the right direction."

They strolled to the door together. "It's a great pity," said Brenzett, once they were out of earshot, "that Miss Herriad should have twigged about Mrs Banks in public like that."

"It was a blasted nuisance. Still, with any luck no damage has been done. It might be a complete red herring."

"And on the other hand, it might not. It's certainly worth following up. I'll let you know what happens about the other business, sir. Good-night."

Philip walked thoughtfully to the study. *Banks... See her*? It certainly chimed in with what John Guthrie had said. But..? He shrugged impatiently and, picking up the telephone, put through a call to the embassy.

When Sir Dennis joined him, with Tommy Leigh in attendance, Philip was sitting on the windowsill drumming his fingers. He looked worried.

Sir Dennis looked at him quizzically. "Is there anything the matter, Mr Brown? Have you contacted the embassy?"

"Yes. I've managed to avoid going to Scotland, thank God. It was a very odd burglary, Sir Dennis. In fact it wasn't a burglary at all. They found a chap lurking in the grounds of the estate armed with a camera."

"Maybe he was a pressman?" suggested Tommy.

"Perhaps." Philip shook himself. "I imagine that's all it amounts to. The bloke ran off, so there's no way of actually telling."

"He doesn't seem to want his picture taken, your boss, does he?"

"He certainly doesn't want a crowd of reporters around."

Tommy laughed. "He didn't mind sounding off when he thought Houblyns had pinched his necklace." There was an outraged gasp from Dennis Storwood. "Oh, sorry, sir. I forgot.... Er, let me show you how I've arranged the papers which you'll need."

Tommy busied himself around the desk. "...And there are Mr Matherson's proposals, sir, together with the projected costs of the railway. This manila folder contains the documents concerning the Kurhaus. You said you wanted to refer to them before your meeting with Mr Sedgwick tomorrow." Tommy straightened up. "It's a funny thing though," he said, looking at Philip. "I saw all that rannygazoo in the papers and they published the President's picture then, all right. You look awfully like him, don't you?"

"A little bit," agreed Philip.

"That will be all, Leigh," put in Sir Dennis, but Tommy Leigh didn't move.

"You know, the more I think of it, the more..." Tommy broke off, staring at Philip. "You're him! You're him, aren't you? I knew you reminded me of someone. You're the President! That's why you're worried about this bloke in Scotland taking pictures. If the reporter or whoever snapped the false president your cover would be blown."

"Leigh!" There was no mistaking the anger in Sir Dennis's voice.

Philip laughed. "Never mind. It's rather flattering in a way. No, Leigh, old man, I'm sorry to disappoint you, but I'm not the President, thank God." He flicked a glance at the red-faced Sir Dennis. "Now I really think you'd better scoot."

"Honestly!" exclaimed Sir Dennis, when Tommy Leigh had left the room. "That young man is impossible at times. I cannot see why it should be so difficult to find a secretary who combines ability, acumen and tact."

"It's not his acumen you have to worry about," said Philip. "He's just shown rather too much of that." He put a cautious hand to his forehead. "Perhaps - I don't know - it would be better to tell him and everybody else the full truth."

Sir Dennis was horrified. "Don't dream of it, my dear feller."

Philip laughed once more. "A true politician's answer. By the way, is that door properly closed? No? I thought not." He walked to the desk and opened the topmost file. "I suppose we'd better make a start."

***   ***   ***

Three-quarters of an hour later they were coming to the end. Philip crushed out a cigarette in disgust. It tasted not

169

of tobacco but old smoke. The figures in the column in front of him moved and he had to blink to steady them. He felt sick, tired and beaten. He put down his pen and rubbed his eyes. "Is there any point?" he asked.

Storwood looked at him.

"To all this, I mean." Philip waved his hand at the mass of documents. "I know the railway will be a success and yet to get the thing started I have to tie up virtually every penny's worth of profit for years."

"I believe we have managed to negotiate the best deal possible in the circumstances."

"In the circumstances!" Philip pushed his chair away and walked to the window, finding relief in the night air. "If we had that blasted necklace then everything would fall into place. My word, it'd be worth doing then."

"Yes...." Storwood seemed oddly hesitant. "That necklace. Quite honestly, I would counsel you to dismiss it from your mind. It seems to have acted as nothing but a distraction from the actual business of arranging a viable scheme to finance the railway. You are still a young man, Mr... er... Brown, and to find the necklace must have a certain romantic appeal but I really think it is a hopeless quest. I would advocate a much more pragmatic, realistic approach, utilizing the conventional means to hand of raising capital. While you still think the necklace may be found, I feel that you are not committing yourself as whole-heartedly as you should to the proposals before us."

"That's because they're rotten."

"They are, Mr Brown, all we have."

Philip nursed his throbbing head. "I suppose so," he said flatly. "Let me sign the damn things and you can start the ball rolling tomorrow." He sat down at the desk once more and pulled a manila folder towards him. The words blurred and danced and he had to shut his eyes for a second.

"Mr Brown?" Storwood's voice sounded very far away. "I'm afraid that's the wrong file."

Philip opened his eyes again and blinked. The words in front of him swam into focus. It was a letter. *Concord of Health and Hygiene, The Kurhaus, Loscombe Dale Road, Thringford, Huntingdonshire. Dear Sir Dennis, With reference to your...* "I'm awfully sorry," said Philip, thickly. "Where's the one I should sign?"

He signed his name in the four places Sir Dennis indicated. It would take the country years to make any money on the railway now. His headache flared. If only they could find the necklace. If only there was some other way. If only... He raised his eyes. Was there something odd in the way Sir Dennis was looking at him? Something very calculating?

"My dear chap, you should be in bed."

"Yes. Thanks." He got up, steadying himself on the desk. "What..." He stopped. Sir Dennis wouldn't know. How could he? But there was something that wasn't quite right...

***   ***   ***

Detective-Constable Colin Airdrie stood in the doorway of the Everight Scales and Weights Manufacturing Co. Ltd., Patents Applied For. He knew who the doorway belonged to, because of the enamelled sign that ran like a dingy banner, white on blue, across the brickwork above him. Keep yourself out of sight, the Sarge had said. That's a good place, the Sarge had said. *Good?* Technically, yes. On the corner of Atlantic Place and Wire Street, the doorway commanded a long view of the alleyway at the back of Hilldrop Road.

A streetlamp threw just enough light to see the back yard wall and gate of number 43. Darkness was greying into dawn now, a chill, comfortless start to the day, bringing with it a soft drizzle of rain. He'd run out of cigarettes two hours ago. It was another hour before he could look forward to a cup of tea... Strewth!

A man came out of the passage that divided number 43 from its neighbour and, with a quick glance round, quietly opened the gate and went into the yard. Airdrie slipped out of the doorway and down the alley. Sergeant Kendall came out of the passage and nodded to Airdrie by the back gate.

"Has he gone in?" he whispered.

"Yes, sir," breathed Airdrie. "Look at that!" In the upstairs window, a torchbeam shone.

"He's giving the place the once-over," said Kendall softly. "We'll get him on the way out. Did he see you?" Airdrie shook his head. "Good. He's a cool sort of customer. He came strolling up Hilldrop Road, looking at the numbers bold as brass, as if he was out for a Sunday stroll."

The torchlight went out of the upstairs room. The policemen waited. The grey light grew paler and the rain got wetter.

"He's taking his time," muttered Kendall. "He's had quarter of an hour. My God!"

Three shots cracked out from the front of the house, followed by a shout and another shot. The brick valley of Hilldrop Road caught and echoed the sound, rolling it like thunder.

"Come *on*!" yelled Sergeant Kendall. He pulled his police whistle from round his neck and, blowing an ear-splitting blast, raced down the passage-way, Airdrie close at his heels. Complete silence met them. Then, up and down the street, curtains were pulled back and windows raised. Sergeant Kendall ignored the shouts from the neighbours.

Colin Airdrie looked up and down in bewilderment. There wasn't a soul out on the street. He tried the front door. It was locked. "Where's he gone, Sarge?"

Kendall gulped. "Stay there!" he commanded and ran back down the passage, skidding to a halt outside the gate. "Oh, hell," he said unhappily. "Oh, bleeding *hell*!"

The back gate to the yard of number 43 stood open. Of the intruder there was nothing to be seen.

Chapter Eight

Detective-Sergeant Kendall and Detective-Constable Airdrie stood stiffly to attention whilst Chief Detective Inspector Hepworth gave vent to his opinions. Inspector Hepworth had, thought Constable Airdrie, an unnecessarily broad, vivid vocabulary and an unlooked for degree of fluency.

"That two officers of Scotland Yard - two of *my* officers, mark you - should behave like a bunch of perishin' Keystone Kops beats the ruddy band. You haven't even got a description worth the name. Dark hat, dark coat, scarf pulled round his face.... Blimey! I think you two better try out for the films because if you carry on like this you haven't got any future in the police. A bloke fires a gun through the letter-box and yells a bit and you two gormless wonders charge round to the front, then stand there gawping at each other. There's some excuse for Airdrie, because he's only been on the job for three months, but *you*, Kendall...! Didn't it occur to you that there was something dodgy going on?"

"Well, no, sir. Not given the way he walked up the street. He wasn't trying to hide or anything. I could have sworn he didn't know we were there."

"Of course he knew you were there. I daresay he couldn't give two hoots if you were or not, knowing he could get rid of you by a simple trick that a kid could've seen through."

This struck Sergeant Kendall as unfair. "What would you have done, sir, if you had heard shots and shouting?"

What Chief Detective Inspector Hepworth would have done was not relevant to the case. What he *wouldn't* have done was let a suspect stroll out of the back door.

"If it was that important, sir, why couldn't we keeps tabs inside the house?"

"Because, my lad," said the Chief Detective Inspector, rising to his feet, his moustache bristling, "there's rules about private property in this country and we didn't have a warrant. And if you, Kendall, are going to start finding fault with the orders you've been given *and* ask that your superiors should relax the law of the land for your convenience, then you'd better look out your old uniform and white cuffs because directing traffic is all you'll be fit for. I've got to go and tell the Chief exactly what happened. Believe you me, he's not going to like it. And if - *if* - he wants to see you himself, you'd better not start making excuses, because you'll have me to answer to."

***   ***   ***

Assistant Commissioner Sir Douglas Lynton was, as Detective Inspector Hepworth predicted, not happy. Superintendent Brenzett, when the news was conveyed to him by telephone at The Bird In Hand, although expressing himself less forcefully than Sir Douglas, shared his distress. The only person who found anything to smile about was, unexpectedly enough, Philip Brown.

Sitting in the saloon of the Bird In Hand, Philip put his hand over his face. Brenzett looked at him anxiously before realising that he was laughing.

"I can't see anything very funny, Mr Brown."

"Can't you?" Philip leaned back in the oak settle. He glanced at Brenzett's solemn face and shook his head. "Ah well, if you can't see it, you can't see it." He picked up his pint of Bass. "It was pretty cool, you know, drawing your men off like that. He - whoever he was - could just as easily have shot them both."

Brenzett's eyebrows crawled upwards. "Shot two policemen? He wouldn't dare. Can you imagine the outcry? He'd have the whole force down on him like a ton of bricks if he'd tried that."

"Which was probably why he took this very neat way out. Tell me, Brenzett, are Scotland Yard treating this case seriously?"

***   ***   ***

"And that, Sandy, is what I think the problem is."

Philip offered her a cigarette from his case and, taking one himself, struck a match. They were sitting with their backs to the cedar tree on the lawn. The only sound which broke the quiet stillness of the summer afternoon was the chakking of a magpie in the branches above. There was nobody else in sight.

Andrew Herriad, his study still barred to him, had retreated to the gun-room. Sir Dennis and Eleanor Storwood had been driven to the station after breakfast, Sir Dennis bound for Houblyns, Eleanor for Madam Vesoul of Bond Street, with a view to adding to her extensive wardrobe. Daphne Marston, was, they knew, at the Vicarage, deep in discussion with Mr Peverell about such matters as self-seeded dogwood bushes, coping-stones and, as she rather painfully put it, taking a firm hand with the nettles.

The only one at a loose end was Tommy Leigh, last seen walking morosely in to the village. Sandy had heartlessly ignored his plea that, granted sunshine and freedom from Sir Dennis, the afternoon should consist of the river, a punt and a girl. Philip, she knew, had seen Superintendent Brenzett that morning and she happily allowed herself to be steered into the garden.

"You see," he continued, "from their point of view there isn't much to get their teeth into."

Sandy was puzzled. "There's the necklace."

"Yes, but that was stolen twelve years ago. If it comes to that, there's the murder of Count von Liebrich, but that was twelve years ago as well. We've industriously worked out that the chief suspect is dead, so in a way the case, as far as the police is concerned, is closed. All that's really happened since then is my performance on the underground yesterday and our friend Mrs Strickland giving false evidence at the inquest. One could be an accident and as for the other - well, false evidence isn't much to get worked up about compared with murder and the like."

"But there has to be more to it than that, Philip."

"Oh, I couldn't agree more. So does Brenzett, but I can't help feeling that if those two bright sparks outside the house in Hilldrop Road had been shot rather than merely led astray, the police would now be acting as if the roof had fallen in. One thing we can be certain of is that, as it was a man who turned up rather than the lady

177

herself, Mrs Strickland isn't working alone. However, we knew that anyway, so it's not much to get excited about. Incidentally, the police have been in touch with the house-agents in Camden Town and managed to work out how the whole stunt with the house was pulled off." Philip turned and smiled. "D'you know, the sun's just catching your hair?"

"Never mind that. What happened?"

"But the sun makes..." He was stopped by a look and sighed regretfully. "Okay. You want to talk business, we'll talk business. The house. First of all, Mrs Emmeline Strickland's name isn't Mrs Emmeline Strickland."

"I'm not surprised. Who is she?"

"She might be Mrs Lily Kelly, but I doubt that too. There *is* a real Mrs Strickland. She's a widow, aged fifty-two, and now lives with her son and his wife who keep a tobacconist's shop in Southsea. Until Friday the 5th of May she was resident at number 43, Hilldrop Road, Camden Town. At noon on Friday, the 5th of May, she gave up her keys and her rent book to the house-agents, Martin and Collier of Camden High Street, and departed, without a stain on her character, to Southsea. The house remained vacant for most of the following week until Thursday, the 11th of May - last Thursday - when Martin and Collier were approached by one Mrs Lily Kelly, also a widow, who was looking for a house which was ready for immediate possession. She paid three months rent in advance and, as far as the house-agents know, still lives there."

"And that Mrs Kelly..."

"Is our Mrs Strickland, the woman at the inquest and the woman, I firmly believe, who tried to push me under a train yesterday."

Sandy hugged her knees thoughtfully. "Did she give a previous address?"

"She did. It's in Belfast and, although the police are checking it, I'm willing to bet it's false."

"So am I. When the police originally called on her, to ask her to attend the inquest, didn't they notice anything fishy? I mean, the house was unlived in and she'd meant to be there for years."

"Brenzett thought of that. Apparently she told the young constable who called that she was turning the place out for spring-cleaning. It didn't strike him as odd at all."

Sandy frowned. "I bet it'd have struck me. How did she pay the three-month's rent?"

"In cash, as you might expect, and as it was banked on the Thursday evening, there's no way of tracing the money." Philip ground out his cigarette and tossed the stub onto the grass. "And that, I'm afraid, is that. The so called Mrs Kelly has vanished into thin air, leaving only a quarter of tea and a bag of sugar. Even that had gone by the time the police eventually got into the house."

Sandy shook her head in irritation. "There must be some way we can trace her. Let's see exactly what we do know. She took the house to provide a false reference for John Guthrie. Yes? Yes. He had a letter in his pocket from Mrs Strickland that was supposed to have been written months ago from that address. If anyone checked about a Mrs Strickland of Camden Town, then the records would show a perfectly authentic Mrs Strickland living exactly where she said she did. It's only when you dig in and ask the house-agents or, perhaps, the neighbours, that it unravels. Now the question, obviously, is why? She took the house on Thursday and we know it was on the Thursday that John Guthrie saw the picture of Sir Dennis in the newspaper and decided to come to Farholt. We're also presuming that it was the emeralds he was after."

"We can take that for granted, I think."

"Where does that get us? Why did he need a letter?"

Philip remained silent.

"I've got it!" Sandy turned to him with shining eyes. "He must have been confident of where the emeralds were, but he needed to get into the house to get them. So he intended to apply for a job of some sort here and for that he'd need a reference, so he produces this letter and bingo! He's got a sister in Camden Town who can say all sorts of nice things about him. Then, when he'd pinched the emeralds, he gives them to Mrs Whatsit to fence, and then they can both disappear back into their own identities, she as Lily Kelly, or what-have-you, and he as Alan Oliver. Then, if we ever decide to chase up that nice assistant gardener or whatever he intended to be, we come against a complete brick wall. What d'you think?"

"I think," said Philip, rolling onto his elbows and picking a blade of grass, "that if the letter was meant to have been a reference, it'd have been a jolly sight easier if it was from a past employer, saying he was a delight amongst the dahlias or a chrysanthemum king or something. I mean, I don't know how you pick your staff, but the fact that some chap's got a sister in Camden Town doesn't seem to be either here or there."

"She might have been going to pretend that he had worked for her. It was only at the inquest she said she was his sister."

Philip chewed his blade of grass in a dissatisfied way. "No.... Rum stuff, this. I can't think why cows like it so much. No. She wouldn't have addressed the letter "Dear Kevin," if she was going to be an erstwhile employer. Maybe..." He paused and sat upright again, looking away from her. "Maybe we've got all this round the twist. Maybe the only reason Lily Kelly took the house was so she would be called upon to attend the inquest."

"But..." Sandy paused. "But it can't be that," she said, an odd note in her voice. "It would mean she knew John Guthrie was going to be killed."

Philip still looked away. "Yes."

"And that would mean that Tommy knocked him over on purpose."

"Yes."

Sandy scrambled to her feet, her eyes blazing. "I don't believe it! Not *Tommy*!"

He did look at her then. "I'm sorry. I didn't know you cared so much about the bloke. It's just that being new here I don't know the first thing about anyone. Have you been friends for a long time?"

"About a year or so, I suppose."

"And who is he? Do you know his family?"

"I believe they came from Westmorland. His parents are dead and they left him very badly off."

"But you don't *know* any of that, do you? Not outside what he's told you, I mean?"

"Well, if it comes to that, I don't know anything about you. Sir Dennis brought you here, just as he brought Tommy. Have you got any family?"

"My parents are dead."

"Just like Tommy's."

"Just like Tommy's, I agree. You'll have to take my word for it."

"As I take his word." She sat down again. "Look, I don't want to be funny, but isn't it all a question of taking someone's word? Sir Dennis Storwood is all accounted for - well, I presume he is - but he met Lady Storwood in America. As for us, we arrived from Canada. No one here knew us from Adam. We could be total impostors. Daddy *says* he was Francis Eldon's cousin. We can't prove it."

"Oh, come on. He talks about the Eldons and, besides that, there's your Aunt Daphne. She's real enough."

"Is she? For all you know she could have been his mistress for years and his first wife has gone mad and is locked up in an attic somewhere."

"Good Lord."

Sandy suddenly grinned. "Don't blame me, blame *Jane Eyre*. I loved that book when I was at school. My point is that you usually trust people to be who they say they are. If we really were impostors of course we'd arrive with lots of tales about the Eldons and an old Aunt or two. It all adds verisimilitude, so to speak, and meanwhile the real owner is weltering in his blood and buried in the kitchen garden or coshed on the head and thrown overboard on the boat back from Canada."

Philip returned her grin. "You've obviously gone into this very thoroughly."

"Well, I would, wouldn't I, if I was an impostor. But you've got to be wrong about Tommy. The letter John Guthrie had in his pocket proves he – John Guthrie, I mean - was hand in glove with Mrs Strickland or Mrs Kelly or whatever you want to call her."

"Tommy Leigh could have planted the letter when he was waiting with him after the accident. He had plenty of time."

"So could you," countered Sandy. "So could I, come to think of it, or Doctor Hayle. It's a rotten idea, Philip. For it to work you have to presume that John Guthrie obligingly collaborated in his own murder by being in exactly the right place at the right time for Tommy to run him down."

Philip still looked unconvinced. "Look," continued Sandy, patiently. "Let's assume, if it's going to make you any happier, that Tommy and Mrs Kelly are plotting together to kill John Guthrie. Why did they wait until he came to Farholt? They could have easily shoved him under a car..."

"Or a train," put in Philip with feeling.

"Or a train - in London and vanished into the crowd. Then all this business would have been unnecessary. Mrs Strickland or Kelly took an enormous risk by appearing at the inquest. We know that all three of them, Tommy, Mrs

Thing and John Guthrie himself were in London on Thursday. It would have been so easy to kill him there that it seems stupid to wait until he got to Farholt and do it in a blaze of publicity."

"Damn," said Philip. "You're right, of course. If they'd played their cards right they needn't even have bothered to make it look like an accident. One of them could have simply sneaked into his rooms at the club, shot him, or left arsenic in his whisky. There's nothing, as far as I can see, to link him to your Tommy. I have to say you're right."

"I'm pretty certain I am. And he's not my Tommy. But all this is a bit academic. To kill someone you have to have a motive, unless you're loopy. Why should anyone, let alone Tommy, want to kill John Guthrie?"

"To stop him finding the emeralds?"

Sandy sighed. "It'd make a great deal more sense if they let him find the emeralds first, then knock him on the head. It's plain silly doing it this way round. And here's another thing. We know that Guthrie had something to hide. As John Guthrie he was wanted for murder, even if he was innocent, and that gives a very pressing reason why he should be working with Mrs Kelly. I think it's obvious she was blackmailing him."

"Maybe she was - is - blackmailing Tommy Leigh."

"She can't have been blackmailing *everyone*. Look, we know, or at least I think we know, that Mrs Kelly and John Guthrie are connected, either willingly or by coercion. If she was blackmailing him she'd hardly want him killed. He wouldn't be any use to her dead. On the other hand, if he

184

was working for her by choice, she'd want him to nab the emeralds for her. She wouldn't knock him over first."

"Could John Guthrie have been blackmailing her? That'd be a motive for murder."

Sandy shook her head in disbelief. "You don't like letting a thing drop, do you? Listen, I'll spell it out. John Guthrie had a false identity. John Guthrie was wanted for murder. John Guthrie couldn't blackmail anyone because John Guthrie was the one with the guilty secrets. Got it?"

Philip laughed and lazily stretched his shoulders. "Got it. There is someone working for or with Mrs Kelly at Farholt, though."

"What? Someone here? How on earth can you be so sure?"

"Because that someone gave her the wink that the police were on her trail yesterday. By the way, I haven't thanked you for your valuable support last night in the drawing-room."

"That's okay," she said absently. "I gathered you were up to something and was only worried in case I wrecked whatever you were doing." She hesitated. "I want to thank you as well, Phil, for not letting on I was in the house in Camden Town. Aunt Daphne would never let me hear the last of it, and even though Dad's pretty tolerant, he would draw the line at breaking into houses. He's funny like that."

"Odd," agreed Philip, gravely. "I imagine most parents would be. No, all that talk last night was directed to letting Mrs Kelly know that there was something in the house she had to go and get. I'd worked out that someone had been listening to that idiot, Colonel Waldrist, telling everyone that Scotland Yard were on their way. As Mrs Kelly then ran for it, that someone must have told her to hook it. My brilliant scheme, which I put into operation last night, was designed to get our Mrs K. back to the house to be met by the police. However, as we know, it was a wash-out. Talking about brilliance, I thought that was an absolute brain-wave of your last night about Mrs Banks."

Sandy looked pleasantly surprised. "Did you? I thought you were rather down on the idea."

"Persiflage, old thing. Don't forget I believe that someone is going to pass on everything we say."

She rubbed her nose thoughtfully. "I don't know about this idea that someone's in league with Mrs Kelly. Can't it all just be coincidence?"

"Hardly. It was fairly obvious that Mrs Kelly had an informant yesterday afternoon. Add in the jiggery-pokery in Camden Town in the wee small hours and I think you've got a certainty."

"I suppose you have." She laughed in sheer light-heartedness. "Oh, Phil, you're right. You have to be."

"Er... yes." He looked at her smile and caught his breath. "Why... why are you so happy about it?" he asked, conscious that his voice was unsteady.

She brushed her hair back from her face. "Yesterday when you rushed off, I knew you were after Mrs Kelly, but I couldn't think how she'd got to be there unless someone had told her."

"Two minds that think as one. We were on the same lines."

"Yes... only, I... Well, I wondered if you had told her."

"Me?"

"I told you it sounded stupid, but I couldn't think how else she'd known. You'd spent ages inside your club. Quite long enough to have phoned her."

Philip touched his forehead. "Have my honourable scars convinced you of my innocence?"

She laughed again. "It's all right now. I can't think how I came to be so idiotic." She glanced at him anxiously. "It is all right, isn't it?"

Philip swallowed. The look on her face was so appealing that he wanted to reach out to her. What he did was to turn away slightly and light another cigarette. "Of course it is," he said softly. "Have you any idea," he added, "who we could be looking for?"

She shook her head. "Not really. I'm innocent, of course, but only I really know that."

"I believe you."

She smiled quickly. "I think that's very nice of you. But as to the others, no. You see, Phil, I'm not quite sure what we're meant to suspect them *of*."

"Well, of aiding and abetting Mrs Kelly, of course."

"And where does that get us? Mrs Kelly, at great inconvenience and some expense, tried very hard to convince us that John Guthrie was Kevin Murphy. But we know who he was and so what? I can't see we're much further on than before. We know he had the emeralds on his mind as he died, and was talking about the Count and so on, but what it all means is anyone's guess. Even if he'd given us a map marked with an X and we'd found the blessed things, we still wouldn't know the why and wherefores of this Mrs Kelly business."

"I'd have the emeralds though," said Philip, with a sharp recollection of the papers he had signed. "And that would make all the difference in the world." He stopped. Last night. There was something about Sir Dennis Storwood and last night that he knew he should remember. In the study...? He clicked his tongue in irritation. There was something important, but he knew better than to try too hard to dredge it up.

He got to his feet, offering a hand to Sandy. "Why don't we walk down to the village? We could look in on the ironmongers and see when Mrs Banks is expected back."

***   ***   ***

Sandy liked Farholt. It had once been an important town, but a Nineteenth-Century Eldon had refused to countenance the railway, leaving Farholt to placidly decline into a little more than a village. It had a jumble of overhanging streets snaked through with lanes and alleys, all converging on Swan Street with its pump and horse-trough, gold-lettered shop windows and cobbles along which the mail-coach had once galloped north.

She especially liked the ironmonger's shop with the astringent smell of paraffin and coal-tar and the clutter of oil-lamps, hammers, mysterious boxes of metal bits, lengths of washing-line, grass-seed and the row of patent packets which, while containing the material for mending

188

kettles and saucepans, promised a thousand uses in the home.

Mrs Enid Stebbing was dexterously sorting a boxful of bolts and wing-nuts into a tray, whilst talking to a heavily-built, red-faced man whom Sandy recognized, with a start of surprise, as Superintendent Brenzett.

He touched his hat to her and nodded to Philip. "Afternoon, Miss Herriad, Mr Brown. I think we're here upon the same errand. Mrs Stebbing has just been telling me her aunt isn't expected back until Saturday."

"Did you want Aunty Dorothy as well, Miss Herriad?" asked Mrs Stebbing. "She's in demand and no mistake." She shot another handful of bolts into the tray. "She's all right, isn't she? I mean, there hasn't been an accident or anything?"

Sandy smiled. "She's perfectly all right. I saw her at Waterloo yesterday. We had a cup of tea together."

"Well, that's a relief." Mrs Stebbing nodded at the Superintendent. "What with this gentleman here asking about her, and that telephone call earlier on, I was beginning to think something had happened to her."

"Don't you worry," said Brenzett, easily. "It's simply that we think she might be able to help us with trying to work out something that happened years ago."

Mrs Stebbing laughed. "Aunty'll be able to tell you. She's got a wonderful memory. Why she can place her hand on anything in the shop, just like that. I don't know where half the things are, and that's a fact."

Glancing round the fantastically crowded interior, Philip wasn't surprised.

189

"And as for the old days," Mrs Stebbing continued, "I've often said to her, I don't think she had time to do any work up at the House. She seemed to spend all her time finding out what was going on." She laughed once more. "You can't get past Aunty though. She's says that's the secret. Take an interest in what's going on round you and it doesn't seem like work." She broke off as the telephone bell rang at the back of the shop. "Do excuse me a minute. I'll have to answer that thing."

Mrs Stebbing went into the little room behind the counter.

"Scotland Yard rang up earlier," said Brenzett in a low voice. "I do wish they'd have a bit more tact. That poor woman's obviously been worrying about it ever since. I'm glad you called in, Miss Herriad. I think you reassured her."

Mrs Stebbing poked her head out of the back room. "Excuse me. Did you say you were called Mr Brenzett, sir? Here's a funny thing. This gentleman on the telephone says he's from Scotland Yard, too. He's asking about Aunty Dorothy as well."

Brenzett raised his eyebrows. "Do you mind?" he asked, with one hand on the counter. Mrs Stebbing invited him through. "It's easier if I talk to them," he said to Philip and Sandy. He went through to the back room. Mrs Stebbing rejoined them in the shop and the door shut behind Brenzett.

"This thing you want to see Aunty Dorothy about," asked Mrs Stebbing hesitantly. "It wouldn't be about those emeralds that got stolen, would it?"

190

"That's right," agreed Sandy. "How did you guess?"

Mrs Stebbing picked up another bag of mixed bolts. "It was Aunty Dorothy who said something about it, Miss Herriad. There was that bit in the papers about a stolen necklace, and she read the name - some foreign one, it was - and said, 'Now fancy that. I knew him when he came to stay at Farholt years ago.' He had his necklace stolen then, too, but they found it afterwards. Some poor man had been murdered for it. He was a foreigner, too, the man who was murdered, I mean. Worth thousands and thousands of pounds, those jewels were. She said she'd always thought there was more to that business than met the eye. But I said to her that it couldn't be the same man that she'd known, because it described him as young and handsome. I mean, he might have been years ago but he wouldn't be now. Not young, anyhow, although some gentlemen do get marvellously preserved."

"This man - the man in the papers - is the other man's son," said Sandy, fighting back a giggle at Mrs Stebbing's description of the male sex as a sort of jam.

"Is he? I'll have to tell her."

Mrs Stebbing broke off as Brenzett came out of the back room. "Everything all right, sir?"

He smiled warmly. "Quite all right, Mrs Stebbing." He touched his hat. "Thank you for your time and assistance. We'll be getting along now."

With a clank from the shop bell, they walked out into Swan Street together.

"What...?" began Philip, but Brenzett shook his head.

"Not here, Mr Brown. Let's walk a bit further on." He ushered them a few yards down the street before stopping beside the horse-trough.

"There's something odd going on," he said, when he judged they were in no danger of being overheard. "That telephone call I took was from the Yard, all right. It was Inspector Hepworth. He's been instructed to find out where Mrs Banks is staying in London and when she's expected back. I was able to tell him that without bothering Mrs Stebbing again. However, he has no knowledge of any earlier phone call."

Philip stopped dead. "But that means..."

"That someone else is checking up on Mrs Banks," completed Brenzett, grimly. "Someone, Miss Herriad, who thought your idea last night was worth following up. Now, before I can act on that, I need to know for certain that the Yard really didn't telephone earlier. Hepworth's going to investigate and ring me at The Bird In Hand."

Sandy felt her skin crawl. "Mr Brenzett, Mrs Banks isn't in any danger, is she?"

"I don't think so." Brenzett was definite. "*If* Mrs Banks knows anything, then she doesn't know she knows it. Whoever our friend is will have to talk to her fairly carefully to find out, exactly as we'll have to. Our advantage is that we can do it quite openly."

Philip pulled a face. "I don't like this. What if our pal does see Mrs Banks and finds she knows something? Won't that place the poor woman in danger?"

Brenzett thought it over. "No," he said eventually. "She's not due back until Saturday. Until then she's at her

192

niece's, and safe enough. If Hepworth confirms that first phone call was false, I'll go up to Town tomorrow and see her myself. Don't worry, Mr Brown. I'll have a good man keeping tabs on her all the way home. If anyone does approach her, we're in business."

"Why don't you go today?" asked Sandy.

He glanced at his watch. "By the time Hepworth's checked on that phone call and I've spoken to Mrs Banks, I'll have missed the last train back to Brosley Dean tonight. However, I can look in at the post-office and see if I can find out where that call was put through from. That might tell us something. I'll be in touch later on to let you know what's happening."

"Join us after dinner if you like," said Sandy.

He smiled and raised his hat. "Thank you, Miss Herriad. I'll look forward to it."

***   ***   ***

Eleanor Storwood was in the grip of an enthusiasm at dinner. "It's the most marvellous plan, Dennis. Madame Vesoul and I spent most of the afternoon discussing it."

"I thought you were going for a fitting for a new frock."

"Gown, Dennis, gown. I did that too, naturally. But really, Dennis, this *is* a good idea. She'll send one of her top assistants down to the Kurhaus twice a week, and there our residents can help themselves by choosing a whole new wardrobe based on the knowledge and principles they've acquired. Depending on who's staying she may very well come herself. It'll add an entirely different dimension to the place, and is based firmly on our idea of health in life outside the Kurhaus as well as within it."

"What," asked Daphne Marston, betraying both a lack of knowledge of the fashionable world and her complete inattention to her guest's conversation over the previous few days, "is a Kurhaus? It sounds," she added with deep disapproval, "German."

Eleanor Storwood blinked but bore up bravely. "It is German, Mrs Marston, but we have, of course, given it an English slant. As you know, the Germans were doing some remarkable work before the war in arriving at a true understanding of what it really means to be healthy in both mind and body."

"Yes, but what is it?"

"It's a high-class looney bin with physical jerks," put in Tommy Leigh with a grin.

"Leigh!" Sir Dennis was shocked. "That is a most misleading description. To give you the essence of the idea, dear lady, the Kurhaus is a place where those of us who are feeling the strain of modern life with all its hurry and turmoil can retreat for a while. There is a highly qualified doctor in attendance to advise upon the more difficult cases, but we have instituted a regime of quiet amongst peaceful surroundings with meticulous attention to exercise and diet, coupled with a complete lack of worry. Even the most careworn benefit greatly after a fortnight of such beneficent attention and we have seen some remarkable cures. At the outset of the enterprise I, too, had doubts as to its efficacy, but I am glad to say these were over-ridden by my dear wife and I have come to genuinely believe that by maintaining such an organization, I am providing a service of very great value to my fellow man."

"I bet you make a bit from it as well, I shouldn't wonder," said Andrew Herriad. "The place sounds like a gold-mine."

Sir Dennis inclined his head. "I am pleased to say that as well as being of physical and mental use, it is also a sound commercial proposition. Eleanor, my dear, by all means ask your dressmaker to submit her ideas for consideration. As you say, it may prove a valuable link between the world within the Kurhaus and the world without."

"For a commission," said Herriad, wickedly.

Sir Dennis refused to rise to the bait. "Naturally, my dear Herriad. I would not entertain the notion on any other grounds." He looked across the table and cleared his throat. "Talking of commissions, I carried one out on your behalf today, Mr Brown. As you seemed somewhat exercised last night as to the fate of the missing jewels, I made it my business to call upon Sir Douglas Lynton at Scotland Yard and find out exactly what progress has been made in the case. I am sorry to have to inform you that he takes a very bleak view of the situation. I know you had reservations, my dear fellow, about the agreement we reached, but I can honestly say I think it is the best that can be offered."

"What about this Banks woman?" asked Tommy Leigh. "There's a clue worth chasing up. Haven't the cops been on to her?"

"Poor Mrs Banks," said Daphne Marston. "I hope the police haven't been bothering her."

"I asked specifically about Mrs Banks, but Sir Douglas seemed to offer no hope that a solution might be forthcoming along those lines. Bearing in mind how energetically you have been following up the slightest lead, Brown, I tried to find out where she was staying in London, thinking that you might want to interview her yourself. However, Sir Douglas either did not know, or refused to divulge, her whereabouts."

"They're at the wash," muttered Tommy, which made Sandy laugh.

"Therefore," continued Sir Dennis, unheedingly, "in your own interests, I think you should put all thought of retrieving the necklace out of your head, as it will only serve as a distraction from the main issue at hand. I am pleased to say that, as we anticipated, Matherson completely approved the proposal for the loan. He intends to join us tomorrow for dinner, by which stage Salvatierra will have made giant strides towards putting its affairs in sound order."

"Oh, thanks," said Philip, bleakly. He stirred himself as his conscience twinged. "I mean it, sir. Thank you for all the trouble you've taken. It's only that it's such a poor offer compared to what we might have had."

"That is precisely what I mean about the necklace being a distraction," said Sir Dennis severely.

"Hang on minute," said Andrew Herriad. "Is that bank chap, James Matherson, coming here?"

196

Dennis Storwood looked at him blankly. "Why, yes. You have no objection, I trust?"

"Er... no. Why should I? You invite who you like, my dear fellow."

"Thank you, Herriad. I knew that I could rely on your unstinting cooperation." He broke off as Larch, the butler, entered the room, carrying a telegram on a tray. "Is that for me?"

"Yes sir. The postmistress sent the boy up with it."

Sir Dennis tore open the telegram, tutting as he read the contents. "I'm afraid this may mean we have hit a snag, Brown," he said, looking up. "It's from Birch at Houblyns. *Urgent see you soon as possible. Cannot discuss on telephone.*" He tutted once more. "I shall have to go to London first thing." He drummed his fingers on the table. "This is very inconvenient."

***   ***   ***

"The phone call," said Superintendent Brenzett, neatly pocketing the red ball, "was false." Philip and Brenzett had the billiard room to themselves, Sandy having taken on the task of distracting both her father and Tommy Leigh. "I called at the post office, but although the girl remembered that there had been a couple of calls for the ironmongers, she couldn't tell me where they were from, more's the pity. And therefore," he said, bending over the white, "I'm going to London tomorrow."

"So's Sir Dennis," said Philip, leaning on his cue. "He was in London today, as well, but he's been summoned back by a late telegram. It came while we were having dinner. D'you know he called at Scotland Yard? He went to see Sir Douglas to find out what progress was being made."

"Did he, by jingo? Did he say why he was so interested?"

"He *says* that he called on Sir Douglas on my behalf. Apparently the necklace is taking my mind off concentrating on the loan to Salvatierra. God knows, he's right there. However, I was surprised he asked Sir Douglas for Mrs Bank's London address. It seemed very keen, don't you think? However, he didn't get it."

"It seems very keen indeed," agreed Brenzett. "I don't suppose," he said, adding seventeen points to the marker board, "you happen to know if anyone else is going to London tomorrow?"

"Just Sir Dennis as far as I'm aware. But he really did receive a telegram, Brenzett. We all saw it."

"Telegrams," said Brenzett, "have been known to be false before now. And they can provide a very welcome excuse for revisiting a place if your first trip has been inconclusive. It's a ticklish job, getting permission to keep an eye on a Cabinet Minister, and I don't know if the chief'll buy it. If this loan of yours goes ahead as planned, will Sir Dennis benefit from it at all?"

"I suppose," said Philip slowly, "as a director of Houblyns he might get a commission on it. In fact, I'm almost certain he will."

"And if the necklace is found, then the loan would be re-negotiated along lines much more favourable to you?"

"Absolutely. He'd still get something, of course, but we'd be in a far stronger position. In fact it'd knock his

198

present cut into a cocked hat. I say, Brenzett, what d'you think?"

"I think," said Superintendent Brenzett, "that it's a motive we haven't even considered yet."

Chapter Nine

Andrew Herriad thought of himself as a tolerant man. All he wanted, as he said to Daphne Marston at breakfast that morning, was to be left alone in peace. He, and he would defy anyone to contradict him, had never taken the slightest interest in politics, world affairs, police matters or high finance. And yet in the last few days he had had to cope with stolen jewels, sudden death, bankers who came and went without a by-your-leave and, on top of it all, was expected to take an intelligent interest in South America.

If it was a question of Canada, now, or farming - and God knows what the Government thought they were doing - had Daphne read this speech in *The Times*? Disgraceful; - then he, Andrew Herriad, would be able to offer an opinion. But no. His opinion wasn't wanted. All that was wanted, as far as he could make out, was for him to offer free accommodation to any of Dennis Storwood's family, household, or business acquaintances that might care to drop in and take pot-luck. If I, he said trenchantly, had wanted to run a hotel, I'd have bought one.

"Yes, dear," agreed Daphne absently. "You know, I really must do something about the spring borders. This warm weather is lovely, but it does mean the daffodils have finished awfully early and it makes them look so ragged."

Andrew Herriad sighed. "I was talking," he said, "about Dennis Storwood's continued presence in the house."

Daphne paused in the act of pouring a cup of coffee. "Sir Dennis? But he's not in the house. He's gone to London. Don't you remember, Andrew? Honestly, your memory is growing quite unreliable. He left first thing this morning. Lady Storwood seemed rather put out that he was going so early. Her idea was that if he waited a little while, he could take Mr Brown with him in the car, but Sir Dennis said that would be completely unsuitable, as he didn't actually know if they would be discussing Mr Brown's affairs. It might be something to do with the internal management of the bank."

She picked up the milk-jug. "I do admire Sir Dennis. He's such a vigorous man who takes a real interest in the world around him. He reminds me of dear Edgar. He always had ambitions to enter public life."

Andrew Herriad winced. Dear Edgar, although a good, upright and honourable man who had made Daphne an excellent husband, had always struck him as an unmitigated bore and just the sort who would want to go in for politics.

"I wish you were more like Sir Dennis, Andrew. It cannot be good for a man of your age to bury himself away as you do."

Herriad looked speechlessly at his sister.

"However," she continued blithely, "I think there's a real chance that we might have the Storwoods as neighbours."

"*What*?" This was the final blow.

"Yes, dear. I had a most interesting conversation with Lady Storwood after dinner. I must say she improves greatly on acquaintance. She fancies a country house, and was most interested when I told her that the Redways' old place in Chesworth Mersey is for sale or let. However, she knows nothing of country life, so I offered to take her round the grounds here this morning to show her what can be done. We'll have to start as soon as I've seen about tonight's dinner - I wonder if we can get sufficient lamb? Perhaps I'd better stick to beef - because I must call in at the church this afternoon. Poor Mrs Horrocks will insist on doing the brasses and I always have to do them again. I do hope the Storwoods choose to settle in the area. It would be so nice, Andrew, for you to have such an interesting man of affairs as Sir Dennis close at hand."

Andrew Herriad drank his coffee. It tasted like the bitter cup. "I'm going to my study," he announced bleakly.

"You can't, dear. Mr Brown's in there at the moment and it's full of Sir Dennis's papers which mustn't be disturbed."

"Damn!"

Daphne Marston blinked. "Well really, Andrew. I've never known you so put out by trifles before. It's high time you developed some more interests. I sincerely hope the Storwoods do take the Redways'. It would be so good for you."

*** *** ***

The library should have been unoccupied at this time of day. Instead Sandy was standing on the steps, earnestly taking out armfuls of books and replacing them whilst apparently having a conversation with the empty air.

"There's nothing in this lot.... Oh, hello, Dad."

"What are you doing?" asked Herriad, peevishly. "Apart from creating a dickens of a lot of dust."

"Isn't it awful? I don't think these books have been touched for years. Mind you," she said, opening one at random, "I'm not surprised. *The Tatler or Lucubrations of Issac Bickerstaff, Esq. London MDCCLXXII*. I can't follow all these X's and L's and things and what on earth's a lucubration? Tommy, do you know?"

"Haven't a clue," said Tommy Leigh, popping his head out from under the library table.

Andrew Herriad, who hadn't known he was there, jumped and bit his tongue. "Exactly what," he asked once more, his hand to his mouth, "is going on?"

Tommy emerged completely and dusted himself off. "We're looking for the emeralds. I had the idea that there might be a hollow book..."

"Or a map," put in Sandy, brightly.

"Or even a secret passage. I've been tapping panels and things and the one beside the window sounds promising. Listen." He crossed the room and rapped on the panel. "What d'you think?"

Andrew Herriad sighed, then, walking to the window, bent down and slid the panel upwards. "There you are. It's not a secret passage. The panel slides back to allow you to get at the sash cords for the window." He looked at his daughter's deeply disappointed face and relented.

"There is a secret passage. I believe it runs from the billiard room."

"Dad! Why ever didn't you tell me before?"

"It didn't seem important," said Herriad.

"Not *important*! How do we get into it?"

"I can't remember. I was shown once, years ago, but I've forgotten."

"Honestly! We'll need torches, Tommy. Come on, let's go and find it."

Sandy and Tommy went out of the room, leaving Andrew Herriad to a fidgety peace. He opened the newspaper once more, but the births, deaths and marriages contained no one he knew and the speech on agriculture was just as irritating when read for a second time. He flung down the *Times* and stalked off to look at his pigs. However, even the pig-sties contained no peace.

Instead of feasting his eyes upon Horace Green, the pig-man, or the comfortably rounded back of his pedigree sow, complete with her five junior editions, he saw the less than lovely sight of Daphne with Eleanor Storwood in tow.

"Would you like to join us, Andrew?" asked Daphne Marston. "I've told Lady Storwood about the great improvements you have made to the sties, but I feel that you should be the one to explain matters thoroughly."

Herriad winced inwardly. Women didn't understand about pigs. Pigs were restful, placid creatures, who didn't go *on* at you all the time. All he really wanted was a bit of peace... "I'm sorry, Daphne," he said, struck by a truly bright inspiration. "I need to see Hutchens. You asked

204

me to do something about the coping-stones on the church wall, remember?"

Daphne beamed. "I thought you'd forgotten about it." She turned to Eleanor Storwood. "We'll postpone the sties until later. Andrew!"

"Yes?"

"I have to call in at the church this afternoon. I'll be able to inspect the work then."

"Oh." In that case, thought Herriad, ruefully, he better really had see Hutchens about the blessed wall. Maybe after that he could be left in peace. The trouble was, he thought, after Hutchens had been duly instructed, that virtually everywhere outside was a danger zone. You never knew where those wretched women would turn up next.

A huge desire for his oldest and smelliest pipe washed over him. With guests in the house Daphne had forbidden it but he could see it in his mind's eye on the mantelpiece of the study as clearly as if he had been gifted with X-ray vision. Brown wouldn't want to talk, would he? A pleasant enough chap, even if he was inclined to collar the conversation and steer it towards missing jewels, but capable, unlike Dennis Storwood, of not gassing away for hours on end when a man didn't want to be gassed at.

In the event, he needn't have worried. The study was empty and the window wide open, the presumption being that Mr Brown had taken this slightly unconventional way of leaving the room.

With his hand firmly clasped round his pipe, Andrew Herriad began to feel his habitual content creep back, when his calm was shattered by the telephone. It was Superintendent Brenzett, in search of Philip Brown. The Superintendent sounded distracted. No Mr Brown? That was awkward. That was very awkward indeed. Mr Herriad had no idea where he might be? No idea at all. Oh. In that case, could he speak to Miss Herriad? Yes, he'd hold the line.

Herriad put down the receiver and crossed the hall to the billiard room. An open panel beside the fireplace showed the secret passage was secret no longer. He put his head inside the dark hole and shouted, but was met with total silence. Sighing, he went back to the telephone. Superintendent Brenzett sounded worried. Perhaps Mr Brown could get in touch with him at the Yard? No, there was no message, only that he'd like to see Mr Brown that evening. With that he rang off, leaving Herriad feeling irrationally irritated at having to take calls for other people's secretaries.

The gun-room called to him. Why on earth hadn't he gone there in the first place? He settled himself in a deep armchair and pulled the tobacco jar towards him. Peace, he thought, as he struck a match and puffed contentedly at his pipe, at last. At least...

He sat upright. They didn't have rats at Farholt, did they? Not in the house, at any rate. Scuffle, scuffle, thump. What the...? A section of panelling swung back halfway up the wall and Sandy peered down at him.

"Hello, Dad."

Herriad managed a frozen smile.

Sandy, looking grubbier than her father had seen her for about fifteen years, clambered out. "It's wonderful in there," she said brightly. "Come on out, Tommy. We're in the gun-room now." Tommy Leigh joined her. "It really is interesting, Dad. I can't think why you never told me about them before. They're not hard to get into. Tommy found the entrance almost right away. The passages run all over the house and one of them goes outside to the old ice-house. You must have a look."

"I'll take your word for it. By the way, that Brenzett chap rang up, pretty anxious to speak to Mr Brown. When I couldn't find Brown he wanted to talk to you, but I couldn't find you, either."

"Did he say what it was about?"

Herraid shrugged. "He didn't tell me. He wanted Mr Brown to ring him at Scotland Yard."

Sandy bit her lip. "Isn't Phil - Mr Brown - in the study? I'd better try and find him."

"Well, for goodness sake, wash your face first. And change. You'll frighten him into a fit if you appear like that."

Sandy looked at her dress ruefully. "Yes, I do look a bit shop-soiled, don't I? I say, Tommy, you're filthy!"

Tommy grinned. "A trifle dusty, perhaps." He smiled at her in admiration. "I don't know how you do it. Even covered in cobwebs you merely look as if cobwebs are in this year." He looked at his hands in distaste. "It's even money whether I should have a wash or just put myself in the bin." He nodded at the gaping hole in the wall. "Have you finished exploring for the time being?"

"I think so. I must find Philip. Goodness knows where he's got to."

"In that case I'll have a wash and brush-up then I'd better have a look at my car. I wasn't at all happy with the ignition."

They went out of the room. Herriad got up and closed the open panel in a marked way, then settled back in his chair. It must have been quarter of an hour later, when his pipe was pulling perfectly and he had had a blissful freedom from interruptions, that the peace was shattered by the roar of a car engine from the open window. Tommy, testing his car.

Feeling that murder was far too harshly dealt with, Herriad got up and slammed down the window. The car roared once more, then the noise of engine receded to be replaced by the somnolent sound of the ticking clock. Quarter past eleven. He should really look at the estate papers for Wistow's Tenancy. If Wistow could only be persuaded to water his cows from the....

"I said," repeated Daphne Marston firmly, "have you seen Eleanor Storwood? She said she would come round the greenhouses with me and if we don't do it before lunch then I shall have to postpone it until tomorrow. Andrew, have you been asleep?"

Andrew Herriad struggled upright in his chair. "Certainly not," he said firmly. Then, as the sound of a Riley engine bit though the air once more, added with more confidence, "How could I? Not with that ghastly row going on. What's the time? Ten to twelve? I must see Green about the new feed. Why on earth should I know where Eleanor Storwood is? She was meant to be with you, wasn't she? How did you come to lose her?"

"I came in to have a word about the butcher. Dinners don't drop down from heaven, you know. They have to be planned. She said she'd wait in the summer-house, but she's not there."

"She's probably got the wrong place and is sitting in the potting-shed or something."

"It sounds most unlikely," said Daphne with a sniff. "Andrew, you've been smoking that awful pipe again. And with the window closed, too." She opened it briskly. "I can't think what you're doing on a lovely day like this, lurking inside with the windows shut."

"I shut it," said Herriad, "to keep out that appalling row. I'm going to have a word with that young man."

Tommy Leigh had replaced dirt for oil. There was a smudge of it on his forehead and his overalls, once khaki, were mainly black. He was so abjectly apologetic that Herriad forgot his bad temper and even allowed himself to be drawn into a discussion on the relative merits of Rileys and Austins, while Leigh replaced his plugs.

"That should do it," said Leigh, putting down the bonnet. "I think I'll take her for another spin. She was sounding a bit rough earlier." He glanced at his watch. "I should just do it before lunch." He climbed in and revved the engine. Andrew Herriad went to find his pig-man and so fascinating were his views on pig-swill that Daphne had to start lunch without him.

209

*** *** ***

Superintendent Brenzett and Sir Douglas Lynton sat in in the granite building overlooking the Thames. Sir Douglas was speaking on the telephone. With a sigh he replaced the receiver. "They missed Mrs Banks at the station."

Brenzett's face twisted. "I was afraid of that, sir."

Sir Douglas walked to the window. "It's a great pity you couldn't get hold of Mr Brown or Miss Herriad earlier on. If we could have had someone at the station who knew Mrs Banks or even Mrs Kelly, then we might have succeeded." He turned and propped himself against the window-sill. "You really think Mrs Banks is in danger, Brenzett?"

"I do, sir." Brenzett counted the points off on his fingers. "Yesterday afternoon, according to her niece, Mrs Gladys Rushton, an Irishwoman turned up to see Mrs Banks. She can't give us much of a description - dark coat, dark gloves and one of these wretched veils which women wear - but the accent was unmistakable. The two women spent half an hour together and they parted on the best of terms. Mrs Banks refused to tell her niece what it was about, saying it was secret, but Mrs Rushton described her aunt as excited and happy. As a result, Mrs Banks changed her plans and announced her intention of returning home the following morning."

"You think she was planning to return home?"

"I think so, sir, but whether she'll ever get there is a different matter. It would be easy enough for Mrs Kelly, to call her that, to meet her at Waterloo and suggest

210

going somewhere else entirely. She may even have had a car waiting. Heaven only knows where they are now."

Sir Douglas shifted uncomfortably. "We don't know she's in danger, Brenzett. Mrs Kelly and her companions don't seem a very blood-thirsty lot to me. The nearest thing to violence we've had so far is the attempt to push Philip Brown under a train and that could be an accident. I think it's at least feasible that all Mrs Kelly wants to do is talk to Mrs Banks."

"She did that yesterday, sir."

"Yes... Could Mrs Banks be showing Mrs Kelly where the emeralds are hidden?" He looked at Brenzett. "Cheer up, man. That business in Hilldrop Road was little more than a farce, but what it tells me is that Mrs Kelly and her confederates don't want to be saddled with a murder charge."

"What it tells me," said Brenzett, glumly, "is that we're dealing with someone who's very clever. And so far, they're winning."

*** *** ***

"I really do wish you make more of an effort to be on time, Andrew," said his sister as he entered the room. "You know lunch is always at one o'clock. Edgar was always so particular in the matter of punctuality and it really does contribute to the smooth running of a household."

She stopped, wrinkling her nose. "Andrew, you have washed, haven't you?"

211

"Of course I've had a wash," said Andrew Herriad, defensively. "Besides that, I *like* the smell of pigs. Good, healthy smell. Not like oil and grease."

He shot a glance at Tommy Leigh, but that young man was sitting placidly finishing his soup, totally free from any trace of the Riley's insides.

"I found it most interesting, seeing the grounds with you this morning, Mr Marston," said Eleanor Storwood, tactfully. "Who was that man I was speaking to when you caught up with us? He didn't seem to mind my interrupting him in the least."

"That was Keating, the head gardener," said Daphne Marston.

Andrew Herriad could only too readily believe that Keating wouldn't mind being interrupted, especially by the glamorous Lady Storwood. "I bet he took his time. Where did you get to?"

"We walked round the rose-garden. I never knew there was so much that had to be done with roses. I thought they simply grew. I'm only sorry, Mrs Marston, we didn't have time to look at the greenhouses properly. Can we do that this afternoon?"

"I have to go down to the church this afternoon. Perhaps you could fit it in after tea?"

"That would be delightful. I am grateful, you know, for your really helpful comments. I know nothing about gardens or running a country-house. I can't help feeling you have to be born to it. Wouldn't you agree, Mr Brown?"

Philip looked up and blinked. He seemed to be passing the meal in a sort of trance. "What? No, I wouldn't have thought so. You can do anything if you're prepared to learn."

"Miss Herriad? What do you think?"

"Eh? Oh, I'm awfully sorry, I didn't catch what you said."

"What is the matter with you, Sandy?" demanded her father. "You've been totally silent all through lunch and you've hardly eaten a thing. What on earth is it?"

Sandy sat upright. "I'm sorry, Dad." She smiled at Eleanor Storwood. "Would you like to live in the country?"

"Yes, I'm quite taken with the idea. I must ask Dennis...."

The voice went on, but Sandy hardly heard it. She was thinking about the telephone call she and Philip had put through to Scotland Yard. Brenzett had sounded rattled - and that was next door to impossible. "I don't like it, Miss Herriad," he had said. "Mrs Banks left her niece's at nine o' clock this morning and she's not been seen since. I don't like this at all."

***   ***   ***

Daphne Marston breathed in and did up the middle button of her blue coat. Really, she must do something about her increasing size. The fashionable preoccupation with achieving a boyish slimness had left her unmoved, but either her coat had grown smaller or she had grown bigger. She had never questioned the fact that her fellow-creatures came in various shapes and sizes. If that was what the Good Lord and nature intended, then that was how it should be. However, she doubted that either the Good Lord or nature should intend that her perfectly good coat should either be let out or passed on when it had years of wear left in it.

The conversation in the garden that morning had not been entirely one-sided. Whilst nothing could shake Daphne's belief that anything calling itself by the German name of a Kurhaus was a lot of nonsense, there was no doubt that Eleanor Storwood's Concord of Health Hygiene had certainly achieved results as far as Lady Storwood was concerned. She would never struggle to do up the buttons of a coat.

And, after all, there was nothing very startling about her ideas. Plain food; exercise. Exercise. Maybe a walk would help? If she walked through the grounds, not only would she be able to see that Keating was applying the correct top-dressing with good, well-rotted manure to the roses as she had instructed that morning (this dry weather was a problem but that *should* do the trick) but she would also be a good mile and a half nearer to the village than if she went by car and took the long way round by the main entrance.

Keating and the boy had, as she expected, needed gingering up. With the satisfaction of a job well done, she emerged onto the road to Farholt. In the distance a black Ford flanked by plumes of white dust drove steadily towards her. The car passed, stopped, then with a grinding of gears, reversed back.

Dennis Storwood put his head out of the station taxi. "Mrs Marston! Can I offer you a lift?"

"No, thank you, Sir Dennis. As it's such a nice day I thought I'd walk into the village." She looked at him critically. Years of experience had taught her to judge when a man was suffering a sense of grievance and Sir Dennis, to use one of Alexandra's phrases, looked hopping mad. "Is everything all right? You are back from London very early."

This was the cue Dennis Storwood needed. "No, everything is not all right! I have been the victim of a disgraceful practical joke. You will scarcely credit this, Mrs Marston, but that telegram was false! False, I tell you. They had absolutely no knowledge of it at the bank and there is no possibility of it having been despatched in error. I have instructed the Post Office authorities to strain every sinew to find out who could have been responsible for such a senseless act. I have my suspicions, Mrs Marston, and if they are proved to be justified, then I will have no hesitation in taking extreme measures. Mr..." He broke off, as if aware he was about to commit himself.

Daphne Marston, however, did not need any more clues. "It can't be Mr Leigh, Sir Dennis. He was here all yesterday. Surely the telegram states where and when it was sent from."

Dennis Storwood stopped, then pulled out the telegram from his pocket-book. "E.C. 1, at 7.23." He put it back with a disgusted frown. "It seems as if I might have been too hasty in my judgement. Then who could..."

"I expect you'll find it's all been a mistake," said Daphne Marston, comfortingly.

"It better had be." He touched his hat to her. "Drive on!" he shouted, and the taxi pulled away.

***   ***   ***

Daphne Marston crunched her way round the gravel path to where the bulk of St Stephen The Martyr formed a dark angle with the wall separating the churchyard from Wistow's farm.

She frowned at the riot of dogwood, nettles and bindweed. This whole corner needed rooting out. Why, the lower part of the church wall was positively green, and as for the wall itself... She gave a sigh of satisfaction. That, at least, had been done.

The dislodged coping-stones were neatly back in place and new cement lay between the cracks. A heap of orange builders' sand stood between two gravestones. It ought to have been moved of course - she could see where children had disturbed it - but perhaps it could be dug in as a foundation for the gravel which Daphne had already decided should replace the weeds.

She retraced her steps and went into the cool darkness of the church, kneeling for a few moments in the rear pew, before going up to the brass eagle on which the huge bible lay open. For some reason the church, in which she was so at home, seemed to have a vaguely sinister feel. She had - deliberately - no truck with feelings and pushed away the little quiver of warning, tutting as she

216

saw the white streaks of imperfectly polished Brasso on the eagle's beak.

What *was* wrong with her? It was as if there was something waiting, just out of sight. She drew herself up sternly and gave her full attention to brass. That would need Doing Again. If only Mrs Horrocks could be persuaded to give up the brasses and Mrs Banks could be persuaded to take them on... In the meantime that white crust had to be removed. The cloths and buckets were in a cupboard in the vestry.

Daphne Marston walked round the altar steps and drew her breath in as she saw the black shadow waiting on the floor between the vestry wall and the front pew. That's what she had seen and refused to acknowledge.

It was like a monstrous spider.

Nonsense! It was a lady's cloche hat, that was all. A lady's black felt hat. Someone must have dropped it. Nothing to bother about. It was only a hat.... But what a funny angle it lay at and what - *what*? - were those spiky black bits sticking out from over the brim?

The spiky bits were black-gloved fingers. Mrs Banks had flung her arm forward as she fell. Daphne Marston had no doubt at all that she was dead.

***   ***   ***

Colonel Waldrist buttonholed Dr Hayle in the porch of the church. "Finished, eh? It's a tragic accident, but can't be helped. I had a call from Farholt. It was Herriad's sister who discovered the body. I thought I'd run down and see everything was taken care of before I called in on her. What caused it?"

"It *looks*," said Dr Hayle, "as if she fell for some reason and hit her head on the stone step of the vestry door." He cut into the Colonel's mutterings of "Tragic" and continued, "However, it might just as easily have been caused by foul play."

"Foul play?" The Colonel's eyebrows shot upwards. "Good God, man, you can't be serious. In the church? That's ridiculous. You'd better be careful, Hayle, before you start making accusations. That sort of thing can be very distressing for the family. I thought you, as a doctor, would have realised that. What earthly reason can you have for suggesting such a thing?"

"The contusions on the head don't match the wound that I would have expected if she had hit her head on the step. I'm far from happy that such a blow could be the sole cause of death."

Colonel Waldrist blew at his moustache. "I suppose you'll do a post-mortem?" he said. He broke off as Philip Brown, together with a large, red-faced man, came into the porch. "How did you get here? I gave orders that no one was to be admitted."

"The constable on the gate let us through when he realised that this gentleman was Superintendent Brenzett of Scotland Yard," said Philip.

"I don't think there's anything for Scotland Yard to concern themselves with here. It's a perfectly simple accident."

Brenzett nodded politely. "I only hope it is, sir. However, if I may have a word with you in private..." He drew Colonel Waldrist to one side. The interview, which was punctuated by clearly audible "Good Lords!" from the Colonel, terminated with Colonel Waldrist walking quickly away down the church path.

Brenzett rejoined them. Stepping outside the porch, he pulled his pipe out of his pocket. "I've asked him to go and telephone Sir Douglas," he said with a smile. "With any luck the Chief'll persuade him to call me in officially." He struck a match. "Tell me, Doctor," he said between puffs of smoke, "are you satisfied that it's an accident?"

"No, I'm not," said Hayle slowly. "I won't say too much now. I'd rather you saw things for yourselves."

It was nearly a quarter of an hour before a very thoughtful Colonel Waldrist returned. "I've spoken to Sir Douglas," he said without preamble. "In view of what he's told me, I think, Superintendent, you'd better collaborate with us. Some of the political implications" - here he glared at Philip - "are out of the sphere of the County Constabulary."

Brenzett straightened up. "In that case, sir, do I have your permission to view the body?"

Waldrist shrugged. "Help yourself. Damned if I know what to make of it, and that's a fact."

***   ***   ***

The three men knelt beside the body of Mrs Banks.

"This is what I mean," said Doctor Hayle. He had unpinned her hat earlier and it lay forlornly beside her.

"If you look at the step, then look at the wound - it may be easier if you touch it - just here, under the hair - then you can see exactly what I'm driving at. The injury is one I'd associate with a heavy blow, whereas if she really

219

had fallen on the step, I'd expect either a puncture from striking her head on the corner or a lateral injury running across the side of the skull. But what we've got is bruising and a fracture to the back of the head. If this was really caused by a fall, then she would have fallen backwards and that doesn't tie up with how she's lying now. Head wounds are funny things and the effects are hard to predict, but I don't think that such a blow, by itself, is enough to cause death. If it was left untreated, then perhaps, but if this is all that's happened, I'd have expected to find her unconscious, certainly, but still alive. As it is, she's been dead for at least four hours and probably five, and not more than three, give or take twenty minutes or so either way. I'm sorry I can't be more precise, but it's cold on this stone and that affects the temperature of the body."

Brenzett took out his watch. "It's a quarter to five now. That takes us back to twenty-five past eleven this morning and five to two - say two o'clock - this afternoon. We might be able to narrow it down a bit more once we find out who's been in the church." He looked squarely at the doctor. "Think the worst," he encouraged. "What else could have happened to her?"

"Suffocation?" suggested Hayle. "If we really are talking about murder, that is. It'd be easy enough to smother the poor woman once she was unconscious, that's for sure."

Philip got up and walked a few feet away, leaving the doctor and Brenzett.

The sun shone through the squat Norman windows, sheening the mellow oak of the pews in dull pewter and turning the ancient stone the colour of thick honey. Dust - was it dust? - glinted in the light in the aisle. Philip stooped down and ran his finger along the floor, then rubbed forefinger and thumb together. The dust was gritty and stained his fingertips orange. He stood up. "Could she," he said quietly, "have been hit with a sandbag?"

Doctor Hayle glanced up sharply. "A sandbag would be the very thing."

"There's a pile of sand outside in the graveyard," said Brenzett. "I noticed it when we were waiting for Colonel Waldrist. Let's go and have a look."

He led the way to the sand heap. On the side facing the church the sand had evidently been disturbed. Brenzett frowned for a few moments before slipping off his jacket and undoing his cuff.

Rolling up his sleeve, he thrust his arm into the middle of the heap. With a look of triumph he brought out a piece of black material, which, when smoothed out, proved to be a man's silk dress sock. "The sandbag?" he said. He laid it out on his hand. "It's obviously had sand inside."

Philip looked at the sock. "It's an awfully good one," he offered. "At least thirty bob a pair, I should think."

"Large, too," added Brenzett. "Mrs Kelly could have bought it, I suppose, but if it belonged to a confederate, then that confederate is a sizable man who's fairly well-off."

221

"Are you thinking of anyone in particular?" asked Philip.

Brenzett indicated Doctor Hayle with an almost imperceptible nod of his head. "I don't want to say anything at the moment, but I have got someone in mind," he said quietly. "And so, Mr Brown, have you."

***   ***   ***

It was past six o'clock before Philip got back to Farholt. Sandy was in the hall to greet him. "How's Mrs Marston?" was his first question.

Sandy pulled a face. "She's bearing up, but it was the most horrible shock for her. She thinks it was all quite natural, of course, which helps, and she's the tough sort who don't show their feelings when they're upset. She's chiefly bothered about Mrs Banks' family." She drew closer. "Phil, there isn't any doubt it was deliberate, is there?"

"None whatsoever. Keep this to yourself, but she was slugged with a sandbag."

Sandy winced. "Poor woman. She was such a nice person, too. All fussy and bothery and gossipy but so kind-hearted. The rotten thing is that I can't help believing that it was so unnecessary. I mean, what *could* she have known?"

Philip shrugged. "Something pretty important, that's for sure. Just at the moment it seems a bit cheap to talk about the emeralds but I'd like to have a good look round the church. It may be that they've been hidden there and Mrs Banks quite innocently showed Mrs Kelly where they were. Gave her the last piece of the jigsaw, so to speak,

222

then, when they got fished out of their hiding place... Well, Mrs Banks couldn't be expected to keep quiet about that." He shook his head. "I'm going to have a bath and change. What time is Matherson expected?"

"About seven. By the way, Sir Dennis is absolutely purple. I thought he was going to go pop. That telegram last night was a fake. Apparently no-one at Houblyns knew anything about it."

"It was *false*?"

The emphasis in his voice took her by surprise. "Yes." She looked at his grim face. "Phil, you can't believe Sir Dennis is involved with all this."

"Can't I? Brenzett said last night that the telegram might be a phoney and he's right." He stopped as Tommy Leigh came down into the hall.

"There you are, old man," said Tommy. "I was just going to the church to dig you out. Your embassy have been on the phone three times now. They're pretty desperate for you to get in touch. They said it was urgent. It's hard to tell with these Latin types, but they sounded absolutely frantic. Didn't you tell him, Sandy?"

"I forgot," she said guiltily.

"Never mind," said Philip. The front doorbell clanged and he glanced out of the window. "Crikey, that looks like Matherson. He's early. Make my excuses, Sandy, but I really should make this phone call before I get involved with anything else."

He walked down the hallway to the study and put through the call. He wondered vaguely what could be so very urgent. Something to do with the loan, perhaps?

But that, he knew, was all in order. The trouble was that "urgent" so very often meant "important" or even "mildly interesting". They got so worked up over trifles. What the embassy had to say, however, wasn't trivial. As he listened, Philip closed his eyes in disbelief.

He put down the telephone and stared in front of him. His mouth was bone dry and he felt slightly sick. He bent forward, resting his forehead on steepled fingers. He had to do something, he knew, but in God's name, what? If only he could *think*!

*** *** ***

He followed the voices into the drawing-room. They were all in there, everyone, even Daphne Marston, talking to James Matherson. They were making conversation, with all the strain the word "making" implied. Did Matherson know or was he stalling? It sounded as if he was playing for time. He consciously pulled himself together and entered the room. Matherson got to his feet and came towards him with relief. He had been stalling.

"I came as quickly as I could, Mr Brown. You've spoken to the embassy? This is quite dreadful news. I can only hope that the police can move swiftly and no actual harm will have been done."

"What on earth's happened?" asked Andrew Herriad. "Are you all right, Brown? You look as white as a sheet."

Philip drew a deep breath. "You'd better tell them, Matherson."

Matherson nodded. "It's President Enrique," he said briefly. "He was kidnapped this afternoon from General Duridge's estate on Loch Skail. Two witnesses saw him hit

224

over the head and bundled into a car, but they didn't get the registration and so far, there aren't any leads."

"He's my cousin and my closest friend," said Philip quietly. "This was his idea and, fool that I am, I went along with it." He put a hand to his mouth. "God knows what they've got planned for him, but it should be me."

Sandy was beside him. "What d'you mean, Philip? Why should it be you?"

Philip turned blue eyes, haggard in a pale face, to hers. "Because I'm the President. Not him. Me. Haven't you guessed? I thought you might. Jerry's been kidnapped. It should've been me. Jerry and I cooked this scheme up to protect me. We knew there was danger and now he's paying the price."

Sandy stared at him. "*You're* the President?" Thoughts tumbled through her head. Why hadn't she known? There had been hints enough. Even on that first evening when he had told them about the jewels and the robbery, Edith Peverell had said Philip looked like the President.

Something else Edith said came to mind. "You? But... but that means you're married."

"Married?" Philip looked at her wretchedly. "I'm sorry. I should have told you but I couldn't. For goodness sake, Sandy, it doesn't *mean* anything." He held out a hand to her but Sandy hit it away, rejecting his startled look of hurt. "Sandy? Please?"

Sandy shook her head and backed away from him, reaching out for the door.

"Well," said Tommy Leigh, when she had left. "That's a bomb-shell and a half. Married, eh? You should have mentioned it, old man. Not quite playing the game, y'know, not mentioning it."

Philip stared at him, all the sick misery inside rising in a solid lump and turning into anger. He felt his hands curling into fists and dug his nails into the palms to stop himself lashing out. "Go to hell," he grated quietly.

"Actually," said Andrew Herriad. "It's about time we were dressing for dinner."

Chapter Ten

Sandy had her dinner sent up to her room on a tray. At ten o'clock a knock sounded on her door and her father walked in. He ambled round the room, eventually ending up at the mantelpiece, where he stood fiddling with a pottery shepherdess. He glanced at his dry-eyed daughter and coughed. "I missed you at dinner."

"I wasn't hungry."

"No." He turned his attention to a basket of china kittens. "I asked, and they told me you hadn't eaten anything. D'you want anything now?"

"No."

He coughed again. "No, no you wouldn't. Er... Sandy?"

"Yes?"

Her voice was flat and Andrew Herriad squirmed.

"Sandy... this is pretty awkward for me. I suppose if I'd been a different sort of father - the sort that Daphne is always telling me I should be - it'd come quite easily, but I'm not and I can't just put it on. You'd see through it right away."

Despite herself, Sandy half-smiled. "What is it, Dad?"

The china kittens teetered, fell and smashed. "Hell! This Philip Brown feller." He saw her lips tighten and hurried on. "Has he...?" He searched desperately for the right phrase. "Damn it, you know what I mean. Has he made any overtures to you? Because if he has, I'm kicking him out, Dennis Storwood or no Dennis Storwood."

"No, Dad, he hasn't." Andrew Herriad breathed a sigh of relief.

She lit a cigarette with shaky hands. "He's never done *anything* but be friendly, but we did things together and he said he relied on my opinion and... I feel so stupid," she finished miserably. "If he had made up to me, I'd have some excuse. As it is, I behaved like a silly schoolgirl, blurting out the first thing that came into my head and dashing out of the room. He's never given me the slightest reason to feel like that, and now everyone knows that I *do* feel like that, I can't possibly face anyone. Especially him."

"Nonsense!" Andrew Herriad was almost hearty. "Everyone understands, Sandy."

"That makes it better?"

"It makes it liveable with. I mean, a good-looking chap like that, he's bound to have dented a few hearts in his time."

"And I'm just another number on the list?"

"No! Well, sort of. But he should have said he was married. It beats me why he couldn't tell us he was the President in the first place. Daphne's clucking about moving him out of the Blue Room to the West Room because it's more fitting for a man in his position - he squashed that, thank goodness - and everyone's treating him with a sort of edgy respect."

A smile nearly surfaced. "He'll hate that."

"Who can blame him? Well, I do, of course. The man should've said who he was and then we'd all know where we were. Storwood knew all the time, apparently, and

228

young Leigh twigged it the other night. Superintendent Brenzett called - dashed if I don't know why *he* doesn't move in - and he didn't seem remotely surprised. Storwood says he told me, but I can't follow half of what he says, he wraps things up so. I think it's a bit much," he added plaintively, "that the whole damn household seemed to know who he was apart from me. And you," he added, remembering why he had come to see his daughter in the first place. "But whoever the wretched man is, you can't stay up here all the time."

"I'm not coming downstairs now."

"No. No, perhaps not." The pottery shepherdess narrowly avoided joining the china kittens in the grate. "Tomorrow?"

Sandy looked at her father squarely. "Do you think I'm a fool?"

"No! Honestly, Sandy, no. I mean, he's a likable man. He'd be exactly the sort of... Damnit, there's nothing foolish about it. I'd have been perfectly happy if..." He coughed again. "But that's not on the cards. Pity. Sorry it can't be helped, that's all." He looked at his daughter helplessly. "There's nothing I can do, my dear," he added softly. "I only wish I could."

He looked so woebegone that Sandy forgot her own troubles for a moment. Going over to him, she kissed him lightly. "Thanks, Dad. Don't listen to Aunt Daphne. I'd rather have you than any other father. And I will come down tomorrow."

*** *** ***

Sandy stood at the top of the stairs and gripped the newel-post, listening. Downstairs, Daphne Marston walked out of the morning-room and down the hall. Good! It would have been more than she could bear to face Aunt Daphne at breakfast, with her well-meant words of warning and kindly advice. She came down the stairs and entered the morning-room. She very nearly drew back at the doorway. Her father was there, buried in the *Times*, but so was Philip Brown.

He glanced up and she unconsciously straightened her shoulders and gave a toss of the head. Going to the sideboard she helped herself to a plate of scrambled egg and bacon, although her stomach was churning, and sitting down across from Philip, forced a smile. Her "good-morning" was as natural as she could make it. His response, she was pleased to hear, sounded strained.

Andrew Herriad glanced from one to the other and gave a depressed sigh. He felt like a well-intentioned dog who had blundered into a meeting between two strange cats. Strapped-down emotion bristled across the table and Herriad was a man who liked a quiet life.

With meticulous courtesy Philip asked Sandy if she would like a cup of coffee; and with upmost politeness she assented. "Milk or cream?" he enquired, as if reading from Chapter One of *Etiquette As A Fine Art.*

It was too much for Herriad. With a muttered grunt he folded up his paper and retreated.

"Why on earth didn't you *tell* me?" demanded Sandy when her father had left. "It's stupid to pretend you don't know how I felt."

Philip met her eyes then glanced away. "I knew," he said quietly.

"Then why the blazes couldn't you say something? It was cruel, Phil - Mr Brown, I mean. I felt so stupid, knowing I'd been building up a complete fantasy."

He looked at her then. "It wasn't a fantasy," he said, still in the same quiet voice.

Sandy drew a sharp breath. "Then..."

"Then I'm to blame." Philip interlocked his fingers and sat looking down at his hands. "I'm not going to talk about my feelings. That would be in rotten poor taste. But those feelings are real, Sandy. I'd hoped, when all this was over, to be able to do something about it. But in the meantime?"

He looked up and shrugged. "I was here as Philip Brown, secretary. Private secretaries aren't married. Now?" He shrugged again. "I've lost the game and Jerry, one of the best men I've ever known, is paying the price."

Sandy swallowed. "It all seems a bit petty when you put it like that."

"Does it? I'm sorry. Because I don't think it's petty." He looked down at his hands once more. "Apart from anything else," he added in a stronger tone, "I found your help invaluable. To talk things over with someone I could trust was enough, but I needed your ideas, Sandy."

He glanced at her with the beginnings of a crooked smile. "I should leave, I know. That would be the decent thing to do. But I'm not going to leave, unless forced, because I firmly believe that the key to the mystery is here. There's something else, as well. I want your help. I

231

want you to talk to me, argue with me, set me on the right lines. I want to know what's behind John Guthrie and Mrs Kelly and the reason for the murder yesterday and how everything fits together. I relied on you. Believe me, I don't really want to ask you this, but can you pretend it's all as before?"

She pushed back her chair and went to stand by him. Putting her hand on his shoulder, she studied his face carefully.

Philip winced and glanced down at her hand. "Please, Sandy. This is very difficult."

She nodded. "You're telling the truth, aren't you, Phil? I wasn't sure and I'm not going to be made a fool of twice."

His hand twitched as if to cover hers but he remained motionless. "Yes."

She sat down once more. "I wish I knew what to do. I believe you, but it's different for you, isn't it? You knew you were married. I didn't, and I can't pretend it doesn't matter. It made me feel raw, Phil."

"Sandy!" He half-rose, then sank back into his chair. "Forget it," he said slowly. He looked at her helplessly. "Forget it. Of course, it matters." He shook himself. "However, I would take it as a great favour if you would talk to me. I'm stuck for ideas and you always seem to spark some off."

She picked up her coffee. "What d'you want to talk about?" she asked carefully.

"Mrs Banks."

"Mrs Banks?" Sandy felt her interest quickening. The trouble was that although Philip apparently enjoyed talking to her, she enjoyed talking to him and that was dangerous. Wasn't it? *Talk won't hurt. It's only talk.* "Do you really think I can help?"

"You might."

She finished her coffee and managed a very small smile. "It's all very well to say you want my help, but I'm stumped. Do I carry on calling you Philip, by the way? It's not your name, after all."

"It'll do. I've got used to it."

"I see.... I wish I had some ideas for you, but I haven't." She ate a slice of bacon thoughtfully. "Why kill Mrs Banks? It seems pointless."

"I wondered if she'd led Mrs Kelly to the jewels." He returned the smile. "Thanks, Sandy. I'm grateful for what you're doing."

"Mrs Banks and the jewels," she reminded him. *Act as if nothing had happened...*

"Yes... If they'd been hidden in the church and Mrs Banks found them, then Mrs Kelly would more or less have to kill her. However, Brenzett was here last night and he tells me that they've been over the church with a fine tooth-comb and there's no sign of any disturbance." He hesitated. "Yesterday, when you told me Sir Dennis' telegram was false, you seemed very sceptical that he might be involved. Why?"

"Why?" Sandy frowned. "Because although he's fussy and pompous, I think he's an old dear, really. I just can't see him doing any harm."

233

"He's a very shrewd businessman and he's no fool as a politician. He likes money, prestige and loves being the boss."

"That may be so, but it doesn't make him a crook. What got you going on his trail?"

"I wish I knew." Philip wriggled in frustration. "There was something the other night and I just can't place what it was. We'd been working in the study on the loan and I signed the papers and then there was *something*. He seemed to look at me oddly."

"Was that the day you got pushed under the train?" Philip nodded. "I'm not surprised he looked at you oddly. When you came back into the drawing-room I thought you were really ill. I know Dad was concerned, because he sent Dutton, his valet, up to take care of you."

Philip smiled faintly. "I wondered what I'd done to deserve it. But that rather bears out my point. I certainly didn't notice anything peculiar about you or your father's manner towards me, so that suggests there was something odd about Sir Dennis's."

"We probably concealed it better. You were in the study, you say?" Sandy finished her eggs. "In that case, let's go there now. It might jog your memory."

"I've tried that," said Philip gloomily. "I was brooding in the study most of yesterday morning. Still, it's worth a try."

***   ***   ***

"I can't pin it down." Philip glared at the study desk in frustration. "This is a waste of time, Sandy." He paused. "Is it all right to call you that? I don't suppose I should."

234

"I don't suppose you should, either, but you might as well. After all," she added in a careful voice, "we've decided it doesn't mean anything, haven't we?"

"I..." He was stopped by a look from Sandy. "Never mind."

"What we've got to do," she said in business-like tones, "is to re-create the scene. You know, like they do in books and things. Now, I'll be Sir Dennis..."

"Good Lord."

"And you be you. Now you were signing papers, yes? Are they still here?"

"They're tucked away in Houblyn's bank."

"Well, we can use any papers. What did Sir Dennis do?"

"He handed them to me," said Philip slowly, "and I looked at them again and went to the window - I was feeling awful - and I said something to the tune of I wish I had the necklace because we'd get a better deal."

"What then?"

"I came back and signed them. That's all."

"There must be..." Sandy stopped as the study door opened and Tommy Leigh came in.

He looked from one to the other in surprise. "I say!"

"I say what?" asked Sandy, icily.

"Well, you know. I wouldn't have thought you two would have... I mean, it's a bit of a... After last night, I mean."

"Mr Brown has explained everything," said Sandy.

Tommy Leigh gave Philip a gaze of undisguised admiration. "How did you get out of that?"

"Tommy!" broke in Sandy, sharply.

"Absolutely," said Tommy hastily. "Least said, soonest mended, eh? Damn smooth work, though," he muttered. "What are you doing?"

"Working," said Philip in uninviting tones, but Sandy had had enough of prevarications.

"We're trying to work out exactly what happened the other night, the night Mr Brown signed the papers for the loan to Salvatierra."

Tommy looked bright. "You were pretty used-up, old man. Trust the old slave-driver to force you in here. What about it? I got the papers out for you, if you remember."

"What papers, Tommy?" asked Sandy.

"Well, the loan papers, of course, and he also wanted a shufti at the Kurhaus things. I've often wondered if that place is all it's made out to be, you know. I put them on the desk and then I noticed..."

"That's it!" breathed Philip. "That's it! I had walked to the window and came back to sign the loan, but I got hold of the wrong file. I'd picked up the stuff for the Kurhaus."

"And?" demanded Sandy.

Philip screwed up his eyes. "And I can't remember," he confessed. "Damn!"

The telephone on the desk rang and Tommy Leigh picked it. "Farholt Hall... Hold the line, please." He put his hand over the receiver. "It's for you, Mr... er... It's for you. The embassy."

236

Philip frowned and took the phone. "Yes? Speaking." His face twisted as he listened. He broke into rapid Spanish, obviously asking questions. Sandy watched him anxiously.

"What is it?" she asked as he put the ear-piece back. "What's happened?"

He took a deep breath. "There's been another kidnapping. Not here. Hollywood. They've got her."

"Her?"

He sighed again, his eyes reluctantly fixed on her face. "Jane. Jane Lehman."

It took a moment for his words to sink in. "Your wife?" she asked slowly.

"Yes."

The word was like a bucket of cold water. He had asked her to pretend and she had pretended and it was all false. At that moment, Sandy hated herself. "No." She spoke very softly. "No." She reached out for the door handle. "I'm sorry, Phil. I really am sorry for you, but I can't help and I can't stay. I'm sorry." The door closed behind her.

"She's upset," remarked Tommy Leigh.

"She's got every right to be," began Philip fiercely, then subsided. "Hell!" He smashed his fist down on the desk. "Are you enjoying this?" he snarled.

"No, I'm bloody well not." For once there was no trace of irony in Tommy's expression. "I'm damn fond of Sandy and hate to see her treated like this." He left out the *by you* but it was clearly there.

"Yes..." Philip dug his hands in his pockets and strode across the room. "Haven't made a good showing, have I? I'm sorry for what I said, by the way. It was unfair. But if only there was something I could do! I haven't a clue what's been going on, or why, and I'm totally stumped as to what to do next."

"Business or personal?" enquired Tommy delicately.

"Oh, business, every time. Jerry's been kidnapped. My wife's been kidnapped. It has to be business."

Tommy sat on the edge of the desk and lit a cigarette. "'Scuse me butting in, but I thought you were on the verge of finding something out when the phone rang. The Kurhaus?" he prompted.

Philip's face cleared. "So I was. I wanted the file I looked at the other night. The Kurhaus one. I saw it by mistake."

"Hang on a jiffy." Tommy walked to the book-case and ran his finger up the shelf. "Those papers should be around somewhere. Here we are." He took out a file and gave it to Philip who opened it on the desk. A letter, the same letter which he had seen two nights ago, was the first document in the folder.

"*Concord of Health and Hygiene, The Kurhaus, Loscombe Dale Road, Thringford, Huntingdonshire,*" he read. "*Dear Sir Dennis...*". Now why is that important?" He looked again and smiled slowly. "Of course! I very nearly saw it at the time."

"What?"

"Loscombe Dale Road, Thringford." Philip looked up. "You said you wondered if the Kurhaus was all it was cracked up to be. Why?"

Tommy shook his head. "You first. You could have got that address at any time. Why is it suddenly important?"

Philip looked at Tommy, then took a deep breath and plunged in. "I'd be obliged if you kept this to yourself, but you know Mrs Strickland who was at the inquest? Well, her real name is Kelly and we think she's either a nurse or used to be."

Tommy looked startled. "How...?"

"Never mind. We worked it out. Anyway, when I broke into the house in Camden Town, I found a bit of burnt newspaper in the grate. Virtually the only bit readable was part of a place-name, and the name ended with 'ngford. Thringford, you see? She's a nurse and there's the nursing-home."

"I say," said Tommy, deeply impressed. "D'you think old Mother Kelly's working at the Kurhaus? That'll stir things up for the boss."

"Will it? What did you mean when you said that you wondered if the Kurhaus was all it was made out to be?"

"I..." Tommy ran his hand through his hair. He suddenly seemed older and far more serious. "You asked me to keep a secret. Well, for God's sake, keep what I'm going to tell you to yourself, because I haven't got an atom of proof. I took this job for one purpose only; to find out about the Concord of Health and Hygiene. It

239

sounds very above-board, doesn't it? But I think it stinks."

"Why?" Philip leaned forward. This was a new Tommy, a mature man who commanded respect. He somehow seemed far more real.

"I had a sister." His eyes were distant. "She was younger than me and I always felt protective towards her. When she got engaged, I was delighted. I couldn't see much of her in the war, but I liked the man she was engaged to. However, he got killed in the September of 1918 and when I saw Mary next, I was shocked. Rather than getting over his death she brooded constantly about him. Then she got in with a rackety crowd and seemed to be the life and soul of the party, but, funnily enough, I was more worried than before. Mary had always been a quiet sort of person and I loathed her friends. About eighteen months ago I decided to take a hand. I told her that she was ruining her life and her health and was very nearly on the verge of ruining her reputation. I'd half expected to be shown the door. Instead she broke down completely. She'd never got over Ronald. Life was empty and pointless and the only solution was to take what pleasures she could. I, God help me, thought I had a different answer. I'd heard about these Health and Hygiene people and thought they could help Mary. She agreed to take a look and ended up staying there for a month. She came back full of praises for the place and happier than I'd seen her for years. What I didn't know was that her happiness was fuelled by drugs. I'm convinced that while at the Kurhaus she contracted a cocaine habit which eventually led to her death." He paused for a moment. "Have you ever seen anyone in the grip of cocaine? They change, you know. It's not pleasant - not when you care about them." He broke off, biting his lip.

"Go on," said Philip, softly.

Tommy shook himself. "Anyway," he continued, "I did some snooping around and managed to find out that she'd had a regular supply by post ever since returning from the Kurhaus. A doctor is a marvellous person to peddle drugs and addicts have no resistance. Mary had money of her own but she died penniless. I swore I'd get the person responsible. My first thought was to get into the Kurhaus myself, but then I had the opportunity of working for Sir Dennis. I had to pull a few strings, but I managed it. For the last year I've been watching and waiting and I'm sure, absolutely *sure* that he not only knows what's going on but is the brains behind it all. The trouble is he's such a respected man that no one would believe me without absolute proof. He's a clever man, too. He knows how to hide his tracks. I could, perhaps, find enough evidence to nail the doctor, but I want Storwood as well."

"What about Lady Storwood?" asked Philip.

Tommy shook his head. "I suspected her, of course, but I honestly think she knows nothing about the true state of affairs. That was a very intelligent marriage he made; Lady Storwood's a real leader of society - fashionable, you know? People like to be seen with her. Her connection with the Kurhaus has brought in dozens of clients of the right sort; rich and gullible. Now you tell me you think there's something dodgy about the place. All I can say is, I'm not a bit surprised."

Philip sat back, weighing up the man in front of him. "I wish you'd told me this before. It would have answered a few questions."

"How could I? I can't start voicing my suspicions, especially about a man like Sir Dennis Storwood. I haven't got any proof. Besides..." He smiled. "I'm just the goofy secretary, remember? It's a useful role. I adopted it to put Storwood off the scent, but I've played it a bit too successfully to be taken seriously."

"I believe you," said Philip definitely. "It chimes in with a few thoughts of my own." He stood up. "I think I'll go and have a look at the Kurhaus for myself. It seems likely I'll find the mysterious Mrs Kelly there and I'm hoping I'll find Jerry. Please God it's not just his body."

"What about your wife?"

"Well, as she was at the studios in Hollywood yesterday it's hardly likely I'll find her in Huntingdonshire today."

Tommy smiled again. "Sorry. Bit of a return to form there. D'you want me along? I might be useful."

"I'd rather go by myself," said Philip. "This is really a scouting expedition. I haven't got a clue what I'll find, if anything, and I'd like someone here who I can trust. What I must do is let Superintendent Brenzett know what I'm up to."

"If you write a note, I can give it to him."

"Thanks. That'll help. Leave it a few hours, though. I don't want lots of policemen to come blundering in." He glanced at his watch. "Ten o'clock. I'll take the car, rather than the train. I don't suppose I'll be back this evening, but I should certainly see you tomorrow."

"And if you're not back?"

Philip grinned. "Panic."

***   ***   ***

Alone in his room, Philip didn't immediately start to pack his over-night bag. Instead he drew up a stool to the dressing-table and lit a cigarette, watching the smoke curl up in front of his reflection in the mirror.

Was his plan working out? He thought so. And yet the speed with which it had developed awed him.

Sandy was well out of it. She hadn't guessed the true state of affairs. That was a bonus, for he didn't underestimate her intelligence for one moment. If she believed him, there was a real chance that everyone else would, too. And Tommy Leigh was here... That flippancy of his had been a front, after all. He had thought as much. He grinned. It was odd how much more likable he was when he wasn't being a fool.

Philip ground out his cigarette and started to pack his case. When he had finished, he opened the wardrobe door and, reaching inside, took out a wooden shoe box. Putting it on the floor, he removed the shoes and felt inside for the catch he knew was there. There was a click and the false bottom of the box sprang back.

A red leather jewel case lay inside. He opened it briefly and, as he saw the shining gold and emerald

243

necklace within, smiled. He tucked the jewel case in the large pocket of his motoring-coat and, picking up his bag, left.

***   ***   ***

"He's gone?" asked Andrew Herriad at lunch. "Damn me if I ever knew a feller like him. Hasn't he heard it's customary to say goodbye to your host?"

"He's coming back again," said Tommy. "Tomorrow, he thought."

"I'll put a tariff up in his room," said Andrew Herriad. "So much for an overnight stay and extra for the use of soap and towels and so on."

Daphne Marston gave Sandy a look so loaded with meaning that it made her squirm. "I imagine that he realises his presence here must be an embarrassment."

"Where's he gone, Tommy?" broke in Sandy.

Tommy shrugged. "Search me."

"I don't believe you."

"Alexandra!" Daphne Marston was shocked. "As I was saying, I would have expected a man, whatever his position, who found himself in such equivocal circumstances, to make arrangements to leave as soon as possible. However, Alexandra, I do feel that you should examine your own conduct..."

"Daphne," said Andrew Herriad quietly. "I won't have it."

Daphne Marston subsided with ill grace. It was a very long lunch.

***   ***   ***

Sandy was horribly restless. She didn't think for a moment that Philip had left for reasons of tact. He's gone chasing after his wife, she thought, in black misery. All that talk about his feelings was so much rubbish. *No, it's not*, another voice insisted. The way he had looked at her - that was real. He had to find his wife. He couldn't just leave her... hang on.

If Jane Lehman was in America, he'd hardly disappear for one night only. Had he gone to the embassy, then? But if that was all, there wouldn't be any need for secrecy. Tommy knew, she was sure of it. They'd cooked something up between them and Phil had left on the strength of it. It must have been something they decided this morning, after she'd left them in the study. *And if I wasn't such an idiot, I'd know exactly what it was. I knew he was married. I can't blame him for mentioning his wife.*

The study. Thankfully no one was there. Sandy circled round the desk, trying to remember what had happened that morning. Tommy had mentioned the Kurhaus. He'd said something there was odd about it, that it wasn't all it was cracked up to be.

She searched on the shelves until she found the Kurhaus file. The name jumped out at her. Thringford. Thringford! She sat for minutes staring at the file, then, her decision made, replaced it on the shelf and took down Bradshaw's Railway Guide.

*** *** ***

Sandy paid off the station taxi at the end of the long drive and looked at the wrought-iron gates of the Kurhaus.

245

She shivered. She was six miles from St Neots and one and half miles from Thringford and felt as isolated as if she was on the dark side of the moon. The place was completely shrouded in trees, as if the house and grounds had been hacked out of the virgin forest. Long forgotten fears surfaced. Trees were creepy things. Lost in the woods. The big, bad, wolf... Sandy took a conscious hold on herself. She hadn't come all this way to think about fairy tales.

Having said that, the Kurhaus reminded Sandy of an illustration to Grimm. It was a massive mid-Victorian gothic pile of a house that looked like a Rhineland castle crossed with a railway station. It stood on a grassy rise surrounded by sloping lawns with slate-covered turrets reflecting the evening sun. Thin coils of smoke drifted up from the chimneys. The doors were open and windows raised. It seemed ugly, innocent and intimidatingly large.

Sandy put her hand on the gates. They were closed, but unlocked. What on earth was she going to do? That was precisely what she had been asking herself all the way here, hoping that the question would answer itself.

Should she leave it up to the police? She'd scribbled a note to Superintendent Brenzett and one to her father (*Back tomorrow. Don't worry, I'm not doing anything silly.*) Just at the moment it seemed a toss-up whether she could do anything at all.

Sandy slipped inside the gates. There was no one in sight. She could have a look round at the very least. She started to walk down the path flanking the inside of the tall brick wall of the Kurhaus.

Rather to her disappointment it was simply a wall and perfectly climbable. It wasn't topped by broken bottles or wire, but ivy. With vague memories of stories she had read, she'd half expected baying hounds, searchlights, electric fences, concealed traps and, maybe, a Nameless Thing in the garden. But this was merely a large house standing in its own grounds. The path led her behind a shrubbery and in the distance she heard music and voices.

Concealed by the trees, she looked out onto what appeared to be a croquet lawn. About twenty women in Grecian costume were doing rhythmic dances to the music of a wind-up gramophone. A large lady in the middle was shouting instructions. Sandy shook her head and withdrew. A growing conviction that she'd made an absolute fool of herself was stealing over her. At the back of the house was a lawn. There were sun-beds laid out on the grass with people lying in them. The gentle hum of voices carried to her. It was all so totally innocent.

She retreated to the wall behind the screen of shrubs. A few yards away was a garden door. She tried the latch and it opened. Just then she heard voices nearby and the crack of a breaking twig. People were coming along the path. She quickly opened the door and got out onto the lane. Some instinct made her cross the narrow dirt road to the trees at the other side.

The voices were clear now on the other side of the wall. "It's open," and the reply "Kids," followed by a laugh. The door opened and two men and a woman walked out.

Sandy crouched down in the grass. Her heart was beating faster and her breath came in a huge gulp. The two men she didn't know, but the woman was Mrs Kelly.

Chapter Eleven

Sandy slid back further into the ditch, praying that she wouldn't be seen. Breathing as quietly as possible, she watched the two men and Mrs Kelly through a screen of tall grass and cow-parsley. She ducked her head as they walked by and then, thank God, they were past.

Very cautiously she looked up. They walked a hundred yards or so down Loscombe Dale Road to where it formed a junction with the road to Thringford, turned the corner and disappeared out of sight. Through the triangle of trees and undergrowth, Sandy could see a flash of something red.

Philip's car, she suddenly thought, with absolute conviction. Moving as delicately as she could, she stood up and crept through the trees towards them. The hummocky ground, tangled with bramble and ivy made horrible going and she had a heart-stopping moment when a magpie flew up from her feet, chakking into the branches above.

She came to a halt about twenty yards from the verge of the Thringford Road, and peered out from behind a tree.

It was Philip's car. The driver's door was open and they were examining the maps and papers in the side pocket. "Nothing here," she heard one of them call.

Mrs Kelly opened up the tiny boot and took out Philip's over-night bag. "We'll have a look at this inside," she said, slamming down the lid. "Let's get the car off the road before anyone spots it. Take it round to the garage."

She started to walk back towards the Kurhaus as the men climbed into the car, started the engine and drove to the junction, turning down Loscombe Dale Road.

Sandy waited for what seemed like hours but was, in fact, only ten minutes by her watch, before coming out of the trees and onto the road once more. It was getting noticeably darker and a chilly breeze had sprung up.

She shivered. Philip was definitely in the Kurhaus and was, presumably, being kept by force. She crossed the road and, summoning up her courage, opened the garden door.

What followed was perhaps the most frustrating and the most nerve-racking half hour she had ever spent.

Shielded by the dusk she walked round the whole of the outside of the Kurhaus. She had hoped that Philip might have managed to drop a message or even be looking out of a window, but there was nothing.

Eventually she ended up at the back of the house, where the kitchen doors stood open, sending a hard-edged wedge of light across the cobbled yard. A little further on stood the low bulk of the old stable block. She toyed with the idea of getting into the house and dismissed it. She'd be spotted right away. Mrs Kelly knew her, and Sandy didn't think she'd be a kindly host.

She shrank into the shadows as a kitchen-maid came out of the door, emptied a bucket down the drain, and went back into the house. The maid shut the door behind her and the wedge of light abruptly vanished.

Sandy slipped across the yard to the stables. They were, as she expected, used as garages, and in the third one she saw Philip's car. Round the side of the garages, tantalizingly close, stood the rear entrance to the Kurhaus. As quietly as she could, she pulled back the old stable door. It scraped on the cobbles and she froze. No challenge came and, after a dreadful few minutes, the doors stood open.

Blood pounding, she sat in the red two-seater and pressed the self-starter. The engine coughed, missed, then roared into life, and Sandy was out on to Loscombe Dale Road, driving for all she was worth.

*** *** ***

It was ten o'clock before she nosed the car across Bridge Street and round the corner into Scotland Yard. There, miraculously, was Superintendent Brenzett.

He waved her to a halt. "We got your telephone call from St Neots to say you were on your way. Miss Herriad, what have you been up to?"

"Didn't you get my note this morning?"

Brenzett shook his head. "I left Farholt first thing. I've been here all day."

Sandy gave a wobbly smile, shaky with relief. "In that case you've got a bit of catching up to do. Would you like Mrs Kelly's fingerprints, Superintendent?"

His eyebrows rose. "Wouldn't I, though."

"They're on the handle of the boot. As far as I know, she was the last person to touch it." She climbed stiffly out of the car and was annoyed to find her legs trembling.

"You'd better come and sit down," said Brenzett, catching her under the arm. "We'll see to the car, don't you worry. You need a cup of tea."

She gave him a grateful smile. "After what I've been through, I need something stronger than tea."

***   ***   ***

Sir Douglas Lynton, summoned from home by Brenzett, ran his hand through his hair. "We're a bit stuck, Miss Herriad. I couldn't agree more that this place in Thringford sounds sinister to a degree, but we've had a note from Mr Brown, via the Salvatierran Embassy, pleading with us to go quietly because of Jane Lehman's sake."

"You've heard from Phil?" The question was startled out of her.

Sir Douglas nodded. "He contacted his embassy at mid-day. That, presumably, is before he visited the Kurhaus. Now we don't actually know, although we can make a good guess, that he's being held against his will. One nasty snag is that the Kurhaus belongs to Dennis Storwood."

"But surely that doesn't make any difference?"

"It means we'd better be right. Sir Dennis is an influential man."

"It's very awkward, Miss Herriad," put in Brenzett. "Particularly in view of Mr Brown's note."

"But we *know* he's there," said Sandy. "And I'm willing to bet this other man, his cousin, Jerry, is too. There's Mrs Kelly, too."

A knock sounded at the door and a sergeant entered, carrying a thin folder. "We've traced the fingerprints, sir."

252

Sir Douglas seized the file eagerly and opened it. "Good God!" He glanced at Sandy. "Those prints you brought us. They belong to Teddy Costello."

"Who....?" began Sandy, but Brenzett was on his feet and looking at the photographs.

"Got her!" he said with great satisfaction. He looked at Sandy. "Teddy, or Theresa, Costello is a real professional. I've never come across her myself, or I'd have recognized her at the inquest, but she's a jewel thief and fence." He looked at the note attached to the file. "Here we are; Irish, lived in America, disappeared from sight for five years and believed to have been in - listen to this - Salvatierra under the previous president, Andrade, and was associated with his wife, Nancy Sterling. Nancy Sterling had a fine collection of jewels. What's the odds they weren't all acquired legitimately?"

"Thin, I should imagine," said Sir Douglas. He ran his finger down the file. "She trained as a nurse - that's one up to you, Miss Herriad - and her speciality was the theft of jewels from private houses where she was employed. She's been quiet for years. Presumably that's the period of her stay in America, North and South." He looked up. "This current crop of jewel robberies, Brenzett. D'you think Teddy Costello's behind them?"

"It would make sense, sir," replied Brenzett. "The method is Teddy Costello's, and now we know she's back in the country, I'd say that there's a very good chance indeed."

He glanced at Sandy. "It's a series of very clever thefts, involving the substitution of fake jewels for the authentic ones. I can't be sure without looking at the records, but I think in each case a nurse had been employed in the victim's house some time previously. That sounds like our Miss Costello, doesn't it?" He frowned. "As far as we know, she's never been involved in any rough work."

"She tried to push Mr Brown off the tube platform," Sandy reminded him.

"That's true enough." He looked at his chief. "Do we make an arrest, sir?"

"We haven't got any choice," said Sir Douglas, in a much more cheerful voice than he had used earlier. "Dennis Storwood ought to be downright grateful to us. Not," he added, "I suppose for a moment he will be."

"And you'll look for Phil... Mr Brown?"

"Don't you worry, Miss Herriad," said Sir Douglas positively. "Just leave it with us."

*** *** ***

After a night spent in the Charing Cross Hotel, Sandy was back at Scotland Yard for half nine the next morning, to be met with disappointment. Despite a careful search of the Kurhaus the police had found nothing.

"Superintendent Brenzett telephoned just before you arrived, Miss Herriad," said Sir Douglas. "The place is a clean as a whistle. However, Brenzett was far from happy. The house is like a rabbit warren and Brenzett believes you could hide an army in there without anyone being the wiser. He didn't like the attitude of the staff, either. Everyone was far too helpful to be natural and he's convinced the manager knows something about it."

254

"But what do we do now?" asked Sandy.

"We'll keep an eye on it." Sir Douglas shrugged. "That's all we can do. It's not quite as hopeless as you obviously think. We know exactly who Teddy Costello is and if she tries to get out, we've got her. As for Mr Brown and his cousin - well, they can't be kept under wraps forever."

"And is that it? Aren't you going to do *anything* else? I'm going back there."

"No, you're not." Sir Douglas looked at Sandy's determined face. "Please, Miss Herriad. Go back home. You've done far more than you realise by bringing us those fingerprints but I can't let you run blindly into danger. There is more we can do, but if you interfere, then it could wreck everything. Let us handle it."

***   ***   ***

Home was a comfortless place. Sandy paid off the taxi and walked up the steps to Farholt with the bitter knowledge of defeat. Yes, she had found out who Mrs Kelly was and that seemed as meaningless as anything else she'd discovered. Phil - *Phil!* - wanted her ideas but she was bankrupt. Where was he? She didn't care if he was married, she just wanted him to be safe. I'm a fool, she thought bleakly. I care horribly and it hurts.

Tommy Leigh was in the hall. As she walked in, his face lit up. "Sandy!" He hurried towards her with outstretched hands. "When your father said you'd phoned from London I was so relieved." He held her hands in his. "I've been imagining all sorts of things."

"What, Tommy?"

His hands tightened on hers and he swallowed. "I thought you'd gone to the Kurhaus." His voice was thick with concern.

She stared into his brown eyes. "I did go to the Kurhaus, Tommy."

She saw his look of alarm. "You silly fool." With a convulsive gesture he drew her into his arms. "Sandy, you don't know the sort of people you've been dealing with. They'll stick at nothing."

She pushed him away gently and his face contorted.

"I know," he said bitterly. "I haven't got the right to worry. But I do worry all the same, because... because I love you."

She drew her breath in sharply. "Tommy... I'm sorry."

He dropped his hands. "It's him you care about, isn't it? Philip Brown or whatever his name is."

She nodded slowly and Tommy's mouth twisted. "I realise there isn't much of a chance for me, but I love you. It was hell, last night. Everyone wondered where you were but I knew, and I knew you were in danger."

"How did you know?"

He laughed harshly. "It was obvious. Yesterday, after you left the study, Brown worked out that's where his cousin must be. I told him what he was getting involved with. I never dreamt he'd drag you into it."

"But he didn't. He didn't know anything about it. I guessed where he was and followed."

"You followed? By *yourself!* You saw him?"

She shook her head. "I only wish I had, Tommy."

He stepped back, thinking. "Have I got this all wrong?" he demanded. "I assumed that's where he was going because he told me so, but if you couldn't find him..."

"He's there, all right. I saw his car. I - I stole it."

"What? Sandy, what exactly have you been doing?" He looked round the hall. "For goodness sake, come into the study with me, before we get interrupted. This is important."

"Now," he said, when the study door had shut behind them. "Tell me what happened." He listened intently as she went through her story, shaking his head at intervals. "So this Mrs Kelly is a criminal? Thank God you managed to stay out of sight. What are the police going to do?"

"I don't know," she said miserably. "They wouldn't tell me and I'm so worried about Phil. Tommy, you talked about the Kurhaus as if you knew all about it. What is it? What goes on there?"

"I've spent the last year finding out." He drew a deep breath. "I've said too much to keep it to myself any longer. Sandy, have I ever mentioned my sister?"

"Tell me about her, Tommy," she said quietly.

After he had finished she drew a deep breath. "I can hardly believe it. Sir Dennis knows, you say? Does Lady Storwood suspect anything?"

"Not a thing. He's used her as he uses everyone. Since he married her, that place has really taken off but she's innocent, Sandy, I'd swear it. I've spent a long time getting my facts right."

257

"But this is awful, Tommy. If this is true, then..." She broke off as a maid came into the room.

"Sorry, Miss," the maid apologised. "I was just hoping to get done in here. I got behind this morning. I didn't mean to interrupt."

"That's all right," said Sandy, absently. "Let's go in the garden, Tommy."

They walked to the back of the house and out on to the stone steps leading down to the lawn. Sandy sat on the step in the sunshine, hands curled round her knees. Tommy offered her a cigarette and sat beside her.

"You're very quiet," he said after a few minutes.

She gave him a quick smile. "Sorry. I was thinking. Tommy, that maid who was in the study just then."

"What's she got to do with it?"

"Well, I know quite a bit about her, what with one thing and another. She's called Rose Price. She dislikes cream but loves sweets, and she has three sisters and a brother. Her mother's a widow who helps in the draper's shop and collects film star magazines."

Tommy looked bewildered by this burst of biography. "So what, old thing?"

"Rose Price," continued Sandy. "I know about her and she knows about me. She knows about all the family. What we do and what we like and who we are. She knows all that because she's a housemaid and if, years from now, she was asked to remember who we were, I bet she could. She wouldn't know it straight away because it wouldn't be important, but she would know."

Tommy shrugged. "So what?" he repeated.

"Mrs Banks was the Eldons' housemaid." Her voice was distant and Tommy remained silent. She turned on him, irritated by his lack of comprehension. "Don't you see, Tommy? Don't you *see?* You know Mrs Banks was murdered, don't you?"

"Murdered?" Tommy drew his breath in sharply. "*Murdered?* But why? Who would want to murder her? Why should they? It seems complete pointless."

"That's exactly it. What was the point of her being killed? The only reason Philip could come up with that poor Mrs Banks somehow knew where the emeralds were, but that's nonsense. I never liked that idea. But when you start to ask what sort of thing she *did* know, then the answer's easy. She knew about the Eldons and she loved gossip and was fascinated by the people they had to stay. When I saw her in the tea-room at Waterloo she was talking about Robert Eldon and she said Philip reminded her of someone."

Tommy sat up sharply. "But..."

"And Mrs Kelly; we know she's really Teddy Costello, but what if she's someone else as well? Someone who Mrs Banks, after a bit of thought, would recognize and wouldn't want to be recognized?"

"Never mind that," broke in Tommy. "What about Philip Brown and Robert Eldon? I've always wondered about that chap. Who is he, really?"

"He's President Enrique."

"Is he, by jingo? Do you know that, Sandy, or are you just repeating what he's said?" He gave a thin smile. "You'd like him not to be, I know. After all, the

259

President's married, but is the President Philip Brown or is Philip Brown someone else entirely? We know he's not called Philip Brown for a start." He scrambled to his feet impatiently. "Do you know?"

Sandy shook her head. "No."

"What if the whole damn thing's a fraud? It'd make a lot of sense. Storwood would have to be in on it, but I can't see that's a problem. Between them they could have enough time to look for the emeralds and - this is just a guess - pocket the money for the loan to Salvatierra."

"No! You're wrong, Tommy. Philip's not like that."

He stopped and looked down at her. "You really do care about him, don't you?" he said quietly. He stooped and, taking her hands, brought her to her feet. "But I love you, Sandy." He moved forward as if to kiss her, but she turned her face away. She felt the tension in his body. "I see..." He relaxed. "What if I can prove to you he's a complete phoney?"

She shook her head, unconvinced. "You can't."

"Oh, can't I? I can get in to the Kurhaus any time I like. I'm Storwood's secretary, remember? With the right letter, which I can write easily enough, I could walk into any room in the place. If Philip Brown, to call him that, is there, I can find him easily enough."

"Well, go and get him, Tommy! Don't stand here talking about it!"

He pulled a face. "What if he doesn't want to be found? I've got a shrewd suspicion he's exactly where he wants to be. He's got the loan money and for all I know he's got the emeralds as well. He's now vanished off the face of the earth in company with a known jewel thief and meanwhile Scotland Yard are wringing their hands and saying he's been kidnapped. He might turn up in South America, but it won't be as President of Salvatierra."

"You're wrong," said Sandy, but without conviction.

"Oh, am I?" He took hold of her hands once more. "Come with me, then. Perhaps if you see for yourself you might believe me."

"What if Mrs Kelly spots me?"

Tommy shrugged. "What if she does? From what you've said it sounds as if she's tucked away out of sight because the police couldn't find her, so I don't think there's much chance of that, anyway. You're with me, so you're a *bona fide* visitor, and no one can lay a finger on you. By yourself you were in danger. With me, granted who I am, you're as safe as houses. And if Mr Brown decides to object... well, not only can I punch but I can shoot as well."

"Philip would never harm me."

He looked at her curiously. "You really have it badly, don't you? Why are you so sure? Are you holding out on me, Sandy? What's he told you?"

"Nothing. Nothing at all. Tommy, would you really take me down there?"

"Haven't you been listening? Yes."

She bit her lip then came to a decision. "Let's go. I'll have to change first, though. I'm feeling awfully travel-stained and I'd better see Dad. Should I tell him where we're going?"

261

Tommy hesitated. "I can't see why not. It wouldn't do for Storwood to find out, though. That'd really tear it. As long as the Kurhaus people think I'm there on Storwood's authority, we're okay. If he knew the truth it could be dodgy."

"I'll keep it to myself, don't worry. I'll meet you at your car in half an hour."

"Good. That'll give me time to write myself a beautiful letter. With that we can turn the place inside out. And then, perhaps, you might believe me." He paused. "Would it be so hard to love me, Sandy? I'm crazy about you." He read the expression on her face and sighed. "I know. The answer is a lemon."

He slipped his arm into hers and they walked together up the steps. "I'm warning you, though. When he's long gone I'll still be around."

"Let's see what happens, Tommy," said Sandy. "That's all I can promise."

***   ***   ***

Sandy sat down on her bed. She should hurry, she knew, but she was very tired. She'd hardly slept last night, and when she did her dreams had been so horrible as to make sleep wretched. Philip was in danger; she'd been sure of that. And now? Philip *was* the danger.

No. Whatever Tommy thought, however black the circumstances seemed, Philip would never lend himself to murder.

Theft? She caught her breath. Theft; a clever, battle-of-wits theft. He might. She blinked and saw once again those dangerous blue eyes. He might....

She wished, more passionately than she'd ever wished for anything, she could talk to him. If she'd told him about her ideas about Mrs Banks's murder they would still be arguing. She smiled faintly. He certainly wouldn't have wasted time suspecting himself.

She got up and poured water into the basin from the wash-stand jug. It was cold, but she didn't mind that. It might wake her up a bit.

Hold on; if Mrs Banks was murdered because she recognized someone and that someone *wasn't* Philip, then who was it? Mrs Kelly had been to see Mrs Banks the day before the murder. Mrs Banks had been excited by the visit. But Mrs Banks had seen Mrs Kelly at the inquest. If she'd recognized her, she would have said so at the time. Damn! Not if she wasn't sure. But what if she had recognized her? Who could Mrs Kelly or Teddy Costello possibly be to warrant murder to keep it a secret? A woman, obviously. Nancy Sterling, the wife of President Andrade? But *that* couldn't be so either, because Teddy Costello and Nancy Sterling had been together in Salvatierra. They were definitely two separate people, weren't they? But what if....?

An answer, so startling and so comprehensive, shattered her thoughts. She gaped at her reflection in the mirror. If that were the case.... Everything seemed to turn inside out. She reached for the towel. She was going too fast. *How fast were you going?* She'd nearly seen it then. Proof. Could she find any concrete, actual proof?

She sat down on the bed again and thought very hard. There was one thing she could check. That would show her she was on the right lines. Not that, she acknowledged, she needed to prove it to herself. For her one insight had explained everything, from the murder of Count von Liebrich twelve years ago to what Tommy had said about twelve minutes since.

It was like the answer to one of those awful old riddles of the "My first is in snow but not in ice" variety. It was all meaningless until you got the right word and then it all dropped into place. But what, she asked herself, was she going to do about it? Go to the Kurhaus, yes. But what then?

She got up, changed her dress, and absently brushed her hair, her mind racing. There must be some way.

She picked up a bottle of scent, a present from Dad on her last birthday, and fumbled the lid. The bottle fell, glugging its contents across the marble wash-stand. She quickly picked it up, her nose wrinkling at the intense smell. The room would niff for weeks.... That was it! All she needed now was another bottle.

*** *** ***

Sandy slipped downstairs and into the study. The proof she wanted was, she hoped, in the Kurhaus file. And there it was. She sat back, wondering at how blind she'd been.

She'd been well and truly taken in and the only consolation was that everyone else had too. Anger mixed with fear. How could he pretend so well? Yet all the signs had been there if she'd cared to look for them.

She shivered, picked up the telephone, and rang the Bird In Hand. Mr Brenzett was expected back that afternoon? Good. Can you ask him to get in touch with Mr Andrew Herriad when he arrives? Yes, it is important. Very important. Thank you.

She put the phone down. There was just one thing left to do, and that was a letter to the Superintendent. Come to think of it, she'd better send one to Sir Douglas Lynton as well. Whatever happened, nothing must go wrong with that side of things.

She swallowed. It wasn't just *her* life she was risking.

***   ***   ***

She tracked her father down in the gun-room.

"Hello, Sandy," he said, then stopped and sniffed the air. "Whatever is that awful smell?"

"It's the perfume you gave me for my birthday."

Herriad was appalled. "The damn stuff must be corked or something."

Sandy laughed. "I'm wearing rather a lot of it, I'm afraid. I dropped the bottle. It's all over my bedroom."

"Dear God, you'll have to evacuate the room. You can't possibly sleep up there with a smell like that. Dash it, Sandy, it's like a gas attack."

She laughed again. "Hold your nose, Dad, because I'm going to kiss you. I'm going away again."

"Again? Sandy, for goodness sake, don't come so close. It's horrible. Where are you going?"

Sandy hesitated. "I can't tell you, I'm afraid, because it's all a secret, but I'm popping off with Tommy Leigh and we'll probably be away overnight."

Andrew Herriad's eyes widened. "With *Tommy Leigh!* Why, the bloke's a complete idiot. Besides that, it was

265

only the other day you were having forty fits about that Brown chap. And," he added as another aspect of the situation occurred to him, "it's improper. I know I let you go your own way, Sandy, but there are limits. You're not eloping, are you? I mean, as a general rule, I'd be the last person to tell, but I never know what you're going to do next, and God knows what Daphne'll say."

"She won't say anything, because you're not going to tell her. I'm not eloping and you needn't worry about me and Tommy. But listen, Dad, and this is really important. First of all, no one, and I mean no one at all, not the servants or anyone, must go into my room."

"With that smell, I don't suppose anyone would go near it if you paid them in hard cash."

She smiled. "I mean it, though. I've locked the door and here's the key which I want you to keep. The second thing is that Superintendent Brenzett's back this afternoon and I've left a message for him to come here. I've got a letter for him which he absolutely must have. I've put another one for Sir Douglas Lynton in the post-bag. If Mr Brenzett doesn't get in touch, you must find where he is, either in London or Farholt, and make sure that he comes to see you. You mustn't, under any circumstances, read out the letter on the telephone to him. Here it is. Put it somewhere very safe and don't tell a soul - I mean it, Dad - anything about it."

Herriad took the letter. "Sandy," he said, suddenly serious. "What's going on?"

She hesitated. "I really can't tell you now. But I'll be all right, just as long as Mr Brenzett gets that letter. Trust me."

He stood up and drawing her close, kissed her. "I do trust you, dear," he said soberly. "But be careful."

"I will."

***   ***   ***

Tommy Leigh was waiting by the car. He sniffed the air and drew back. "What on earth is that smell?"

"It's my perfume."

"Your *perfume?* Sandy, darling, let me break this to you gently. A dab behind the ears, fine. I've never known anyone run a bath of it before. It's positively decadent. And," he added, moving hastily to the other side of the car, "overwhelming."

"I spilt it," she said with a giggle. "Then, when I tried to clear it up, some splashed on me."

"Holy mackerel. Get in, old thing. Strewth," he added as another wave of scent drifted towards him. "Thank God it's an open car."

***   ***   ***

They had dinner, which Tommy had insisted on eating in the garden of a pub, on the way to the Kurhaus. To be in a closed room with Sandy, was, he explained, rather more than flesh and blood could stand.

They arrived at the wrought-iron gates just after half-past six, which was, thought Sandy with a shudder, about the time she had got there the day before last. However, her entrance this time was very different. Tommy roared

267

up the drive and brought the car to a halt outside the main entrance.

A man - one of the men who had taken Philip's car - came down the steps to greet them. "Mr Leigh, how nice to see you again. Is Sir Dennis coming down?"

Tommy got out of the car and stretched. "No, I'm afraid not. Mr Keston, this is Miss Herriad, who has accompanied me down here." Mr Keston gave a small bow in Sandy's direction. "I've got a letter of authority from Sir Dennis," continued Tommy

"Oh, you won't need that, Mr Leigh."

Tommy gave a quick smile in Sandy's direction. "I've got it, all the same. Sir Dennis was concerned about the visit you had from the police this morning. He wanted me to check if there was any substance in this extraordinary story that there's a wanted jewel-thief on the premises."

"I can assure you, Mr Leigh, there is not. I, naturally enough, allowed them to look around, but I believe that Sir Dennis should write a strong letter of complaint."

"He certainly will," said Tommy, walking up the steps into the house, "but he wants me to have a dekko at the place first. I'll start with the attics, if I may."

With Mr Keston leading, they walked up five flights of stairs to the very top of the house. The first three floors, from what Sandy could glimpse of them, were luxuriously fitted out. The fourth floor was plainly, if adequately, furnished and clean. These were obviously the servants' quarters. The fifth floor however, looked as if it was only used for lumber. There were no carpets or oil-cloth and the bare boards were dirty. Even though she was used to

Farholt, Sandy found the scale of the house oppressive. No wonder the police search had failed.

Mr Keston took them along the top corridor and into a sky-lit room that boasted no more than a few old trunks.

"Nothing here," said Tommy.

Mr Keston smiled. "Not here, no. But if you would like to observe, Mr Leigh..." He went over to the far wall and, finding the right place, pressed down on a floorboard with his foot. There was a click from the wall.

Tommy walked over to where the click had come from. "I say, Sandy, come and have a look at this. I think there's another door here."

She stood beside him, examining the wall carefully. "You're right!"

Tommy reached out and pulled the door open. Sandy looked in. Then there was a shove in her back and she was sent sprawling forward. The door slammed closed behind her.

From outside the door she could hear Tommy's muffled voice. "Well, this is a turn-up for the books, isn't it?" And he laughed.

Chapter Twelve

Gentle hands came round her shoulders to help her to her feet and a voice came close to her ear.

"*Careful,*" it whispered. "*They can hear and see everything we do.*"

Sandy looked up and for a second she thought the man was Philip. He had the same blue eyes and dark hair and the shape of his face was similar, but it wasn't Phil. Her disappointment must have showed, for he drew back slightly.

"Are you hurt?" His voice was warm and concerned.

"No." She scrambled to her feet. She nodded to show she'd heard his warning. "Who are you? Hang on, you're Jerry, aren't you? Phil's cousin."

He smiled. "Well done. And you are?"

"Sandy Herriad."

His smile widened to a grin. "Are you, by Jove? I've heard no end about you." His smile faded. "Miss Herriad, you shouldn't be here. We're up against it and I can't pretend otherwise."

She looked round the room. It was long and narrow and obviously ran along the eaves of the attic. The floor was carpeted and a table with chairs stood at one end. Another door was set into the wall at the back of the room. Against the wall was a huddle of blankets on which lay Philip. At the sight of him her heart seemed to stand still. He was fast asleep.

She went and knelt beside him, taking his hand in hers. There were livid bruises and an open gash on his face and even in sleep he looked haggard. Jerry knelt beside her. "How did this happen?" she demanded in a low voice, pointing to the bruises.

"They beat him up. I think the police must have come, because that man Keston and two others came in here. They tied us up and gagged us. Philip managed to break free." Jerry's eyes shone with anger. "They beat him unconscious. I was trussed up to that filthy chair." He broke off as Philip stirred and his eyelids flickered.

"Sandy?" He sat up slowly. "*Sandy?*" He reached out his hand incredulously and then she was in his arms, held close to his chest, his hands gripping her.

She turned her face up towards his and he kissed her hungrily. She felt a shudder go through his body and he opened his eyes. His hands still holding her arms, he pushed her away slightly.

"I'm sorry. Sandy, I'm so very sorry, but I've been wanting to do that for so long." He glanced round and saw Jerry. With a shamefaced laugh he dropped his hands.

She reached for his hand again. "I'm not," she said softly and his smile was all she could have hoped for.

He winced and nursed his face. "That hurt. Smiling, I mean. I feel like I've been put through a mangle." He stopped and sniffed the air, then looked at her with a puzzled frown.

"I know, I know," she said hastily. "I had an accident with my perfume."

He got to his feet stiffly. "Sandy, how on earth did you get here? Are you a prisoner too?"

271

"Tommy Leigh brought me."

Philip raised an eyebrow. "That's one gentleman who's going to get what's coming to him. How did he persuade you to come? And why, for heaven's sake?"

"I'll answer the "why" first. I think I scared him, Phil. I started to guess the truth and it rattled him. You see..." His eyes narrowed a warning, and she nodded. Her lips framed the words *I know*. "You see, I came down here yesterday. I found your car and took it to Scotland Yard, then I went back home."

"And the police raided the house first thing this morning," put in Jerry.

"I know they did," said Sandy. "Superintendent Brenzett was with them and he reported their failure. I went home, desperately disappointed, and Tommy Leigh met me. I believed him at first. He seemed so worried I'd been here. Then, as I said, I think I started to guess the truth about Mrs Banks. Suddenly he changed his tune and offered to bring me down. He said all sorts of things about you, Phil, how you were in this for your own ends and weren't the President and so on, and how he could prove it by letting me see you here. He said you were a thief."

"Did he, by George," said Philip, grimly.

"It was all very plausible and I fell for it. Some of it, at any rate. He said as Sir Dennis Storwood's secretary he could search the entire house and if you were here he'd find you."

"Have you..." began Philip, when a door at the back of the room opened. Tommy Leigh, accompanied by Keston

272

and another man walked in. They were all holding automatics.

"Now that," said Tommy, "was a very affecting reunion." He brought the gun up sharply as Philip started forward. "Steady as she goes, old man. You probably wouldn't be killed, but just think of having an untreated injury up here. Nasty, eh? Painful too, I shouldn't wonder. Sandy, I would never have thought it of you. Letting a married man make up to you, and you such a nice girl, too. Rotten bad form, I'd say. Which part of my story didn't you believe, by the way?"

"The part where you said you loved me," said Sandy stonily.

Tommy laughed. "S'funny that. That's the part which happens to be true. Oh, not in the Love, Honour and From This Day Forward sense. Dear me, no. But I did want you. Quite badly at one time. I still do, as a matter of fact. Now Mr Brown here does, I think, suffer from a sense of honour. Beastly inconvenient thing. Especially when he has a wife already and is, I imagine, a Catholic. Salvatierra would want a Good Catholic President and the church rather frowns on divorce, doesn't it?"

"We were married in a civil ceremony," said Philip tightly.

"How very far-sighted. Your wife is perfectly all right, by the way. How long that happy state of affairs continues depends on you. If she is your wife, that is." He looked at Jerry. "Or is it to you we should be offering our sympathies? I realise you've had this conversation

273

before and I hate to be tedious, but which one of you is the President?"

"I am," said Jerry and Philip together.

Tommy Leigh sighed. "You can't both be. Don't be silly. You've managed to keep us guessing for this long, but affairs are coming to a head. We've sent cable photographs of your two smiling faces to Miss Jane Lehman. She'll be able to pick out which one she's actually married to easily enough. And then? Well, the party really is over."

"Jane would never help you," said Jerry.

Tommy nodded. "Oh yes, she will. She's rather frightened at the moment, I understand. But all she has to do is pick out the right picture, and off she goes. It's a publicity stunt, don't you know, and will remain so as long as she keeps quiet. If she doesn't... Well, there are so many suicides in Hollywood these days. However, that will take some time and I think fate might have sent us a shortcut. Sandy, my darling, I did resent you turning me down."

He came very close to her. So close his breath was in her face and she could see the muscles round his mouth working. She was suddenly very frightened. He sensed her fear and grinned with enjoyment. "This is part - a small part - of what I want."

He swaggered over her then, without letting hold of the gun, forced her to him. His mouth sought hers and his fingers bit painfully into her shoulders. The stubble on his face scraped against her cheek. He twisted a hand in her hair, pulling her head back, knocking his teeth on hers in a

274

bruising, loveless kiss. Sandy struggled in his arms and, getting an arm free, slapped his face as hard as she could.

Tommy drew back with a broad grin. "Naughty. You'll pay for that slap, by the way."

Sandy felt as if she were choking. She rubbed her hand across her mouth, trying to get rid of the taste of that dreadful kiss.

Philip had all three guns pointed at him. For a moment he looked as if he was going to brush them to one side, then stopped, breathing deeply. "If you touch Miss Herriad once more," he said evenly, "I don't care how long it takes but I'll hunt you down and break your neck."

Tommy grinned. "Really?" He pulled her to him again. Sandy twisted desperately to avoid him and to her horror saw Philip crouch to spring.

"No, Phil!" she screamed as the guns levelled. Philip stopped and Tommy thrust her away.

"Mind you," said Tommy, "before you favour me with any more attentions, Sandy darling, you really ought to have a wash. You smell like a cheap tart."

Philip, moving very deliberately, walked towards her. Tommy raised the automatic, but Philip ignored him. He opened his arms and Sandy fell against him, burying her head in his shoulder. To her fury, she realised she was sobbing. She was terrified and very angry with herself. Philip held her close and kissed her hair. In the comfort of his arms, her fear subsided, and with its going, thought returned.

"Leave her alone, Leigh," Philip said quietly. "Your quarrel isn't with her." His arms tightened. "Easy, Sandy, easy." He bent his head over hers as another sob racked her body. "I won't let him hurt you."

A very faint whisper came to him. *"Buy us time. We need time."*

Philip looked at Tommy over her shoulder. "What do you have planned for us? For her?"

"For her? I'm sure you can guess." Despite herself, Sandy gave a little cry. The sound seemed to please Tommy. "Looking forward to it, my dear?"

Philip held up his hand. "Enough. I can't let this continue. What do you want, Leigh?"

"What has already been asked. Sandy, darling, will you please stop draping yourself all over Mr Brown. I find it quite intensely irritating."

He walked a few steps back and sat on the corner of the table. "Now come over here like a good girl and sit down." Sandy didn't move. "Now!"

"Let me go, Phil," she said quietly. He dropped his hands and Sandy, nerving herself, went to sit at the table. "Tommy, what's all this about?" she asked. Her voice cracked and she shook herself, trying not to show how scared she was.

She had never realised how strong a full-grown man was. Tommy was tall, powerful and very broad-shouldered and the brutal desire in his eyes brought the sick taste of fear into her throat. "You can't keep us here." She willed her voice under control. "Not for long, anyway. The police are bound to find out where we are.

276

They already know about Phil and Jerry and it won't take them long to guess where I am."

"Long enough. But if these gentlemen would like to co-operate you can leave at any time."

"What do you want them to do?"

Tommy looked towards Philip and Jerry. "Why don't you explain things? It might interest Sandy here to find out exactly why she might be... inconvenienced." He stretched out and ruffled her hair. "Wouldn't it, darling?" She flinched away and instinctively drew her dress a little closer round her. Tommy Leigh laughed out loud. "Over to you, Brown, old man. Don't keep the lady waiting."

Philip moved restlessly but said nothing.

Jerry shrugged. "It's one of the nastiest little schemes I've ever come across, Miss Herriad." For the use of her surname and the respect it implied, she was intensely grateful. He acknowledged her look of thanks with a little bow. "Incidentally, Phil and I are of the same mind. Whatever this scum -" his words were like the flick of a whip "- says, you will not be harmed." Tommy Leigh grinned lazily.

"As you might know the people who killed my father, President Ramon, were called the Haciendistas. After ruining the country they were finally chucked out, but they're greedy for more. Mr Leigh and the rest of his gang want me to appoint Haciendistas to the government. Now we've got this loan, there's something they can steal, you see? They'll take the lot and leave us sucked dry. To make sure I don't kick, they've got a stack of letters for me to write admitting I've been a total fraud, am in league with the Haciendistas, have bought my way to power and am paying them regular bribes. The loan will come in three instalments over the next two years and for the next two years I've got to pretend to govern the country honestly whilst handing over every penny to this bunch of murderous thieves. I won't be able to do a thing about it, because they'll have the letters, written by me, to hold to my head. I won't be able to say they're false because I'll have been forced to do precisely what the letters say I'm doing."

Tommy casually ruffled Sandy's hair again, letting his hand trail down her face. "That's rather well put. You'll do it, of course. We haven't, more's the pity, managed to work out exactly which one of you is the man in charge, so to speak, but we will. There'll be a funeral fairly soon *if* those letters aren't written. To say nothing of what will happen to Miss Jane Lehman and, of course, our own darling Sandy." He put his hand under her chin and forced her to look at him. "I think I can promise you won't enjoy it." He grinned as she tried to squirm away. "I will."

"Stop that," said Philip. His face was grey. "I'm the man you want." Jerry glanced at him, horrified. Philip swallowed. "I'm sorry, Jerry. It was a good game and we played it for all we were worth, but the stakes are too high. I can't risk either you, Jane or Sandy any more. For God's sake, Leigh, leave her alone! I'll do what you want. I'll write your letters."

"Now this," murmured Tommy, "is interesting. I must admit I'd like to actually know if you were the President

278

before you start the letters. Not that it really matters, of course, because we'll find out as soon as we get an answer from Jane Lehman."

Philip buried his head in his hands. "Of course I'm the President. And the thought of having to go through with your filthy plan makes me heave." He looked up and Sandy saw a sudden gleam in his eyes. "Leigh, you and your crowd want money, don't you?"

"Rather a lot of it, yes. Expensive tastes an' all that."

"What if I gave you half a million? Five hundred thousand pounds? It might be more. Would you keep your fingers off the loan and let us go? We wouldn't be able to say anything. It'd be too dangerous. I'd love to nail you and your gang, but I care too much about the people in this room to chance it. If I paid up, you'd have the money without the risk of being around me for the next two years. Two years is a long time."

Tommy drew his breath in. "You haven't got half a million, Brown."

Philip nodded. "Yes, I have." He looked at Sandy. "I'm sorry. I haven't told you the truth about lots of things. I wish to God I had done, because everything might have worked out very differently. I was trying to be clever. Leigh, you can have the money. I've got the emeralds."

"Phil!" Sandy's voice was a shocked whisper.

"Where are they?" asked Tommy sharply.

"At Farholt." He gave a little shudder. "Sandy, please! Don't look at me like that. It was a grubby little plan, but I was desperate. You would have hated it and I cared what you thought. I've known where the jewels are for days. My first idea was to tell you and I wish to God I had. Try and imagine how I felt. The loan was secure but I saw a chance to make more money. All I can say is that I didn't want it for myself. We were so broke, you see, and this was going to be money, real money at last. I was going to find the stones, insure them, then arrange another theft. We would have struggled with the loan. The terms are ruinous but this way I could have made it work."

"It's... it's so dishonest, Phil," she said shakily.

"It's damn clever," said Tommy Leigh. "Where are they?"

"Not so fast," said Philip. "Before I tell you that, I want to know what's happening to us."

Tommy Leigh sat back and, without letting hold of the gun, took a cigarette out of his case and lit it. "That rather depends. You see, I can't deny that it's awkward to keep you here." A glint came into his eye. "If this is just a scheme for getting me back to Farholt, forget it. *I think* I can persuade my boss to let you go if we not only get the emeralds but the loan as well. Those loan papers are our security, you see. All that you'll have suffered is a couple of days in the country. We're a big organization, bigger than you could dream. Any attempt to put the police on our track would have disastrous consequences."

"You killed my father," said Philip, flatly. "I might have been stupid but I'm not so stupid to disbelieve you."

"In that case, we're in business. Where exactly are they?"

"In the library." Philip glanced at Sandy. "It gave me quite a stir the other day when you said you'd been looking in there. Count von Liebrich was a collector of rare books. When he came to hide the emeralds, the library was an obvious choice. That's all I knew, but I was haunted by John Guthrie's last words. Incidentally, Leigh, you did murder Guthrie, didn't you?"

"Very neatly, although I say so myself. He didn't die right away, so I slugged him with the monkey-wrench from the car. I did wonder if that fool of a doctor was going to give the game away by insisting he couldn't have spoken with those injuries, but I got away with it." He yawned. "But this is very old history. Back to the emeralds, Brown, old thing."

"It was his last words, as I said. *Banks.* I went looking in the library for any book to do with banks and I found one. It's a collection of Scottish verse, called something like *Yon Bonnie Banks and Braes.* A few spaces along is another book called *From the Sierra Nevada to the Sierra Mojada: Travels From Spain to Mexico.* That was the *Sea Air* bit. I put my hand in behind the books and found - well, I found the emeralds."

"And you left them there?" Tommy Leigh was scathing.

"Of course I didn't. I hid them in my wardrobe. However, I was worried about them. I didn't trust Storwood. I thought he might search my room."

"I did," said Tommy with a smile.

"That never occurred to me. Anyway, I put them back in the library. I thought if they'd been safe there for twelve years, they'd be safe for a little while longer."

Tommy Leigh stood up. "My darling Sandy, I'm afraid you're going to have to wait." Once again a hand like a vice closed round her jaw, forcing her face upwards. "Look at me," he said with the suggestion of a snarl. "That's better..."

"But there is one thing," said Philip. "If you touch Miss Herriad, I will kill you." He spoke in a quiet conversational tone, but his eyes blazed.

Even armed with a gun, Tommy couldn't face those eyes. He dropped his hand and attempted to smile. "In that case, gentlemen, I'll leave you to have the pleasure. You'll have to be locked in together overnight and real men... Well, real men would."

He backed out of the room, followed by Keston and the other man.

Sandy put her face in her hands and burst into tears. Her jaw hurt where Tommy had held her and she felt dirtied and used. She was aware that Philip had his arm round her but she broke away. "Don't! Not you. Phil, how could you?"

She looked up and saw the oddest expression in his eyes. It was as if she had bitterly hurt him and the sight racked her. "Oh, Phil!"

He held her close. *"Have I bought you enough time?"* It was the gentlest of whispers.

"I'm not sure." She tried to whisper in return but it came out with a gulp. "I don't know."

282

Jerry dipped his handkerchief in the jug of water that stood on the table. "Perhaps, Miss Herriad, you'll feel better for a wash." He smiled encouragingly. "It's the best I can do."

"Thanks." She mopped her face and unconsciously screwed the handkerchief into knots. "Why..." (*Think, why can't I think? Not of him - it - but think*) "Why is he going to leave us overnight?"

"He'll have to contact Farholt and Sir Dennis," said Philip. "He daren't risk a telegram or a telephone call, so my bet is that he'll do it by letter. Sir Dennis'll receive it first thing tomorrow. There won't be any problem about the answer. Everyone would expect Storwood to telephone here and all he has to say is, 'Go ahead'."

"Phil, are the emeralds really there?" Stupid question. What could he answer? But she believed him when he did.

"They're there all right. I wish I could have saved the loan. I might, even now."

There was a long silence. There didn't seem anything to say.

The sun, which had turned the attic room into a stifling box, had long since passed over the roof of the house and the sky had turned to deep, star-pricked blue. Sandy wondered if they were going to get fed, or if starvation was part of the treatment.

The rear door opened and Keston, armed as before, came into the room followed by Tommy Leigh, holding a torch in one hand and a gun in the other. Two more men, also armed, came in and stood by the back wall.

Tommy came and shone the light in Sandy's face. "We're going to tie you up. Don't try anything, Brown," he said without looking round. "This gun is aimed directly at your girlfriend. She's not important to us and if I have to shoot I will. If she's lucky it might only wound her."

He put the torch down on the table and pushed her into a chair. Keston came forward, a length of thin rope in his hands. He forced her hands to the back of the chair. Sandy gave a yelp.

"Please, I'll do what you want. My shoulder hurts. Please, Tommy, let me have my hands in front. I'll do what you say." She cried out as her arms were pulled back. "Please!" She struggled under Keston's hands. "It hurts."

"Do as she says," said Tommy quickly. "Only for God's sake, get on with it."

Sandy subsided and allowed herself to be tied and gagged. With a murderous look at Tommy Leigh, Philip sat in a chair while the rope was securely fastened round him. Jerry looked at the gun pointing at Sandy and submitted.

"Off you go, Keston," said Tommy, when they had all been secured. "I'll stay here and keep an eye on things." He stood listening, his head on one side. Voices came faintly through the open sky-light. "It sounds as if they haven't got inside yet. You should be able to get downstairs before they do."

He sat with his back against the wall as the men left. "As you will have gathered," he said conversationally, "we're about to be favoured with another visit from the

284

rozzers. They may come up to the attics. If you have any foolish ideas of trying to make a noise, forget it." He looked up as Keston came back into the room. "Yes?"

"Come downstairs," said Keston briefly. "That Brenzett character is back and he's asking for you by name." He nodded towards Sandy. "He knows she was coming here with you. You'll have to think of some story to explain her disappearance."

"Damn!" Tommy got to his feet. "So you told Brenzett where we were going, did you, Sandy? And I thought you trusted me. Never mind." He grinned wolfishly. "Be good, everyone. I'll be back." He went, leaving them in darkness.

Sandy's hands were tied at the wrist and her arms were lashed together. It was painful to move, but she managed to wriggle so that her fingers got to the pocket of her dress. Careful with this bit. I mustn't drop it...

Her hand closed round the small bottle and, keeping it in her pocket, she managed to unscrew the cap. An intense, opulent, smell filled the room.

She heard a puzzled grunt from one of the men - she couldn't tell if it was Philip or Jerry - and then, from very far away, came the sound she had been waiting for.

It was the excited howl of a dog. There was what seemed like an endless wait and then came muffled shouts as feet pounded on the stairs outside. A scrabbling, whining noise came from the outer door, and a sharp, quick bark. Three tremendous crashes shook the outer wall, followed by a flood of light as the door was broken down. A brown and white Springer Spaniel rushed in and, flinging itself at Sandy, barked triumphantly.

Superintendent Brenzett followed the dog in, and as he saw them, his face creased in a smile.

"In here!" he yelled over his shoulder, and, taking out a clasp-knife, knelt beside Sandy and cut her free. "Miss Herriad, that was the cleverest, bravest trick I've ever come across. Thank God you're all right."

"I'm fine," she said, rubbing the circulation back into her arms and legs. "Have you caught Tommy Leigh? He's responsible for all of this."

"He's safely downstairs in the care of my men," said Brenzett, cutting free Philip before moving on to Jerry. "And that Keston chap. Far too pleasant for his own good, that one. He's in the bag together with a choice collection of villains."

Philip stood up. "Sandy? What did you do?"

She laughed. "It was my perfume. I knew Tommy was the man we'd been looking for and when he suddenly became so keen to get me down here, I guessed he was going to lock me in with you. I hoped I'd find Jerry as well. There was no point in simply being another prisoner, but if I could let Mr Brenzett know exactly where we were, then I was quite happy to let myself be captured. Quite by accident, I spilled my perfume while I was thinking. It suddenly struck me that a dog, a police dog, could track down that scent, so I left some perfume in a bottle in my bedroom and took the rest with me in another bottle. It was in the pocket of my dress. I put as much on myself as I could, just in case I couldn't open it. I really do smell awful, don't I?"

"When I got your letter telling me what you'd done, I could hardly believe it," said Brenzett. "Your father was worried stiff and wanted us to come earlier, but you said ten o'clock in your letter, and I stuck to it."

"I wanted to be sure that there had been enough time for things to develop."

"And I thought the least we could do was follow your instructions. I do hope, Miss Herriad, that you haven't been harmed in any way."

"Miss Herriad has had to listen to some of the most loathsome suggestions I've ever heard a man make," said Philip. He came up to her, hands outstretched. "You were brilliant, Sandy. I've never hated anyone quite as much as I hate Tommy Leigh."

"I was really scared," she admitted. "It never occurred to me that he'd suggest... well, what he suggested. That was stupid," she said with a little frown. "It was so obvious, but all the men I've ever had anything to do with have been like you, Phil, and Jerry and Dad. I can't think how I came to be such a fool."

"A fool?" Philip grinned broadly and kissed her fingers. "That's not a word I would ever use about you. Fool indeed!" He turned to Brenzett. "Superintendent, did you say Tommy Leigh was downstairs?" The light of battle came into his eyes. "Right. This is where Mr Leigh and I have a few words."

"Stop!" shouted Brenzett as Philip went out of the room and down the stairs. "Mr Brown, you can't *do* that."

"The only way you can stop me is to arrest me," called back Philip.

They caught up with him in the hall. Tommy Leigh, Keston, and one of the other men who had been in the concealed room were standing chatting to four stolidly respectful policemen.

"You're certain to find there's been some mistake," Tommy was saying, when he turned and saw Philip, followed by Jerry, Brenzett and Sandy. He looked at them with horror, which as he saw Philip's face, turned to naked fear.

He backed down the hall. "You can't touch me," he stammered, then, finding a policeman's hand on his shoulder, spun and lashed out. The policeman, taken by surprise, crumpled and Tommy ran.

He made it to the door, wrenching it open before anyone could stop him. Philip gathered himself and sprang forward in a flying tackle. The two men sprawled down the steps together, then Philip hauled Tommy to his feet.

"This," he snarled, "is for me." A right hook crunched into Tommy's face. "And this is for Jerry," - a left jab followed - "and this, you absolute bastard, is for Miss Herriad."

It was a smashing piledriver of a blow, a short right uppercut which travelled eight inches before it connected with the underneath of Tommy's jaw. His eyes rolled back, his knees sagged forward and he fell, unconscious.

"I say, Phil, old bean, you left out Jane," said Jerry mildly.

Philip dusted his hands together. "I'm sorry, old son." He poked Tommy with the toe of his shoe. "He'll have to wait for that one until he wakes up."

"I think you'd better let us deal with him, sir," said Brenzett. "We can't really allow that sort of thing to happen, you know. I suppose, as he was resisting arrest, I can overlook it, but..."

Philip, who seemed not to have heard, came back into the hall and seized Keston by the collar. "You're another one I owe a debt to." Keston licked nervous lips, judging the distance between Philip's fist and his own face. "Where's Jane Lehman?" Philip demanded. "How do we get her released? And she'd better be unharmed."

Keston looked wildly at Brenzett who was standing in the door. "Stop this maniac," he croaked.

Brenzett placidly stroked the angle of his jaw. "I can't see any maniacs," he said thoughtfully. "Perhaps I should leave Mr Brown in charge while I go and look for them."

Philip shook Keston like a terrier with a rat. "Tell me!"

"All right, all right!" Keston whimpered. "There's a coded message we can send to release her." He stared, terrified, into Philip's face. "She'll be fine, I promise you. I mean it!" he added in a near-scream as the shaking continued.

Philip released his grip and Keston fell grovelling to the floor. "In that case, Mr Keston, you'd better send it."

"Hold on," said Brenzett. "I want a word with the American police before we do. The more of this lot we can get behind bars the better. And, Keston, I want to know where Teddy Costello is."

"I'll take you to her," said Keston sullenly. "It's all over now, anyway."

"Yes, it is," agreed Brenzett with a smile.

"Not quite," put in Philip. "Superintendent, is there someone you can leave in charge to finish things off here? We need to get back to Farholt as quickly as we can."

***　　***　　***

It was nearly seven in the morning. Little pockets of mist lay like milk in grassy hollows. Doves and wood-pigeons cooed in the great elms of Farholt and the entire world seemed stilled. Philip, Jerry, Sandy and Brenzett caught the mood and when they spoke, it was in low voices.

Philip glanced at his watch. "We'd better be making a start," he said, throwing away the butt of his cigarette. He glanced towards the squat, stone building, whose roof was covered in turf. "What's this place again, Sandy?"

"It's the old ice-house. It's not used any more. Shall I lead the way, Superintendent?"

"You better had, Miss, as you're the one who knows the lie of the land, so to speak. You've got your torch? After you, then."

***　　***　　***

They had been sitting in the secret passage for what seemed like hours. Sandy, oddly enough, wasn't bored. The anticipation edged her nerves and in the dim light of the now faded torch she could see Philip felt the same.

290

He smiled at her. "It can't be long now," he whispered.

There was a click as the library door opened. Someone had come in. Sandy tried to breath as quietly as possible. Another click. The door shutting. There was silence for a time, interspersed with little noises of movement. Then came a series of short, flat, sounds which Sandy recognized as the sound of books being moved on the wooden shelves.

There was a little cry of triumph and a click. Philip and Jerry nodded to Brenzett. "Now," Philip mouthed and with a crash, shocking in the silence, flung back the panel of the passage and strode into the room.

Eleanor Storwood, a red leather box in one hand and a glittering string of emeralds in the other, screamed.

"Eleanor Storwood," said Brenzett, impervious to her scream, "I arrest you on charges of attempted theft, kidnap, conspiracy to murder and actual murder. You do not have to say anything, but anything you do say may be used in a court of law."

Jerry started forward. "I know you!" He glanced at Philip. "Didn't you recognize her, Phil? We've never seen her in the flesh, and she's made herself look different, somehow, but you've seen photographs, too. This is Nancy Sterling."

"Prove it," said Eleanor Storwood, recovering herself.

"I think you'll find," said Sandy from the rear, "that she's got another name, too. She was married to John Guthrie. This is Adela Guthrie and she's tried to steal the emeralds again."

Chapter Thirteen

The study door opened softly and Daphne Marston came into the room. Dennis Storwood, sitting with his head buried in his hands, didn't look up.

Daphne put a hand on his shoulder. "Dennis..." He turned to face her with a look of such numb anguish that she drew her breath in. "Dennis, I'm so very sorry."

He continued to sit rigidly for a few moments, then gave a little shudder. "She was too good for me," he said in a flat voice.

Daphne's hand tightened on his shoulder.

He shuddered again and slumped back in his chair. "I'm a fool. Everything I've worked for, everything I've thought important... What's it worth?" He raised his hands then let them drop back in his lap. "I realise what people like Herriad think of me. *Pompous ass*... I can hear him saying it. Herriad's content to be what he is. I always needed to be someone. The bank, the government, it's all nothing but arrogance. I'm nothing without what I do. Arrogance. Arrogant enough to think that she really cared."

"Why..." Daphne hesitated, trying to find the words. "Why did she marry you, Dennis?" Somehow it seemed right to put it that way round.

"Why?" He looked at her again. "For protection. For cover. No one would suspect that my wife was really -" he swallowed "- Andrade's wife. She said as much, didn't she? She pretended very well, but that's all it ever was. Everything she wanted, I gave her. I knew she didn't care.

But she pretended. I thought it was good enough. She was always too good for me."

She squeezed his shoulder again. "Dennis, you can't want to live with pretence."

"No? I haven't any answers anymore. Perhaps you're right."

***   ***   ***

Philip glanced at the grandfather clock. Half past two. Surely, *surely*, Sandy would wake up soon. After Eleanor Storwood had been taken away, Sandy had gone up to wash and change. In reply to his anxious question half an hour later, her maid had told him that she was fast asleep.

A step on the stairs made him look up. "Sandy!"

She came down the stairs rather self-consciously. "Hello, Phil." She looked round the hall. "Where is everyone?"

"Goodness knows. Jerry's asleep on my bed."

"Where's Sir Dennis?"

"Again, goodness knows. Did you want him?"

"Not really, but I felt sorry for him, Phil. That was an awful scene when his wife was arrested. She didn't have to say all those things to him and he was - well, noble, in a way. He simply stood there and took it and she was horrible to him."

"She," said Philip thoughtfully, "is the most vicious piece of goods I've ever come across. She and Andrade simply murdered anyone in Salvatierra who got in their way. I don't mind admitting the thought that Nancy Sterling might be at large scared me rigid. I never dreamed she was under my nose, so to speak. We've got a chance, now. Salvatierra, I mean."

"And you've got the emeralds."

"Yes," he said thoughtfully. "Sandy, I need to speak to you. Can we go in the garden?"

She drew back. "I'm not so sure, Phil. Yesterday was different. I mean, you were in danger and I had to try and help. I was overwrought, I know, and so were you. But now..." She was standing on the second step and her eyes were level with his. She took a deep breath and squared her slim shoulders. "I know how things are. Is there really anything left to say to each other?"

"I think you'll find," said Philip, "that's there's a great deal to say to each other." He reached out his hand to her. "Please."

They walked out onto to the lawn in silence until they came to the cedar tree. Sandy felt ridiculously nervous. He had said nothing, but she was acutely aware of his presence. She guessed, from the way he carefully avoided taking her arm or standing too close, that he felt the same. She glanced at him and saw him watching her with a little crooked smile.

He moved restlessly, then was still. "Sandy, it's no secret how I feel about you."

"What's the point?"

"Listen." He made as if to hold her hand, then drew back and drew a deep breath. "I've had to deceive you from the beginning. Jerry and I knew there was danger, so we came up with a plan. He went to Scotland, I came here as Philip Brown. It was a bluff. Some things were true. I had to negotiate the loan and I wanted to look for the emeralds. What I - we - also wanted to do was cause the Haciendistas enough doubt as to who was the President to make them hesitate. As you know, it worked for a time."

"And then they found out the truth."

He laughed. "Not quite. You see, Sandy, I'm not the President."

She gazed at him. "You're not the President?" she repeated.

His smile widened. "No, thank God. I'm just me. I'm not married, I never have been married, but Sandy, darling Sandy, I'd like to *be* married."

He reached out his hands to her again. "I wanted to tell you last night, but I was damned if I was going to ask the most important question of my life with a hoard of policemen looking over my shoulder. Can you trust me now? Because I love you, Sandy, and I hated deceiving you. Despite all that, please? Will you marry me?"

She took his hands. Strong, brown hands. She remembered how that strength had fed her courage last night when she was so desperately frightened. She wanted, with a sudden, savage hunger, to feel his arms round her once more but a little hard lump of self-respect made her hold back.

His hands tightened on hers and she looked up into his worried blue eyes. "Sandy? Sandy, you've got to say yes." His mouth trembled. "Because if you don't, I don't know what I'll do."

Still she hesitated. "Why did you lie to me about the emeralds, Phil?"

The worry vanished and he threw his head back and laughed. "I didn't, idiot! Those weren't the real jewels I put in the library. God alone knows where they are. The ones that Eleanor Storwood found were the fake ones from Houblyn's Bank."

"*What!* Phil, that was brilliant!"

"I know." His smile faded. "Sandy? Please?"

"Of course I'll marry you, Phil. I love you far too much not too."

He reached out and brushed the hair away from her eyes, then drew her close and kissed her.

*** *** ***

"Phil..."

"What?" he mumbled, kissing her eyes, her mouth and her hair.

"We'd better go and tell people."

"Why?"

"Because Dad's looking at us from the terrace."

He broke off. "I suppose we'd better had."

Arm in arm, they walked back across the lawn. Andrew Herriad was waiting for them. He looked acutely miserable.

"Sandy," he said as they approached. "What the dickens is going on?"

"It's all right," she said happily. "Phil and I are engaged. He's not the President."

Herriad's face cleared. "Congratulations," he said heartily, and stuck out his hand to Philip, before drawing

Sandy to one side. "Who is he?" he asked in a carrying whisper.

Sandy laughed. "You know, I never thought to ask." She turned. "Phil, Dad wants to know who you are. I wouldn't mind finding out, either."

"My name?" said Philip, with some embarrassment. He scratched his ear. "I hardly know how to break this to you, but as a matter of fact, it's Philip Brown."

"*What?*" said father and daughter together.

"Well, sort of. The Sunday Best version is Felipe Jorge Xavier Artiaga. But quite honestly, Sandy, I was blest if I was going through school and the army and so on with a label like that. My mother was English and called Brown, and the two surnames always get put together in Spanish, so my parents were called Artiaga y Brown, and in England I always use her name. As a matter of fact, in England it *is* my name. Officially, I mean, as "Brown" comes last on all the documents with my parents' name on. You can't expect a bunch of civil servants to cope with how the Spanish arrange their surnames. Jerry's the same."

"Your cousin?" said Andrew Herriad.

Philip grinned. "As a matter of fact, he's my brother. His full name is Javier Roberto Ignazio Artiaga, known to all and sundry as Jerry Brown."

Andrew Herriad was frowning. "Hold on a moment. That's who you are sorted out, but if you're not the President, what are you?"

"Er... yes." Philip scratched his ear again. "This is going to sound so dull. I'm actually a Chartered Accountant."

"You're a *Chartered Accountant?*" said Andrew Herriad. "Good God, Sandy, you're marrying into the middle classes. It sounds quite horribly respectable."

Philip gave a crack of laughter. "I told you it sounded dull. I am, or will be, the Minister of Finance for Salvatierra when we've got any finance to minister. It's because I understand figures that I came to Farholt to work out the loan with James Matherson. Jerry would have been hopeless at coping with the detail."

"And your brother, Jerry," continued Herriad. "I suppose he's the President?"

"Er.... no. The President is our cousin, Enrique Ramon Alfonzo Artiaga, otherwise known as Harry." Philip glanced at his watch. "I hope you don't mind, sir, but I telephoned him this morning and he should be arriving shortly."

Herriad sighed. "D'you know, m'boy, for the first time I can actually believe you're in government, even if it's the Salvatierran version. You're acquiring the same techniques as Dennis Storwood. Keep at it, young man. By the end of the week you'll have got over adding, "Do you mind" when telling me to expect one of your guests."

"Dad," said Sandy reproachfully. "You can't honestly object to Phil asking one of your relatives-to-be to dinner."

"No?" Herriad looked down the terrace and his eyes widened. "What's the climate like in Salvatierra?" he asked casually.

Philip looked puzzled. "It's not bad. Why?"

Herriad nodded to where Dennis Storwood and Daphne Marston had come out onto the terrace and were strolling arm-in-arm onto the lawn. "Daphne nearly landed him a couple of years ago before he went off to America. I don't think he's got any chance now. It might take a little time, but she'll have him hooked, netted and gaffed. I saw her expression when she went to find him this morning, and for grim determination and womanly sympathy it couldn't be matched. Goodness knows why's she's so keen on gardening. She ought to take up fishing." He smiled at Sandy. "And quite honestly, my dear, if Storwood's going to move in, which I'm sure he will, I'll appreciate a bolt-hole at the other side of the world."

Daphne Marston looked up and, leaving Sir Dennis, came up the steps towards them. "Andrew! Sir Dennis has to leave us for a couple of days, but he'll be back after the weekend."

Andrew Herriad gave her his most charming smile. "I'm sure he will. Tell him we can't run to a salmon river but there's some good coarse fishing to be had."

Daphne frowned. "I don't know what you mean."

Herriad's smile widened. "Don't you? You will, Daphne, you will."

***   ***   ***

President Enrique Ramon Alfonzo Artiaga raised his glass to the assembled company. "Here's to you all, and especially to you, Phil, and you, Jerry, and, of course, most of all, to you, Miss Herriad. That trick with the perfume was nothing short of brilliant."

"It certainly was," agreed Superintendent Brenzett. "And brave."

"It was horrible," said Sandy. "I was really frightened, you know? Tommy had always seemed so nice, and then I realised what he was really like and what he was capable of..." She shuddered. "I knew who he was, you know. That should have warned me, but it didn't. Stupid of me."

Philip covered her hand with his. "I've never hated anyone as much as I hated Tommy Leigh. I honestly think I could have killed him."

"You looked as if you were going to," put in Brenzett.

"Hang on a minute," said Herriad. "What d'you mean, Sandy, that you knew who he was?"

"Haven't I told you, Dad? Tommy Leigh is Robert Eldon."

Herriad put down his glass and stared at her. "I think," he said in a controlled voice, "that you'd better tell me all about it. From the beginning, mind. That's the only way I'm going to make head or tale of it."

Philip looked at his cousin. "Will you kick off, Harry? After all, the first part of the story's yours."

"Okay. My father started the ball rolling by coming up with the idea for the railway. He employed his friend, John Guthrie, and was going to fund the project by raising money on the Serpent's Eye. That was dealt with by his financial advisor, Count von Liebrich, who, as we know, was a wrong 'un. The Count was also having an affair with Adela Guthrie. We know as much from his private papers."

"I've seen a photograph of him," said Sandy. "He radiated power. That can be very attractive."

"I can see I'm going to have to watch it," muttered Philip.

"Anyway," continued Harry. "The negotiations were conducted here. We know the Count was a crook. Nancy Sterling, as Adela became, was most certainly a crook and I don't have to remind you what Robert Eldon was capable of."

"No," said Herriad, with distaste. "What about this Guthrie chap? Was he a crook too?"

Harry shook his head. "He swore to my father he was innocent. I'm sure he was."

"If he had found the Serpent's Eye and handed it over, that would prove it, wouldn't it?" said Sandy.

Brenzett nodded. "It would go a long way. I've got no doubt of it, knowing what we know now."

"That's right," agreed Harry. "I think it's obvious that the three of them, Adela, Robert and the Count were in it together. Adela wore the necklace at the ball and she was perfectly placed to substitute it for the paste copy that had been made."

He opened the flat red leather box on the table in front of him. "Here it is."

He took the necklace from the box and looked at it for a long moment. "It's a wonderful thing, isn't it? If only we could find the real Serpent's Eye...."

He shook himself. "The Count hid the necklace and our three staged a robbery. The false necklace had to disappear, you see, otherwise when the final valuation was carried out for the loan, it would be shown up as false and suspicion would fall on Adela, who had worn it, and the Count, who had access to the safe. That's where things began to go wrong."

He picked up his whisky and took a thoughtful sip. "This is guesswork, but it chimes in with what we know. As the real necklace is, we think, still here, that implies Count von Liebrich double-crossed Adela and Robert Eldon. Either Adela or Robert must've shot him, but it was John Guthrie who was arrested. Then another plan of the Count's came into operation. The rebels, the Haciendistas, began their revolution. My father went back to Salvatierra as quickly as he could, leaving me here in England. I never saw him again." His lips tightened. "I loved my father."

"He was a great man," said Jerry quietly. "Our father - Uncle Ramon's brother - died in the fighting, too. We three boys were brought up together."

"John Guthrie," went on Harry, "escaped the police, went to Salvatierra, and fought alongside my father. As I said, they were friends. It was reported that he'd been killed, but he obviously managed to get back to England. Meanwhile, Adela re-named herself Nancy Sterling and married Andrade. Robert Eldon faked his own death and

302

turned up in Salvatierra. Together with Teddy Costello, they ruled Salvatierra like the pack of thugs they were. God knows how many they robbed and killed, but eventually, as you know, their time ran out. Andrade died of natural causes, and the whole rotten edifice of power fell in. I was asked to become President. I didn't want the job, but the thought of my father spurred me on. And, of course, I had Jerry and Philip as my right-hand men. I couldn't have done it alone. Pretty tough going, wasn't it? We'd all been in the army during the war, of course, and Jerry, in particular, has a brilliant grasp of strategy and tactics."

"Leave it out, Harry," said Jerry, flushing.

Harry grinned. "Take my word for it. We managed to knock the country into something resembling peace and the three of us were able to start thinking of building on what was left of my father's work."

"The railway was the obvious place to begin," said Philip. "But, like my Uncle Ramon before us, we were faced with the problem of finance, and like him, decided to use the Serpent's Eye as security for a loan. However, when Harry turned up at Houblyns and found that the necklace was a fake, he went pop."

"I was blistering," agreed Harry, with a wry smile. "I made a huge fuss. Then we received some sinister news. Nancy Sterling had disappeared but a report came from Estrada that she'd contacted what was left of the Haciendistas. By announcing so publicly that the jewels in Houblyns were fake, I'd also announced that we were a great deal weaker than they'd supposed. It was Phil who spotted that I'd be in danger, and he came up with a plan."

"We had to keep you safe until we'd tried to get a loan together," said Philip.

He looked round the table. "We made Harry go into private life for a time, and Jerry and I set out to throw dust in the eyes of the Haciendistas. I'd seen Sir Dennis, and led him to believe I was really the President, but had adopted an alias for safety. Scotland Yard were allowed to pick up that impression too, while Jerry put himself about at receptions and so on, also pretending to be the President. Sir Dennis had given a cautious go-ahead to the idea of a loan without the Serpent's Eye, and I suggested that we could come to Farholt, so I could have a look for the original necklace whilst hammering out the loan."

"Your technique is getting smoother," remarked Herriad. "Storwood himself couldn't improve on the way you phrased that."

Philip had the grace to look abashed. "Sir Dennis assured me there wouldn't be any problem, sir."

"And there wasn't," agreed Herriad, gloomily. "Not after he'd fed me whisky at the club, that is."

"Anyway, I arrived, and at the same time John Guthrie, poor devil, put in an appearance. I'd give anything for a few minutes with him, you know. Not only would I want to shake his hand, for he was a fine man, but it's obvious that he knew where the Serpent's Eye was hidden. Sandy, you had an idea about that, didn't you?"

304

"Yes," she said. "I don't believe he *did* know beforehand, if you see what I mean, but once he'd heard the Houblyn jewels were false, then it was fairly certain he'd done some thinking. He must have seen something, perhaps on the night of the ball that, once he knew the jewels really had been stolen twelve years ago, made him think he knew where they were. He was very definite in telling us the Count had hidden them. I only wish he'd got round to telling us where. He tried to, but he died."

"And you say Tommy Leigh - or Robert Eldon - murdered him?" asked her father.

"Yes, Dad. He boasted about it. Not only did Tommy - Robert - knock him over, he hit him over the head with a monkey wrench as soon as Philip and I left to drive to the house."

"But why, Sandy?"

"Because John Guthrie knew who Eleanor Storwood was. He'd been married to her, after all. We found a cutting in his room with a picture of Sir Dennis and Eleanor Storwood. I think poor Mr Guthrie must've tried to contact Eleanor after that was published, and her first thought would've been to get rid of him. That picture was in the *Daily Express* on the Thursday, and the next day John Guthrie cancelled his fishing-trip with his friends and set out for here. Because of what happened next, it's obvious that Eleanor Storwood was expecting him. I got confused about this part of it, because I thought that *if* it was murder, then Tommy would have had to have had split-second timing to be in the right place at the right time. Actually, it needs nothing of the sort. All Tommy

305

needed was the intention to kill John Guthrie as quickly as possible. Tommy saw his chance and took it. By the way, Phil, if we'd been on the ball, we could have spotted Eleanor Storwood and Tommy Leigh were in partnership at the time."

"How?" asked Philip.

"When the Storwoods came into the house we'd got the gun-room all ready for poor Mr Guthrie. I explained to the Storwoods there'd been an accident, and Eleanor straightaway rounded on Tommy. "How fast were you going?" she asked. But we hadn't said it was a car accident - and as we were in the gun-room, a shooting accident was at least as likely - and we hadn't said Tommy was responsible. I knew something had niggled at the time, but I couldn't think what it was."

"Then came the inquest," said Brenzett, "and you, Miss Herriad, spotted Mrs Strickland was a phoney, which led you to the house in Camden Town. Was that the same day you met Mrs Banks at Waterloo?"

"Yes," Sandy swallowed. "It's horrible what happened to her. She was such a good, harmless, soul. She'd been at the inquest, and the sight of Eleanor Storwood had clearly jogged her memory. However, I was still all steamed up about Robert Eldon. She told me she wouldn't know him now, but she also said it was the inquest which had brought him to mind. She'd seen Tommy there, you see. Meanwhile, Phil, you were chasing Mrs Strickland, as we then knew her."

"I was," said Philip, grimly. "And violent record or no violent record, she very nearly saw me off. She must've arrived on the same train which brought Mrs Banks. She'd obviously been warned to clear out, and that told us there was an enemy in the house. I was puzzled that no-one made any attempt to contact the outside world after I'd announced that Mrs Strickland had left a clue in the house in Camden Town, but what we think must have happened is that Tommy Leigh used the secret passage to sneak out in the night and get a message to one of the gang. He knew all about the passages, of course."

He looked at Sandy. "I imagine that's why he was so careful to show you where they were. If you'd have got into them off your own bat, you'd have seen his tracks in the dust and realised they'd been recently used. Two more things happened that day; Sandy decided that Mrs Banks was the "Bank" that John Guthrie had talked about...."

"Which she wasn't, poor woman."

"And I very nearly spotted that Thringford, where the Kurhaus was, was the place we were looking for. However, it was the discussion about Mrs Banks which really set the cat amongst the pigeons. Suddenly our precious pair, Eleanor Storwood and Tommy Leigh, realised that there was one woman who could identify them both. Not only that, but she'd kept a scrapbook of all the famous people who'd been to Farholt in the Eldons' time. What's the betting that Eleanor, at least, was in it?"

"They both are," said Brenzett. "Mrs Banks was in London. Someone, probably Tommy Leigh, to call him that, got her address from her niece by pretending to telephone from the Yard, and Eleanor Storwood paid her a visit. I wouldn't be at all surprised if she admitted to being John Guthrie's wife and fed her a romantic tale about clearing her husband's name and so on. Whatever she said, the end result was that Lady Storwood was convinced that Mrs Banks suffered from an inconvenient memory. She arranged to meet her the next day. She planned the murder very carefully."

"She certainly tried to implicate Sir Dennis," said Sandy. "Poor man. There was that false telegram and then, Phil, you found one of his socks in the sand-heap by the church."

"She'd used it as a sandbag to slug Mrs Banks," said Philip. "It made a good weapon."

"I don't understand," said Daphne Marston. "How could this dreadful woman possibly have killed Mrs Banks? She was with me in the garden all morning and then we were all together at lunch."

"Tommy Leigh did the running around," said Philip. "That's what we worked out, isn't it, Brenzett? They knew when Mrs Banks would be arriving at the station. He went to pick up Mrs Banks and dropped her off at the church, where she'd agreed to meet Eleanor Storwood. He came back here, and collected Eleanor from the gate at the rear and drove her to the church. I don't know how she managed to give you the slip, Mrs Marston."

"I came in to see about the butcher," said Daphne Marston, thoughtfully. "Now I come to think of it, it was Lady Storwood who asked me if everything was ready for that evening. I believe, although I'm not certain, that she gave me the idea that I'd better go and check that things really were all right. It was very well done."

"It would be," said Philip. "Tommy Leigh came back here and, after a suitable interval, went to collect Eleanor again."

"Damn me," said Andrew Herriad. "I went and talked to him. He said he'd been having trouble with his plugs or something and I waved him off to test the car."

"I assumed she'd been in the garden the whole time I was in the house," said Daphne. "I can hardly credit how I was taken in."

"You were dealing with an expert, Mrs Marston," said Brenzett. "She's a very clever woman. The next thing to happen was that Mr Brown," - he nodded at Jerry "- was kidnapped."

"I didn't stand a chance," said Jerry ruefully.

Philip lit a cigarette. "When I got the news, Jerry, I was stunned. I knew Harry was safe, though, which meant they'd guessed wrongly who the President really was. I hoped that if I declared myself to be the real McCoy, I'd be kidnapped in turn. I assumed that once I was with Jerry, we'd be able to get out of it in one piece. I underestimated them. If it hadn't been for you, Sandy, things would have been very different."

Sandy blushed with pleasure. "Did you suspect Tommy before you went to the Kurhaus, Phil?"

Philip nodded. "Yes, but I couldn't be sure. Before I left Farholt though, I took the false jewels and put them in the library. I arranged the books to coincide with John Guthrie's last words. I thought it might be useful to have some sort of bribe to offer. As it happened, it proved the key to the whole thing. I'd hoped to rescue Jerry. Instead, I walked straight into a trap. Although I'd posted a note to Superintendent Brenzett to tell him where I was going, when the police did come, they couldn't find us."

"We were worried about Jane, too, weren't we?" put in Jerry. He nodded towards his cousin. "I know you've had your differences, Harry, but the thought of her in their hands was not pleasant."

"Fortunately," said Philip, "Sandy decided to take a hand." He looked at her warmly. "You were terrific."

She smiled. "I was worried sick. When I heard you'd gone and didn't come back, I knew something was wrong. I worked out the Thringford clue easily enough but the police couldn't find you. I knew you were there, because I pinched your car, but I felt utterly beaten. I came back home and Tommy Leigh was very, very nice to me. It didn't seem quite real. Then, thank goodness, I saw Rose Price, our housemaid, who made me think about Mrs Banks and what she knew. She knew about the Eldons. Had she recognized Robert Eldon? Not for certain, no, but she had thought about him. Was Robert Eldon at Farholt? If he was, and I ruled Philip out of it - because I'd actually asked Mrs Banks when we were at Waterloo if Philip was Robert - there was only one person who he could be, and that was Tommy."

Andrew Herriad took a deep breath and poured himself another glass of whisky. "You went off with that scoundrel knowing who he was?"

"Yes, Dad. He was so keen to take me to the Kurhaus, I suspected that I was the next on the list of kidnap victims."

"Dear God," muttered her father. "Dammit, Sandy, these people had just murdered Mrs Banks!"

"I know," agreed Sandy. "I guessed why, too. Mrs Kelly was at the Kurhaus so she hadn't visited Mrs Banks. But if it *wasn't* Mrs Kelly, it had to be Eleanor Storwood. She fitted. I mean, she *really* fitted. Mrs Banks would be happy and excited by a visit from her. But if Eleanor Storwood had murdered Mrs Banks, I wanted to know why. And that answer, too, was staring me in the face. She'd recognized her. But who, in this whole business, could Mrs Banks have recognized her *as*? The wife of the murdered man, of course, John Guthrie. That explained everything. If John Guthrie had identified his wife, then Eleanor Storwood would be ruined."

"That was only a guess," said her father. "I can't credit you put yourself into such danger on the strength of a guess."

Sandy shook her head. "I had proof, Dad. Tommy had told me that the Kurhaus was a front for a drug-ring, run by Sir Dennis. He talked as if the Kurhaus was a going concern when Sir Dennis had married Eleanor, but I was fairly certain we'd been told, on the first evening they arrived, that the Kurhaus was Lady Storwood's pigeon and they'd bought it after their marriage. I went to the study and looked at the Kurhaus file and there it was in black and white. I'd been right; the Kurhaus *was* bought after their marriage and Tommy was a liar. As for the rest of it?" She shrugged. "Well, it was the worst evening of my life. I was really frightened, even though I knew it was only a matter of time before the police arrived."

"I was nearly beside myself," said her father. "The Superintendent insisted on following your directions to the letter but I wanted to go and tear the place apart." He looked at Philip. "You hit him, did you? I only wish I'd had the chance." He picked up the necklace. "And this is what it was all about. We're still no nearer knowing where it is, are we?"

"No," said Harry regretfully. "We're not."

*** *** ***

The moon was full and the night was warm. "This," said Philip, "is perfect." He slid an arm round Sandy's waist. "You are so lovely, Sandy. I keep on thinking of all the trite songs I've ever heard about love. Every single one of them is true."

"What's the moon like in Salvatierra?" she whispered.

"I'm looking forward to showing you."

*** *** ***

It was another half hour before they came indoors. Sandy snuggled up on the sofa and looked with great affection at her father. Poor Dad! If he was right about Aunt Daphne and Sir Dennis, she suspected she and Phil would be seeing quite a lot of him. It would be a wrench to leave. She loved Farholt. At this moment she even loved Aunt Daphne without any twinge of irritation. She hoped Aunt Daphne would be happy. She looked happy, deeply absorbed in a seed catalogue. Dad was talking to Jerry and Harry and as for Phil... Her heart turned over.

312

"I'm sorry," she said, putting her hand on his.

He raised his eyebrows. "Whatever for?"

"We didn't find the necklace. I wish I could guess what John Guthrie meant. It seems meaningless, and yet he knew. *Banks. Sea Air.*"

"I must have it moved," said Aunt Daphne, without looking up. "It really is taking over all that corner."

"What is, Aunt Daphne?"

Daphne Marston put down her catalogue. "The Banksia, dear. The candle-tree. It's got quite out of hand."

"The... the *what? The Banksia*! And John Guthrie loved plants! He'd know what it was!"

"And call it by its proper name," added Philip. His eyes were alight.

***   ***   ***

There was a loose stone at the bottom of the wall which had been built round the candle-tree. Philip prised it free and put his hand in the hole.

"Can you feel anything?" asked Harry, anxiously.

With a broad grin, Philip drew out a cloth bag. There was a gasp as he opened it and tumbled the contents into his hand. The necklace, the Serpent's Eye, gleamed dark green fire at them.

"I've never seen anything more wonderful," breathed Sandy.

Philip stood up and ceremonially clasped it round her neck. Stepping back, he took her hand and kissed her fingers. "I have," he said.

Made in the USA
Monee, IL
29 January 2021